Chickering & Sons

Richard Schubert

PublishAmerica

Baltimore

ISBN: 1-59286-481-3
PUBLISHED BY PUBLISHAMERICA BOOK PUBLISHERS
www.publishamerica.com
Baltimore

Printed in the United States of America

CHAPTER 1

"Bring me the tray with the scalpels," the surgeon said.

Marcy leaned forward. "What did you say?

The surgeon stopped. Motionless. The already taut face sharpened to starched creases, the redness in the neck rising to the stony lips, now the nose, now the narrowed eyes.

"Bring me…" he said, "… the… goddam… scalpels," the low hoarse voice barely escaping from the clenched teeth.

Marcy nearly tripped in her rush to get the tray. She had never heard the surgeon lose control before. Never. Cold, distant, abrupt. But always – *always*! – in control.

She set the tray down. The surgeon didn't move, locked in place.

"Are you alright?" Marcy whispered.

"Alright," he repeated. "Incompetence at every level in the hospital. Absurd new regulations in the OR. An inexcusable traffic jam. Bumbling police. Idiots abound. And you ask me if I'm alright."

And, he could have added, he had to fight the recent signs of aging, the decreased stamina, the increased fatigue.

* * *

A single horn blew insistently. Seemingly unaware of the winter cold, the driver stepped from the car and shook his fist.

But the traffic on Massachusetts Avenue still didn't move. A policeman came over, briefly spoke to the driver, and walked away. When the driver reached into the car and leaned on the horn again, the policeman whirled around and the two got into a shouting match.

Mr. Collins watched from the third floor window, its thin mullioned panes marking the boundaries of the two worlds – cold on the one side, warm on the other. "Is it always look this?" he asked.

Marcy shook her head. "No. The President rarely comes up here, but he's the guest of the British Prime Minister at the embassy today. Lunch, I think." She looked at her watch. "With any luck, he'll be leaving soon."

Massachusetts Avenue was deadlocked. No cars moved; pedestrians were restrained behind cordons; blue and red police car lights swirled in every direction.

Mr. Collins smiled and stepped back from the window. "We don't get this kind of excitement in Warrenton," he said. He was weak and walked slowly back to the examining table. "I've always been glad to live out there," he said, gesturing towards 'out there.' "Never liked the city."

Marcy looked over the top of her half frame glasses.

"He should be with you soon," she said.

The older man sitting on the examining table nodded slowly. A full head of white hair atop a lined face, he looked too small for his frame, the clear loser in his life long struggle with gravity. The gown tried unsuccessfully to hide the sagging shoulders. His eyes, slightly sunken, were so weary that the lines surrounding them looked permanent, as if he'd been born with them.

Had he ever smiled?

Marcy closed the door gently, catching one final glimpse of the man on the examining table, sitting almost motionless. Outside she could hear the unrepentant horn blower.

She'd seen so many types over these twenty years. The high-strung, the fidgety, the nervous, the terrified, the over-concerned, the under-concerned, the arrogant, the insecure. And the resigned, like Mr. Collins. Even though he hadn't seen the surgeon yet, he knew. The posture gave him away. Some of them already realized they were playing the final hand.

Marcy walked down the hall, vaguely focusing on the gray carpet, one slow step after another.

"I need a suture removal kit for room 3," the surgeon said as he passed her. Marcy's stride quickened at once, eyes straight ahead, back erect, shoulders upright. The lines on her face were frozen again, chin thrust slightly upward, stiffened corners of the mouth ending in a slight frown.

For the thousandth time, for the ten thousandth time, Marcy had searched the surgeon's face, but his eyes were already focused past her, fixed on infinity. He had recovered his poise, his demeanor. The sharply pressed white coat, crisply creased and glacially white, covered his arms and torso, only the gleaming golden cufflinks peering out from the end of the sleeve, dark gray slacks coming out below the lower hem atop the burnished black of his shoes.

"Mr. Collins," the surgeon said, opening the door, "I'm Dr. Brink." The right hand was extended from under the white sleeve. The patient looked at the surgeon; the older man sat stooped, the crinkles of the face still lifeless; the surgeon stood straight, every contour in his face mirroring the razor-sharp creases of his white coat.

4

"Dr. Jefferson told me your story," the surgeon said. "Did you bring the CT scan with you?"

The patient nodded, and bent down to pick up the folder with the X-rays. He leaned on the side of the examining table for a moment before getting back up.

"How long have you had the pain?" Brink asked.

"About two months."

Brink motioned for the patient to lie down. At once, the hands lost their rigidity, became soft and pliant, as the surgeon pushed and poked and probed the abdomen. He shut his eyes. Never once looking at the patient, he continued his exploration. "Breathe," he commanded quietly. "And again."

Brink carefully placed the CT scan on the X-ray view box.

"I was lucky to get here on time," Collins said. "That's quite a mess on Massachusetts Avenue."

"Yes," Brink said without turning around. He leaned forward to look at one of the CT images.

For five minutes, as if he were alone, he scanned one film, then the next. Mr. Collins sat up, watching, saying nothing.

"Here," Brink said at last, pointing to a black spot on the X-ray. "This is the pancreas. It's enlarged. Over here," he pointed higher up, "is the liver. There are a few holes in it, of a density that suggests a cancer."

"From the pancreas?"

"Precisely."

Brink walked over to the examining table. "I believe you have a cancer of the pancreas with metastases," he said, now engaging the patient's eyes.

The patient nodded, returning the surgeon's fixed stare. "What can you do to help?" Collins asked.

"I can operate to divert the bile ducts into the small intestine, but I can't remove the tumor."

"Why?"

"It's stuck to all the tissues around it."

"Would the surgery improve my life?"

"It would probably prolong it for a few months."

Collins smiled. "But would it improve it?"

"I don't think so."

"Can you give me any good reason to have the surgery?"

Brink didn't hesitate with his answer. "No."

"Only television doctors can make predictions."

Collins sat forward sharply, suddenly filling out the space his body occupied. "How much time, Dr. Brink?"

"Three to six months," the surgeon answered.

"Thank you," the patient said softly.

Brink shook his hand and left. He would write a brief note to the referring physician. The patient refused surgery. The surgeon strode down the hallway. A brave man, he thought, with the courage to make the right decision.

Brink's office was at the end of the hall. A large desk, a white top above two lean black pedestals, had commandeered the center of the room. Apart from a telephone and a high gloss wooden model of some type of red sports car, the desktop was bare. Angular white drapes covered the sides of a large window overlooking a courtyard. On the walls were several diplomas and surgical certificates.

Brink walked into his office and nodded to the couple seated in the straight backed armless chairs opposite the desk. Dressed in a plain black suit, the almost pudgy late middle-aged woman shifted in her seat and squeezed the man's hand even tighter.

In her free hand was a bunched up lace handkerchief. She sniffled through an overly broad nose. Eye liner ran irregularly across the lids, a casualty of frequent dabs to the eyes and forehead. Thickly applied red rouge cracked across the facial bones.

"It's pretty exciting," the woman said, as Brink walked in.

"What is?" the surgeon asked.

"The President's visit. I've never seen him in person before, but I caught a glimpse of him when he rode by."

Brink stared at the woman for several seconds, then sat down in his high-backed silver and black chair.

"Have you ever seen the President?" the woman asked.

Brink shook his head from side to side.

"There might still be time," the woman said, "if you look out the window."

Still Brink said nothing, drumming his fingers lightly on the desk.

"What is your decision?" he asked after several seconds.

"Pardon my prattling on," she said. "I know you understand. I'm, well, pretty nervous." She stopped.

When Brink said nothing, she went on. "So you think a mastectomy is the only option," she said.

Her nails dug into the husband's hand. He turned towards her, the small

6

tight knot of his thin tie pinching his neck, accentuating the Adams apple.

"We're so frightened," the man offered.

Brink drummed his fingers across the desk top for a moment, then brought his left hand up underneath his chin, appearing to support it with the thumb, his index finger curling over his lips.

"Mrs. Miller," he said slowly, "it's very important that you listen closely to what I tell you. I never said that a mastectomy was the only choice." The thin lips squeezed into an even tighter line. "What I said was that it is the most reasonable choice." He flicked some dust off the sleeve of his white coat.

Mrs. Miller's eyes didn't seem to focus. "Tell me again why a lumpectomy isn't just as good. I hate to sound stupid, but..."

Brink held up his hand. "Because," he said, "I think there is some unevenness to the skin near the nipple. Even though the mammogram didn't show anything there, I think there's a good possibility of an additional malignant focus." He cleared his throat. "As I already explained to you."

"Isn't it possible you're wrong?"

The surgeon's eyes widened as he leaned across the desk.

"You came to me for my best opinion and I've given it."

Mr. Miller struggled with the chair to bring it closer to his wife, then put his arm around her waist, pulling her closer.

"What would you recommend to your wife?" Mrs. Miller asked.

"I'm not married."

Sweat beads began pooling on her forehead. She wiped them off with an abrupt motion and turned to her husband. "You remember how Marge had just a local excision. She did very well."

"Yes," Mr. Miller replied, "but Dr. Brink feels your circumstance is different." He turned to the surgeon, who had resumed an erect posture on the other side of the desk. "Isn't that right?"

The surgeon looked at his watch. "Well, I have to go now. If you're not sure, I'd urge you to get a second opinion. If you decide to have the surgery with me, please tell Marcy and she'll arrange it."

Brink stood up and extended his hand, first to Mr. Miller, then to the patient.

"Dr. Gaston said you're the best," Mrs. Miller said, her voice trailing off as the surgeon walked out the door.

Marcy looked up from her small desk in the hall to watch the surgeon head out, shoulders stiff, arms swinging tightly at his side. Marcy knew her boss: Dr. Brink had not liked this patient.

Marcy sighed. She'd wait a few moments, then go in and talk to the Millers. When she was finished talking, Mrs. Miller would probably sign on for the surgery with Brink. How many times had she covered Dr. Brink's abruptness? Did he ever realize how often she'd smoothed over his defects?

Nah, she thought, people like Brink never even ask that kind of question.

For the first time that afternoon, the surgeon looked out the window, just in time to see the last police car pull away. The traffic was beginning to move freely.

Putting on his sportscoat, Brink walked down to the basement garage. It was raw and cold between the concrete pillars, with a few puddles lying on the floor where ice had melted off some cars. He started the engine and headed up the ramp. Dirty mounds of crystallized snow on the roadsides seized sunlight from a clear blue sky and focused it into the surgeon's eyes as he pulled the Porsche out onto Massachusetts Avenue. He set the shades down over his glasses. Passing the British Embassy and the Vice Presidential mansion on the left, the great towers of the Cathedral rose on his right, but the surgeon paid them no mind as he made an illegal left turn onto Wisconsin Avenue, then a quick left into the parking lot of Cleveland Park Hospital.

The old hospital with its huge gray granite blocks at the main entrance had recently undergone an interior renovation. The cavernous ceilings of the domed foyer were lowered with acoustic tiles, and faux wooden paneling now covered the old stonework in the halls.

The cold late afternoon January sun was quickly setting as Brink walked into the unremodeled doctor's entrance and headed for the teaching conference room on the fourth floor. The surgeon invariably took the stairs, and was slightly short of breath by the time he reached his destination.

Just as Brink reached the conference room, a medical student was blowing a huge pink bubble of gum. Brink tilted his head slightly and stared at the Magritte-like image. The bubble burst abruptly, the student quickly wiping it off his mouth.

"What is your name please?" Brink asked him.

"Ted."

Brink continued staring at the student. The room was still, an electric clock humming on the wall. The house officers shifted from one foot to the other. The student twisted slightly in his chair and looked to his left and right, but not at the surgeon.

"Dr. Brink wants your full name," one of the residents volunteered in a very quiet voice.

The student looked up at the unblinking Brink. "Ted Schwartz," he said.

Brink lowered his head slightly and continued to stare at the student for a few seconds more, then he turned his attention to the seniormost resident.

"How many do we have today?" he asked.

"Ten," the resident answered.

Brink nodded and began walking down the passageway to the Surgical Intensive Care Unit. The housestaff and students fell into a loose line behind him. Through a hall window the sun was setting, the temperature outside dropping quickly, the water on the street preparing to spend the night as ice. The only sound as they walked in the corridor was the clicking of heels off the tiled floor.

Brink entered the ICU, slowly turning his head from left to right, then back again. The entire ICU stopped – froze - as the surgeon surveyed the expanse. Two nurses, as if responding to some hidden cue, arose simultaneously from their seats and hurried over. The Unit Secretary stopped writing to look up, the maintenance man quit mopping a section of floor. A small knot of physicians on the other side of the ICU turned towards Brink, and a couple of them nodded to him. Only at a nearby console did a man, dressed in blue scrubs and intently watching a bank of heart monitors, fail to note Brink's entrance.

Then the apparent pause button was released and the ICU returned to its routine. The group of physicians turned back to their patient, the Unit Secretary began writing, the janitor resumed his mopping. The man in the blue scrubs continued to watch the monitor, surveying each patient's vital force, represented by little green blips on a television screen.

It was nearly dark outside, but the ICU was brilliantly lit, recessed fluorescent light pouring out from behind plastic ceiling covers. Patients' charts lay scattered on white formica counters. The janitor pushed an empty stretcher out of his way and began mopping the vacated area.

"Who's first?" Brink asked.

"DeMandeville," the junior-most resident answered. He lead the way across the ICU. One of the nurses picked up a clipboard with all the patient's vital statistics and handed it to the surgeon. Temperature, blood pressure, respirations, pulse, fluids in, fluids out, respirator settings, oxygen saturation... The list went on. Blood test results, antibiotic dosages...

Brink folded his arms over his chest, closed his eyes and rocked back on his heels.

The junior-most resident poked the medical student.

"Mr. DeMandeville is a 74 year old man," the student began. He was a kid, no more than 23 or 24 years, with an unruly head of hair, wearing a rumpled pair of chinos, and blinking frequently. Brink remained quiet, his eyes closed.

The resident poked the student again.

"Um, he was in his usual state of good health when he was creamed, I mean, hit head on by a drunk driver." Brink opened his eyes and looked at the discomfited student. "He was wearing a seat belt." The thinnest hint of a smile appeared on Brink's lips. "He never lost consciousness," the student continued, "but began complaining of excruciating abdominal pain, so the Rescue Squad brought him to the ER."

"Thank you," Brink said quietly, holding up his right hand and turning his attention to another medical student.

"Alright," he said, "you're on call in the Emergency Room and this man is wheeled in on a stretcher. What's the first thing you'd do?"

The student averted his gaze, shifting her weight from one foot to the other. She swallowed hard.

"Well," she said, drawing out every sound, "I'd probably get a CT scan of the abdomen."

Brink stood straighter still, his presence now overwhelming the surrounding space. His eyes opened wider, focusing on the student. Well into her forties, she had dark blond hair pulled into a short ponytail. Her hands were in front, but they stiffened as she searched for a place to put them, settling on folding them in front of her chest for a moment, then clasping them behind her back.

"She'd get a CT scan of the abdomen," Brink said, raising his eyebrows and looking at one of the surgical house officers. "A CT of the abdomen," he repeated. "Dr.... what's your name?" Brink asked, looking back at the student.

"Ellen."

"Do you have a last name?"

"White."

"Dr. White," Brink said, "have you ever heard of taking a history and examining the patient?"

"Of course. I didn't think…"

"Dr. White, if this patient had no blood pressure or were cyanotic, do you think sending him for a CT scan would be a good starting point?"

"Of course not I…"

"Let's try again. Dr. White, the patient has just arrived by ambulance.

Three or four people come running into the ER with this man on a stretcher. What are you going to do?"

"Take a history."

"Very good, *Dr.* White."

The surgeon turned back to the initial presenter, the kid with the rumpled chinos, who still had a few pieces of bubble gum stuck to one cheek.

"Please continue."

"In the ER, it was felt he had an acute traumatic abdomen."

"Bravo!" Brink said. "Most astute. Dr.... what's your name again?"

"Schwartz."

"Dr. Schwartz, Dick and Jane see Spot run. Run Spot run." Brink leaned forward. "You don't need to go to medical school to reason that a man in a car crash with abdominal pain has an acute traumatic abdomen."

"Yes sir," Schwartz said, blinking furiously.

"How did the ER geniuses figure that out?"

"They examined him sir."

"Excellent! What perspicacity! Now, tell me, Dr. White," he said, turning his attention to the student who appeared to have gone into hiding behind one of the residents, "what might the doctors have found?"

Ellen White, 45 years old, was starting a second career following her divorce. She wore only a hint of eye shadow and pale pink lipstick. Pens and papers and notecards were jammed into the pockets of a short white coat that had long ago forgotten where the creases were supposed to be; a stethoscope hung around her neck. She stepped out from behind the resident.

"They probably found his abdomen was very tender, with guarding and rebound," she said. "Most likely he had no bowel sounds."

Brink nodded.

"Dr. Schwartz," he said, "what was the patient's blood pressure in ER?"

"I'm not entirely sure, sir. I only picked him up after he arrived in the ICU."

The nurse next to Dr. Brink coughed.

"You're not sure?" Brink asked. "Schwartz, how did you get into medical school? Can a doctor function in a vacuum? This man's blood pressure is critical." Brink looked across the top of his sharp nose and over his thin almost-frameless glasses, his vision landing on one of the surgical house officers.

"He was hypotensive, sir," the house officer said, "with a blood pressure of 70/40."

11

Brink turned to Ellen White. "Still want to get a CT scan?"

"Of course not!" she said.

Brink's eyes widened slightly and the vaguest hint of a smile wavered for a moment on his thin lips.

"I'd give him fluids to support his blood pressure, and put in a urinary catheter," Ellen said.

Brink nodded. "There may be hope for you yet."

The rounds went on for three hours, a typical teaching exercise for Roland Brink. The surgeon questioned, probed, demanded, never wavering in his attention to the smallest detail. By the end of teaching rounds, he usually knew the patients better than their own physicians did. It was Brink's custom to remain standing for the entire length of the exercise, often causing weary house officers and students to increasingly fidget and shift around, always apparently unnoticed by Brink who continued on with his rounds. Today, however - much to everyone's surprise - Brink sat down on a number of occasions between some of the patients.

The sun had long fled the heavens by the time the surgeon was finally finished. With only a curt nod, Brink left the last patient and walked over to the elevator. "Where the hell is the damned elevator?" he said half aloud, looking around for a chair. Roland Brink never sat on rounds, never took elevators. But recently, he'd been feeling tired, needing more sleep, not exercising quite as easily. So far it hadn't affected his ability to stand in the Operating Room, but he was wondering -- just a bit.

"Growing old," he muttered as he reached the parking lot.

The Porsche headed for Chain Bridge and crossed the Potomac River to his house in McLean in suburban Virginia. As always, the house was immaculate; living alone, there was hardly ever any mess. Whatever did occur was quickly repaired by the weekly visit of the cleaning lady.

Brink pulled the Porsche in the circular driveway and got out at the front door. After briefly scanning the mail, he walked to the living room. Furnished in intersecting angular blacks and whites, a free form glass table in the middle and a large abstract canvas on the longest wall, the decor – very similar to his office - had been chosen by a Georgetown decorator with Brink's strong input. The surgeon loosened his tie, undoing the top shirt buttons, and went over to the bar and poured himself a couple of ounces of Johnny Walker. Sitting down on one of the overstuffed white couches and kicking off his Italian leather shoes, he slowly sipped the scotch. For several seconds, he looked at the chess board on the adjacent table, the players in black and white cut glass, poised for their next move. The surgeon had been thinking about the next move all day; it would have to wait. Brink turned to stare blankly at the ceiling. The piercing rawboned beam from the pointed Plexiglas lamp shone into his eyes.

But, for the first time he could ever remember, he fell asleep on the couch, sleeping deeply even with the light shining on him.

CHAPTER 2

"Trust me, Alyssa," Ellen said, "someday you'll know what I'm talking about."

"I already do," the younger woman answered. "I have this pair of jeans I bought last year, and they shrunk in the drier. I have to diet a week before I can fit into them now."

Ellen smiled. "Just wait until *everything* in the closet doesn't quite fit. Look at this skirt," she said. "It fit perfectly when I bought it, well....maybe ten years ago. Now I have to suck it in to keep it from strangulating my waist....and *I* never put it in the drier."

Ellen adjusted herself in the seat. At times she still had a youthful insouciance, sometimes mixed with an impishness, a boyish smile. She would still giggle after a glass of wine, still flirt in front of a mirror when she was wearing a jogging outfit.

But with age and experience she could also be mature, sensible... even cynical.

A tray crashed to the floor somewhere on the other side of the cafeteria, glasses and plates shattering everywhere. Someone clapped a few times; the noise level dropped for a second only to start up again when the myriads resumed talking. Chairs scraped against the floor as they were pulled out and pushed in, knives and forks clattered on the plastic trays and plates. A metallic clamor enveloped everything, coming from no one place but from everywhere. All the tables were taken up with students, house officers, physicians, nurses, and many others whose identities eluded Ellen.

The two medical students continued eating.

"Yogurt and a banana?" Ellen said. "No wonder you're so thin." Ellen looked down at her plate. "The sign said this is meatloaf." She cut off a piece. "Does this look like meatloaf to you? Does it even look edible?"

Alyssa shrugged. "Sorry, but I'm sort of a vegetarian, so I really can't say."

Ellen looked at the younger woman, the expression so animated, the smile so overwhelming; even the diamond engagement ring was struggling to match the glow of her face.

"When are you getting married?" Ellen asked.

"In June, as soon as I finish my pediatrics rotation." Alyssa burbled on about her marriage plans, her fiancé ("he's been offered a job by a big engineering firm"), the plans for children, the home. She didn't even know where she'd be living, "but I already know just how to decorate the living room."

Ellen loosened the button on her skirt. Nobody would notice under her white coat, its pockets under siege by the stethoscope, pens, papers, notecards. Frowning, she courageously looked down at what remained of the meatloaf, gracelessly covered by a splash of nameless tomato sauce. Alyssa continued, animated, excited. And so sure of her future.

I was young once, Ellen thought, admiring more the gestalt than the details of what Alyssa was saying.

"Sorry," Ellen said, "what did you ask?"

"I wondered why you decided to go to med school when you were so, um, so.."

"So old?"

"Oh no, no, not that at all," Alyssa blushed. "But you already have kids and it's unusual, you know, to want to, um…"

"Let me bale you out," Ellen laughed. "I got tired of the book clubs, the church volunteering, the flower arranging courses. My husband left me, and I decided to try and do something with my life." *Not to be an ornament.*

Alyssa blushed again. "I'm sorry. I didn't mean to intrude."

"I'm the one who should be apologizing," Ellen said, "for sounding sour at a time that's exciting for you." She glanced at the wall clock. "The last thing I..... oh my God," she said, jumping up, "I'm late for my surgery lecture."

* * *

Running, tripping, tumbling slightly down the hall, Ellen pushed open the door, and erupted into the lecture hall room.

A few of the other students smiled and greeted her as she tripped over an assortment of legs and shoes on the way to her seat.

"I thought I was late," she panted, wiping off her forehead. "Sorry. Was that your foot?"

"If we're lucky," someone said, "he'll forget to show up."

The door opened and a large man walked in. His basketball shaped head rested snowman-like on a round torso. The arms had clearly been designed for a shorter, thinner man and stuck out at an angle from the sides. Quite likely

15

the suit had fit in an earlier life, but now it pulled at the middle, challenging the limits of the jacket button. Stretching across the belly, the jacket fought unsuccessfully against horizontal creases. The pants were pulled up to nearly one-third the way up his calf, where white socks showed.

"Do you think his arms are long enough to reach the operating room table?" one of the students whispered.

After arranging some papers on the lectern, the professor walked along the side of the room to the slide projector in the back. Saying nothing and still not making eye contact, but periodically coughing and blowing his nose, he sorted the slides while trying with variable success to insert them into the carousel. After a couple of minutes, he turned on the light and pushed the remote control button a few times.

Satisfied that he had assumed mastery of the projector, he walked back along the side of the room to the lectern, rustled a few papers, and then, for the first time, lifted his head and looked out at the twenty or so students.

"I'm Dr. Haynes," he started. "I'm here to lecture about the proper metabolic care of the surgical patient."

"I can hardly wait," someone behind Ellen whispered.

Haynes rearranged his notes again, then, pushing a button on the remote, the first slide maneuvered smartly into position, but couldn't compete against the overhead light. The surgeon pointed to a student and flicked his index finger up and down several times.

The student got up and turned off the lights.

The slide was now visible.

Proper Metabolic Care of the Surgical Patient
By Wilfred J. Haynes, MD, FACS
Associate Professor of Surgery

"It is often assumed," Dr. Haynes began in a curiously high voice, "that the surgeon's responsibility ends with the final closure at the end of the operation. Nothing could be further from the truth because, in fact, the surgeon's responsibility has only just started. Let us consider some of the types of..."

Oh my God, Ellen thought. An hour of *this*?

"As the second slide shows," Haynes continued, "there are multiple concerns every surgeon must think of. It is the surgeon's responsibility to be alert to all the various ramifications...."

Ellen shifted in her seat, crossing and re-crossing her legs several times. To her right, the student had already closed his eyes.

"The importance of electrolyte balance cannot be overstated. On this next slide," he pushed the button, "we see that the body can be considered as a large fish tank with fluids coming in here," he pointed with his laser light, "and coming out over here. Clearly it is essential that..."

The room was too dark to take any notes. Ellen yawned and forced her eyes open.

Haynes continued to run through the slides.

I have no one to blame for this except myself, Ellen thought. I didn't *have* to go to medical school. Paying good money to sit in ridiculous lectures like this, stay up all night in the OR, take killer tests designed to humiliate me. For what?

"...and that was an important surgical lesson learned by the American Army during World War I." Haynes blew his nose. "Another key point is the importance of weighing the patient. In this modern era, when we have so many hi-tech machines, sometimes we overlook the...."

The student to her right began snoring.

This would be funny, Ellen decided, if it weren't so pathetic.

Ellen closed her eyes, listening to Dr. Haynes babble on. And on.

She tried to picture Haynes in the operating room. Would the scrub nurse fall asleep? At least the patient wouldn't have to listen to the surgeon; the anesthetist would see to that.

Or maybe they didn't need an anesthetist – just let Haynes start talking and the patient would be asleep in no time.

Trying to picture Haynes in an army uniform during World War I made Ellen smile. Buttons on the Army green uniform pulling at the middle, with ol' Wilfred J. himself weighing the patients and drawing fish tanks, looking so important and pontificating.

World War I. American Army. *Be all that you can be.* Ellen opened her eyes. What was that from? *You can do it in the Army.*

Be all that I can be? Or maybe 'anything I want to be?' like my father used to say when I was growing up. Is that why I'm at this dreadful lecture? Hmmph! I never wanted to be a divorcee, a used model, a veteran of lunches with the ladies.

"I always emphasize to the students that the *quality* of the urine is as important as the *quantity*," Haynes said as Ellen tried to rejoin the lecture. "I always look at the urine *first*. Is it cloudy, is it dark and concentrated or.."

Somewhere behind Ellen, someone chuckled. The student on her right abruptly snorted, didn't breathe for ten seconds, then resumed his snoring.

Anything I want to be. I went to medical school to learn to look at the urine. Before looking at the patient.

Ellen heard someone yawn.

"Our time is running short," Haynes said, "so I'll have to rush through the last twenty or so slides."

"There is a God after all," someone whispered.

The slides scurried through the projector and soon the overhead lights came on.

"I hope you've all now learned some fundamentals of caring for the surgical patient," Haynes said as he tapped the notes on the lectern and walked out.

For a moment, the students all sat dazed. One stood up.

"Any questions?" he asked, trying to imitate the surgeon's voice.

"Professor, I have one," called a student from the back. "If a patient comes in with a hangnail, should I examine the urine or weigh the patient first?"

Everyone laughed as the class broke up. Ellen had to scrub on a late afternoon case, then see all her patients. With luck she'd get home by ten o'clock.

* * *

Ellen trudged into the kitchen. Ten thirty. She hadn't eaten since breakfast. After scraping a few moldy speckles off the bread, spreading on some peanut butter and jelly, pouring a large glass of orange juice, she sat down at the kitchen table.

Through eyes too tired to care, she focused haphazardly on nothing as she ate, periodically pushing droopy hair off her eyes. Looking down at her blouse randomly, she winced when she saw a brown stain; where did that come from?

In recent months, she'd stopped looking at the kitchen, once so bright, cheerful. Ellen had worked hard in choosing wallpaper and paint, getting new track lighting and counters. It had been fresh once, a place where she could really enjoy spending time, cooking, visiting with friends - not just a place to eat, but a destination. And now? It was grungy, almost dingy. Stained wallpaper with a browned-over floral print. The yellow paint, so badly faded, made a mockery of sunlight. One of the burners didn't work, the sink dripped.

18

Two overhead lights were broken.

The kitchen: once youthful and vibrant, now tired and old, long past its prime.

She lifted the trash out of its bin and put a twistie on it. "Why can't my kids do this for me?" she muttered. "Instead of watching television." She put in a fresh plastic bag. "Maybe if I took a baseball bat to the television....Hmmph. That's the best idea I've had all day."

"Did you say something?" Brent said, walking in.

"What are you doing up?" Ellen turned abruptly. Freed from its restraining elastic band, her hair swung in front of her face. "I thought I sent you to bed half an hour ago."

"Mom, I'm fifteen. I don't need a curfew anymore."

"And I say you need to go to bed, right now!"

"Did you read my Civil War paper yet?"

"Oh my God," Ellen said. "I completely forgot. Bring it to me."

"Mom, if you're too busy, I can...."

"No, bring it to me."

Brent returned a minute later with the twelve page paper. Ellen looked at it for a moment and closed her eyes.

"It's kinda long," Brent said. "You can read it some other time. I'll understand."

For just a moment, Ellen sat immobile, then she reached out and grabbed Brent. and began to cry. As her neck bent forward, the hair covered her face. Ellen sniffled and pushed the hair back.

"Did I do something, Mom? You really don't have to read it now."

Ellen hugged Brent tighter. "No," she said, sobbing quietly. "It's nothing you did. It's just that...." She sobbed again. "Everywhere I turn...." Leaning back, Ellen turned around and found a tissue on the counter. She blotted her eyes, then blew her nose. Tears re-formed instantly and dripped onto her blouse.

"Can I help?" Brent asked.

"Nothing's going right," she said. "I forget to read my son's paper. Deb is annoyed because I didn't get to a poetry reading she gave at college. The surgery rotation is awful. Today I heard some pompous old fool give a lecture that would put a cup of coffee to sleep. But even worse is the senior attending, some guy named Brink. Arrogant, hostile - he really has it out for me." She sighed. "I don't know why. I'm doing the best I can." She nodded side to side. "I wish I had more time to read my surgery book, but I'm too tired." She looked at Brent. "I'm *always* tired. I get up tired. I'm tired on rounds. I'm tired at lunch. I'm tired in the Operating Room."

"Really Mom, you don't have to read my Civil War paper. Deb looked at it and had a couple of good suggestions. It's fine, really."

Ellen kissed Brent on the top of his head. "It's past your bedtime. You head right upstairs now. I'll read your paper before I go to bed." The reluctant scholar said goodnight and headed upstairs.

Ellen looked at the Washington Post on the counter and shook her head. Not tonight. She was *so* tired.

She wiped her eyes again.

Walking into the study, Civil War paper in hand, Ellen found her reflection waiting in the window. Almost transparent, framed by the outside darkness peering through her image, Ellen was unprepared for the apparition of a middle-aged woman. She couldn't make out the face in the thin reflection, but the body shape was all too clear. To be sure, it was more ample than even ten years ago, but the way the clothes hugged her was different tonight. Maybe after some rest, she'd rediscover her vigor and the clothes would greet her body more cordially.

Picking a newspaper off the floor, she stood up and looked again at the window. The middle-aged shape followed her up.

Ellen pulled down the window shade.

On a bookshelf she saw the mail, some from a few days ago, still unopened. The electric company - past due. A credit card payment - past due. Better do them first. She got out the check book, crying silently as she wrote out the checks. She didn't even bother to review the MasterCharge bill. She'd just assume it was right. Too tired.

Ellen sat down with Brent's paper and looked at the title sheet: "Economics and the Civil War." The Civil War. Hmmph. The army again. *Be all that you can be.*

She adjusted the sofa cushions behind her and changed the angle of the light. It felt so good to sit down.

Some people thought slavery was doomed, war or no. More recent research suggested that it was a lot more economically viable than had been thought until now.

Ellen leaned back in the cushion. It felt so soft, so good.

Extension of slavery west of the Mississippi provided whole new challenges to the economic assumptions of both the south and the north.

Maybe she'd just close her eyes for five minutes. That would refresh her enough to finish the paper. Just a few minutes.

An hour later, Brent walked quietly into the study. Ellen was sound asleep, hand still on the second page of the term paper. He kissed her lightly on the cheek."C'mon, Mom. Let's get you upstairs to bed."

CHAPTER 3

"Please pull more gently on the retractor," the surgeon said, peering over the top of his green mask. "This is living human tissue. If you want to push and pull vigorously, you can scrub pots in the kitchen."

Ellen White looked over the top of *her* mask at the surgeon, then with some help from the scrub nurse, repositioned the retractors, lessening the tension a small degree.

Dr. Brink took another brief look at the medical student, then turned his attention back to the surgery. Only a shade under six feet tall, he was not physically any larger than some of the others, but his presence dominated the OR. In front of the open abdomen, he controlled everything. His fingers moved so quickly that it was hard for the student to follow. He cut, cauterized, sutured, sometimes making a knot with one hand. Brink frequently looked over at the EKG monitor next to the anesthesiologist. This was a very sick patient with multiple medical problems; the surgeon would have to work quickly.

Ellen leaned forward, pulling the abdominal wall tissue apart with the retractors. Her arms ached from the constant tension; now her upper back ached; now the discomfort spread all the way to her lower back. The operation was in its third hour. Ellen's muscles screamed out in pain, but she held fast, scarcely daring to breathe, holding the retractors carefully.

Ellen could feel the heat from the brilliant OR lights as the sweat continued forming under her green operating room gown. She sensed the globules congealing, then dripping down along the sides of her chest, across the back and abdomen. At the same time, her glasses steamed up until she could barely see the operating field. And now, she began to focus on the two cups of coffee she'd had before the surgery; her bladder was full and the pressure was increasing by the minute.

If only she could just roll over and die.

"Will you please be more gentle?" Brink snapped. "This is a living human being."

"I'm doing the best I can," Ellen answered sharply, matching his tone and volume.

A barely audible gasp from the scrub nurse.

Brink looked over his mask at Ellen, then resumed his cutting, cauterizing, sewing.

Ellen could think of nothing now but the unforgiving throb of her aching muscles, the fogged glasses, the drenching sweat, the full bladder.

The eye glasses began to slowly slip forward on her nose, creeping ever further towards the tip. She scrunched up her facial muscles, trying to arrest the downward slide but to little effect. At last she turned to the scrub nurse, speaking in an almost inaudible whisper.

"Please put my glasses on before they fall into the abdomen."

Although no obvious signal was given, another OR nurse came over and, removing the glasses, wiped the student's face, then replaced them.

The anesthesiologist sat on his stool, eyes closed, while one of the nurses opened a glass cabinet and took out some sterile equipment. The heart monitor continued its quiet beeping; a soft buzzer went off in the corner and the anesthesiologist opened his eyes. An OR supervisor came in and spoke quietly to one of the nurses for a moment; then left as noiselessly as she came.

The surgeon continued his rapid work, stopping for a moment to talk with the anesthesiologist about a slight change in the patient's blood pressure. He turned back to the operating field.

"Dr. White," he said, this time without looking up, his voice harsh, quiet, "I trust you will be more careful in the future. If those glasses had fallen into the operating field, it would have contaminated everything. Being a medical student does not excuse incompetence."

Ellen leaned her head over the open abdomen and slowly looked up at the surgeon.

"First of all," she said, her voice also very low, barely above a whisper, "it is not *Dr.* White. I am still a student. Second, although I am only a student, I'm still entitled to be treated with respect. I am doing the best I can."

Another gasp - this time quite audible - from the scrub nurse.

But Roland Brink continued his work, saying nothing.

The surgery went on nearly one hour longer. Ellen tried to stand straight, but periodically caught herself slumping. She'd never known how much pain contracting muscles could give; she held tight onto the retractors. And she waited for Brink to slow down for an instant, so she could – even momentarily – relax her grip on the retractors. But the man never even paused. It reminded Ellen of one of those robots she'd seen during a tour of an automobile factory; the guide had pointed out how the robots never stopped, never needed a rest. They turned, moved back and forth, welded, screwed, hammered.

Brink cut, sewed, cauterized.

At last the ordeal was over. Brink finished stapling the abdomen, snapped off his latex gloves and removed the green operating room gown. He pulled the mask down over his chin and walked out.

Ellen helped the nurses move the patient off the table and onto a stretcher, then practically ran out of the OR to the bathroom. She was stopped at the door by one of the nurses.

"'Atta go, girl," the nurse said.

Ellen said nothing.

"Don't forget to take off those gloves before you leave."

Ellen fumbled to get them off.

"Why does anybody tolerate him?" Ellen asked as the nurse helped her pull off the green gown.

"Because he's such a damned good surgeon. Plain and simple, there's nobody who can do what he does."

Never had a bathroom looked so good. Emerging a few minutes later, her face washed with cold water, Ellen decided life might be worth living after all. She quickly pulled her hair back, but several wisps still stuck out over the forehead. The starch having quit the fight long ago, the jacket hung lifelessly, its pockets jammed with pens, stethoscopes, notecards and papers, and a small calculator.

Ellen looked at one of those scraps of paper, the one with her schedule on it. There were still a few routine hospital chores before she was done; then she'd head for the dressing room, take a shower, and try to feel like a human being again.

"Dr. White," a familiar voice called out behind her. She turned around to look at the surgeon. "We were all medical students once," he said, "but that's no excuse for incompetence."

Ellen began to say something, but Brink held up his hand.

"Come. I'm going to meet with the family. Maybe you'll learn something."

Ellen fell in step behind the surgeon, striding down the hall. Brink seemed fresh and clean, every hair in place, white coat immaculate, sharply creased. His black shoes looked newly polished.

The windowless OR waiting room was aglow in fluorescent yellow-green light, a selection of nondescript couches clumsily covering the tile floor, stacking plastic chairs filling unused spaces. A coffee pot on a small scratched table in the corner steamed away next to styrofoam cups, beneath a handwritten sign that said "Help Yourself."

Two people were seated in the waiting room, an older woman next to a younger man. Mother and son, they shared the same body form, each sitting hunched over, face drawn, flesh hanging over the jowls, their complexions matching the glow of the fluorescent lights. The almost dulled expressions on each face changed instantly to one of apprehension as Brink walked in.

"How is he?" the woman croaked out. She cleared her throat.

"He seems fine," Brink answered. "It was very difficult surgery, but it went as well as could be expected."

"Everyone said you are the best," the son said, looking up at the surgeon. Brink nodded.

"I had a lot of plumbing repairs, but so far...."

"Plumbing?" the wife interrupted, scrunching her forehead.

"Yes, you know, diverting the intestine."

"Oh," she said, "medical jargon."

"Any questions?"

"How long will he be in the hospital?"

"Not sure. Assuming he survives, probably ten days, maybe two weeks."

"He might not survive?" the son asked.

Brink sighed, opened his palms and shrugged.

"I did the best I could," he said, turning around to leave.

"Thank you for everything," the woman called out after him as he left.

Ellen followed him out, turning around briefly to look at the forlorn pair. How on earth could they thank this miserable SOB?

"They seem pretty upset," she ventured.

Brink shook his head. "Look," he said, "I'm just a human. If they wanted God to operate on him, they should've gone to church or hired a monk. But they hired me, so they got the best surgeon." He turned into the men's dressing room. "And they were damned lucky to find me."

"May I talk to them?" Ellen asked the disappearing figure.

"I really don't care," he answered. "You going to be a psychiatrist?" he said and left.

Ellen went back to the waiting room. The pair was still there, just where she'd left them moments earlier. They looked bewildered. Ellen sat down next to them.

"I helped at the operation," she said. "Dr. Brink was amazing. He's the best, you know." She fumbled for words.

The mother and son looked at her. At forty five, Ellen wore a settled patina of early middle age, the veneer coming with her years, not her experience.

She might not have paid her dues yet but age alone gave her credibility.

"You're a doctor too, aren't you?" the son asked.

Ellen looked down at her running shoes. "No," she laughed gently, looking back up, "just a medical student."

They spoke for a few minutes. Ellen might not have known much but she sure as hell knew more than these two people. They asked a host of questions she couldn't answer completely.

"Remember," she said at one point, "I'm still a medical student."

"Oh yes, of course. Well, it was wonderful of you to try and explain some things to us. And we're so pleased with Dr. Brink," the wife went on. "He's such a fine surgeon. And very nice. Don't you think?"

Very nice, Ellen repeated to herself as she walked out. Hmmph. He's a crude mean-spirited son of a bitch. It wouldn't have killed him to show a little humanity to these two frightened people.

Very nice. She kept hearing the woman's voice as she drove home. Very nice.

CHAPTER 4

Ellen leaned back in the leather chair. The study had always been her favorite room. When she and Jeff bought the house nearly twenty years ago, it was this room, more than any other, that sold them. Small but not tiny, a fireplace to one side, lots of bookshelves, real paneling - like some exclusive club; and it had taken less than a year for all the residual cigar smell to disappear.

Even with the deterioration of the house, much more pronounced since the divorce, this room had held up well.

Ellen rested her feet on the ottoman. This room was her sanctuary, her "secret garden," her place to run and hide. She poured herself sherry and watched the gleam of the light off the liquid.

The interview with Dr. Lorne Smith earlier in the day hadn't gone very well.

"I understand your reasons for wanting to transfer to another surgical preceptor," he'd told her, shuffling and reshuffling the papers on his desk, "but Dr. Brink is extremely well respected and has a great deal to teach."

"I agree he's very smart," Ellen had said. "But, as the head of the surgery teaching program, you must have had complaints before about his abusive behavior."

"I'd rather not discuss that. Look, Ms. White," he'd gone on, "you only have a bit more than three weeks left on this rotation. And, to be honest," Smith had lowered his voice, "I think Dr. Brink would be offended if I let a student change to a different preceptor."

"*He'd* be offended?" Ellen had said. "What about me?" She'd risen to her full height, then leaned forward over Smith's desk. Her face had reddened; even her golden hoop earrings seemed to redden. "I have to listen to him spew out misogynist nonsense. Did I tell you he suggested I should go back to washing pots and pans? And *rude* to the patients? I don't see how they can stand him?"

"He's probably the best surgeon in Washington."

"So that's how you judge a doctor? By his hands? Aren't physicians supposed to be compassionate and humane? Didn't I read something about that in the medical school catalogue?"

"Look," Smith had said, standing up to indicate that the interview was over, "everybody knows you're one of our best students; lesser students have survived Brink."

Lesser students have survived Brink. Ellen leaned back in her leather chair once again and closed her eyes. So that's how it is in the real world.

She took another sip of the sherry, and looked at the wooden clock on the shelf: *4:35.* Of course it always said 4:35. It hadn't worked properly in years; the last time Ellen tried to wind it, the wooden gears had grated and clunked. And so it was always 4:35 in the study, at least in spirit.

She glanced at her watch, less charming than the wooden clock with its small painting of Mt. Vernon, but certainly a lot more accurate. 8:00 p.m. She'd better read Brent's paper now.

She picked up the Civil War paper once again. Having gotten an excellent grade on it, Ellen was reading it now in her role as the proud mother, not the exorcising critic.

After the first page, her eyes wandered. She looked at the bookshelf to her left. A half-dozen books on flower arranging. How long ago had that been? Nine, ten years maybe. She'd taken an adult course at Montgomery College. Wasn't life so simple then? She'd wait for Jeff to come home at the end of the day. She'd help the kids with their homework, read to them, sing to them. Brent was five, Deb was ten. There was soccer practice on Tuesdays and Thursdays, softball on Mondays. She still could almost fit in her wedding gown then, and never needed makeup to hide anything. Jeff would tell Ellen he loved her "super extra much" when she laughed and her golden hoop earrings would jangle. And she laughed all the time, her face getting a pinkish flush, eyes sparkling. She was happy and she loved Jeff so much. And he loved her.

And Ellen was taking a course on flower arranging. Hmmph.

One more sip of sherry and she plunged back into the Civil War.

A moment later and Ellen looked up again. She'd walked with a bounce then, sometimes almost skipping, pleated skirts swirling about her. And once or twice, men had whistled at her; she'd pretended not to hear. But it sure had been nice.

And she still could almost fit in her wedding gown.

The Civil War, she told herself. Concentrate on the Civil War.

She glanced out the French doors into the living room, where the ancient Chickering grand piano in the corner was collecting dust. Nearly six feet long, the ebony frame sat atop three heavy Victorian legs with curlicues at their apices. Once, Deb had practiced vigorously. Mozart, Chopin, Joplin.

During crescendos, the sounding board sent the music to every corner of the house; during pianissimos, quiet liquid sounds barely reached the hallway.

And then she'd quit. Too hard, she'd said. All those years of scales and exercises, all that preparation – for what?

The Civil War. Pay attention to the Civil War. She looked at the typed sheets.

Brent wrote very well. He obviously had Jeff's talent for words. Jeff could write a brief or speak to a convention ex tempore without any apprehension, often with scarcely any preparation. A highly successful attorney, he was always in demand at dinner parties. Ellen had always gone as *Mrs.* Jeff White.

Now she was *Ellen* White, determined to make it on her own. No more flower arranging courses. She was going to be a physician, in spite of the Roland Brinks of the world.

The Civil War finished at last, it was time to learn about that thyroid operation tomorrow. She groaned lifting the massive surgery textbook and began to read, but only briefly. A look at the bookshelf: *4:35.* Was that a.m. or p.m.? And that book on the end of the shelf was very artsy, beautiful pictures of floral arrangements, but no practical information. The book next to it....

Light must be too dim, Ellen decided, hard to concentrate. She turned it up another click. That's better. Develop a subplatysmal flap, then identify the recurrent laryngeal nerve and isolate the parathyroids.

Damn! Not one word was going in. Wasn't there a Cliff's notes for this? Or a "Surgery for Dummies."

Try again. Develop a subplatysmal flap.

Perhaps a subplatysmal flap would have been more exciting two years ago, when she was a freshman. In her early forties, she'd looked around at all the kids who were her classmates. At first she'd even, probably unconsciously, tried to imitate them. She'd worn Reeboks to class, jeans that were just a bit too tight, and maybe walked with a little too much bounce. She'd even once tried to match her classmates' schedules – classes all day, study in the evening, then go out to "party" after midnight.

That lifestyle hadn't lasted long. "That's a cute idea, dressing like the kids," the wife of one of Ellen's professors had said at a Halloween party.

Slightly frumpy, Ellen thought as she closed her eyes, her finger still pointing to "subplatysmal flap." She'd changed her shoes and jeans, put on a few pounds, and couldn't stay out late even if she wanted to...except for those nights on the wards. But, she was more like the "kids" than she'd expected.

The toil of studying ....studying ....studying had worn them down too. Their clothes were perhaps more fashionable, but the eyes and cheeks sagged a bit, and there were a lot fewer beers and late nights...except for those interminable nights on the wards.

"Chickering & Sons" the ancient piano read atop the keyboard. Who was Chickering? Did Chickering's wife have a first name, or was she always introduced as "*Mrs.* Chickering?" Did she volunteer at church and take flower arranging courses?

Why wasn't it "Chickering & Daughters?"

Why had Deb quit, thrown in the towel, when it got too hard? How could she let Chickering's piano conquer her? Was it the scales? A weak left hand?

A failure of spirit?

Deb had banged her fists on the keyboard. "Chopin wins! Chickering wins! I quit!"

"You can't just quit!" Ellen had said.

"No? Watch me then," Deb had said, storming out.

Ellen opened her eyes, staring at the finger pointing to "subplatysmal flap."

"You okay?"

Ellen looked up. "Deb. I thought you'd be out late tonight."

Her daughter came over and gave her a kiss. If Brent looked like his mother, Deborah was a re-creation of her father. Thin, almost wiry, ears set close to her head, slightly curly hair.

"Save any lives today?" Deborah asked, sitting on the small desk chair.

Ellen shook her head. "No. Monkey work all day. I'm going to put this book under the pillow tonight to see if I can learn by osmosis. I'm sure not learning anything by reading." She slammed the book shut. "Too tired."

"We're proud of you," Deborah said, picking up a small empty vase, turning it over and over.

Ellen smiled. "Thanks. I wish I were proud of myself, but I have to listen to that scum of a preceptor. Not only does he hate women, he hates people. But all the muckety mucks defend him. Great hands, you know."

Deborah got up and stood in front of Ellen. "Mom, you've been moaning nonstop about this creep for two weeks. Why don't you just go in and tell him off. What are they going to do? Take away your stethoscope?" She sat down in the desk chair again.

"They could lower my grade."

"What do you care?" Deb asked, rolling her fingers on the side of the chair. "You don't want to be a surgeon anyway. Aren't you the person who told me to take a stand in high school when that teacher was harassing me?"

Ellen laughed. "I'll think about it," she said.

"No you won't," Deborah said, standing up again. "I recognize that patronizing put-off. But really, think about what I'm telling you."

Maybe she's right, Ellen thought, climbing the stairs a few minutes later, but now she was too tired to think about anything but the bed. She'd say goodnight to Brent, then be under the covers in five minutes. Never would a bed feel so good.

"Okay Mom," Brent said as she walked in. "Here's the stuff for my history exam. You read the questions on the left side and I'll give you the answers. Ready?"

She'd completely forgotten. "Let's go," she said, sitting down.

CHAPTER 5

Eight a.m. and Ellen was just finishing her morning rounds. She ran over to the OR to scrub for the thyroidectomy. At least Brink wouldn't be doing the case; this surgeon was much more genial.

A dumpy little guy with a five o'clock shadow somehow even visible through his mask, the surgeon was an affable fellow who tried to explain some of what was doing to Ellen.

He worked slowly, methodically, creating a subplatysmal flap, isolating the laryngeal nerve, dissecting the parathyroids free. But by comparison with the reviled Brink, his hands were slow, clumsy, stiff. Even Ellen could see that. Whom would she want to operate on her? The affable surgeon or the bristly SOB?

"Thanks for your help," the surgeon said to Ellen as he finished closing the wound. She took off the green gown, washed up, and got ready to see some of her patients. During the thyroidectomy, the whole atmosphere of the OR was much friendlier, much more relaxed and genial. Was it less sharp as well?

One of the junior surgical residents who had befriended her winked as she left the OR. Just a friendly gesture. Ellen straightened up slightly, her pace quickening. She took a fleeting look into a mirror on her left.

Ellen didn't much like looking in mirrors these days. But scooting by this time the glimpse was so brief that she didn't see the fuller face and the more ample hips. There was only the briefest flash of an image before the mirror had passed; the skin seemed younger, more supple, the hair more vibrant, the face softer, resonant. She was twenty five again.

Ellen stopped and looked again to her left. A gray wall looked back. She did nothing for a moment, then, taking a few steps back to the edge of the mirror, turned slowly and looked in a second time.

She stared for several moments, then moved on. The image was very much a forty-five year old. Hmmph.

A faint smile. It had been nice, ever so briefly, to be young again, or at least look that way. Her smile broadened. It *had* been nice.

And, it was nice to be winked at, even if the kid who did it was closer to Deb's age than her own. What would Deb say? Did she even know that older people found attention appealing, even if just a common wink. A wink tossed off and forgotten. Tossed off by a kid.

She passed a ladies room, went in, and took a real look in a mirror, bringing her face over the sink and peering closely. This time her reflection wasn't in such a mischievous mood. Ellen could see the slightly taut lines about her mouth, the hair a bit thin, the less elastic skin around the cheeks, and the ears sticking out in front of the ponytail.

Well.... maybe it wasn't so bad for an old lady.

Once Ellen got out to the hall again, she passed a clock on the wall, and immediately felt her pulse speed up. Closing her eyes for a second, she swallowed and took a deep breath. She'd procrastinated long enough. The time had come.

Ellen quickened her stride down the corridor to the elevator, then to the Surgery Department.

The time had come.

"I'd like to speak with you," Ellen said a few moments later, crossing the threshold to Roland Brink's tiny hospital office.

The surgeon didn't lift his eyes from the chart he was reading.

He pointed to a chair. "Sit down, Dr. White," he said, still not looking up.

Ellen pulled the chair out and seated herself. She looked around at the spartan room. Black pedestals, white desk top. White walls with a few diplomas. A spotlight on the ceiling. A window looking out onto the street, only barren tree trunks and branches visible in the bleak light. The lone color in the office was a small wooden car on the desk, beautifully carved, carefully lacquered, with a tiny plaque: "1937 Jaguar SS 100 Roadster."

Brink turned a page in the chart and continued reading.

Ellen felt her ears reddening, seeming to stick out further than ever, all the moreso because of her ponytail.

Brink continued to read. He picked up the phone and made a call, never acknowledging Ellen's presence.

"I'd like to speak with you," Ellen repeated when he hung up.

"So you've said. Twice. Speak."

"I find your manners appalling. I'm nearly as old as you are and I deserve your respect for that alone. I deserve your respect because I'm a medical student. I deserve your respect because I'm a human being. I'm tired of being treated like dirt by you."

Brink set his papers down and slowly looked up. The lips were pinched. His glassine blue eyes bore down on the student who was sitting upright in the chair, her shoulders straight. She didn't yield under his stare. She matched his demeanor.

"So," he said, "you don't approve of my doctoring?"

"That's right."

Brink continued to stare at this adversary, barely blinking, his face hardened to bronze.

"Is there anything else?" he asked.

"Yes," Ellen said. "I think your behavior towards women is inappropriate. Offensive."

Brink nodded. "And what else?"

For a moment, Ellen's composure faltered. "Isn't that enough?" she stumbled out.

"Thank you for your input," Brink said. He looked at his watch, then at Ellen.

"Dr. White," he said, "please close the door behind you on your way out."

CHAPTER 6

"There's the doorbell," Ellen said into the mouthpiece. "Gotta go."

"I hope everything's perfect," Jill said.

Ellen hung up. A flick of the right hand to push back an errant bit of hair, a look in the hallway mirror to be sure that the stickpin was in the right place. Then a deep breath, and off to the front door.

At first, Ellen hadn't known whether to be annoyed or excited when Jill had called her the night before.

"He's gorgeous," Jill had said.

"I thought you hadn't met him."

"Well, Rick said that he's..."

"Your husband? You trust his judgment in these things."

"Of course not, but I told him how important it was that he check this guy out carefully. After all, you're my best friend."

"And..."

"It's like I already told you. This guy was the most successful lawyer in their Denver office, and they've transferred him to Washington to handle some incredibly big case."

"You're sure he's not married?"

"Rick's secretary checked it out. I wouldn't trust Rick on this, but I *do* trust Connie. She told me he got a divorce recently."

"How long is he staying in Washington?"

"Nobody's sure, but apparently he might move here if things turn out well."

Ellen turned the door handle. A real live blind date, she thought. My first date in a very long time.

The man at the door was, well, gorgeous. He appeared to be nearing fifty, had wavy brown hair combed straight back, a strong jaw, broad shoulders. His winter coat unbuttoned, white scarf around the neck, he was wearing a blue blazer over a maroon sweater with gray trousers and tasseled loafers, the hands in his pockets.

"Ellen?" he said, taking out his right hand and extending it. "Dave Longacre." A broad smile showed off gleaming white teeth.

Ellen stood motionless, then slowly extended her hand.

"May I come in?" Dave asked. "It's cold out here."

35

"Oh yes, yes, of course," Ellen said quickly. "Please come in."

For a moment, she didn't move, then stepped back, tripping slightly on the edge of the foyer rug.

"Hi," said a voice, coming around the corner. "I'm Deborah, Ellen's daughter. Nice to meet you." She stuck her hand out. Dave returned her firm handshake.

"So what are you guys doing tonight?" Deborah asked.

Dave laughed. "Nice to meet you Deborah."

"Actually, everyone calls me Deb."

"Well, Deb, I thought I'd take your mother, Ellen that is, to an art gallery downtown to see an opening and meet the artist, then go out to dinner."

"Cool. Is that your BMW out there?"

Dave smiled and nodded yes.

"My dad used to have a Beemer, but after the divorce, he gave it up and...."

Ellen shot daggers at her.

"Excuse me Dave," she said, a sudden permanent smile on her face. "Say, Deb, would you come with me for a moment."

She pushed Deb down the hall, then turned back to Dave.

"Make yourself at home in the living room. I won't be a moment."

"Mom," Deb said when they were in the next room, "he's gorgeous!"

"Deb, would you please keep your big fat mouth shut. He's my date, not yours. This is my first date in a very long time. I don't want you to screw it up. Okay?"

"Sure," Deb said, giving a big wink.

"Kids sure are funny," Dave said as Ellen returned. "I have two teenagers of my own back in Denver. Always putting my foot in my mouth." He laughed, a deep gentle laugh.

"That's a beautiful piano," Dave said. "You play?"

Ellen shook her head from side to side.

"Here, let me get that for you," Dave said, coming over to hold the coat for Ellen.

"So we're going to an art show?"

"An opening actually," Dave said, opening the front door. "It's a long story, but the gallery owner's an old friend of mine who has a knack for really showing some of the better artists."

The quickening arctic wind, rushing recklessly from the blackness above, impaled the skin; even the moon looked chilled. Ellen pulled her coat around her, already regretting that she'd worn a skirt instead of pants. A shiver overwhelmed her briefly when she got into the still warm car.

"How long have you been in D.C.?" Ellen asked a little while later as they headed to the gallery. The BMW moved smoothly over the pavement.

"Only a few weeks."

"You drive like you've always lived here."

The BMW cornered at nearly full speed onto Canal Road. Through bare tree branches, lights from Virginia shone across the Potomac. Brilliant sparks of starlight on crystalline spheres came out of the blackness to pierce the bitterly cold wind.

Deftly avoiding the potholes, they arrived at the gallery on M Street in Georgetown. Dave drove up and waved to a man on the street who ran right over.

"Mr. Longacre?" he said. "Welcome to Hopewell Galleries. I'll take your car. Mr. Hopewell is looking forward to seeing you."

Dave got out and opened the door for Ellen. The shrill wind cut across M Street.

"I feel underdressed," Ellen said, looking at a very well dressed couple entering the gallery. "Nobody told me this was a fancy affair.'

Dave laughed. "Hardly," he said, but said no more.

Mr. Hopewell came out and introduced himself.

"It's too cold out here," he said. "Let's go inside. I have somebody I want you to meet."

A balding man with a partially trimmed beard approached them. He was wearing a cross-hatched brown and yellow flannel atop jeans held up by a rope belt. Looking down at his feet, Ellen was almost surprised to find him wearing shoes.

"This is Mike Regules, our artist," Dave said.

With Hopewell hovering over them, calling for drinks, Regules took Ellen and Dave on a brief tour of the show. Lines - up, down, sideways - in a variety of colors, but always with significant reds and whites, dominated his perfectly square canvasses.

"Mike's known for the very strong interplay of horizontal and vertical elements," Hopewell explained.

Ellen sipped her sherry, nodding her head up and down from time to time as Hopewell or Regules explained some feature. Sometimes Dave asked a question.

After a while, the artist and the host left to greet other art lovers. As studio began to fill up, it became harder to move around. A man serving hors d'oeuvres somehow slipped effortlessly among the guests.

"What do you think?" Dave asked over the background noise.

"It's very interesting," Ellen said raising her voice slightly, taking a bite of smoked salmon on black bread.

Dave laughed that gentle deep laugh again.

"No really, what do you think?"

Ellen finished swallowing the black bread.

"Actually, I didn't follow a word of what they said and I have no idea what I'm looking at," she said, coming closer to Dave to make herself heard. "This kind of art always makes me feel so stupid." She pointed to a painting on an adjacent wall and shook her head. Coming still closer to Dave, she dropped her voice, and tried to match Regules' cadence." 'Do you see how the green intersects the yellow while containing the red but not constricting it?' Or something like that. Now what on earth does that gobbledygook mean?"

The deep laugh again.

"Bravo for you," he said. "I don't like it either. Why don't we leave early and go to dinner."

Hopewell was terribly sorry they couldn't stay longer but understood completely that they had another commitment. The artist was off with some others, and Dave darted off to shake his hand and leave.

More guests were crowding in as Ellen and Dave walked out. A parking valet, mysteriously wearing only a very light green coat on the frigid night, ran off at their appearance; shortly after, the BMW appeared. Ellen wrapped her scarf one more time around. The sky was clear and cloudless and a bright three quarter moon shone cold on the streets of Georgetown. During the short ride, Ellen watched scattered pedestrians leaning into arctic gusts of wind.

The warm restaurant felt good when they got inside. An old crystal chandelier hung in the center of the high-ceilinged room and ersatz Argand lamps decorated red velvet walls. Chippendale chairs with red velvet seats were placed around tables with ball and claw feet just visible under linen tablecloths. Waiters in tuxedos stood quietly by. Hidden speakers overhead quietly played music from Don Giovanni.

"It looks like an old opera house," Ellen said.

The maitre d', in formal tie and tails, greeted Dave like an old friend and seated them at the best table in house. "Welcome to Le Opera," he said.

"May I make some suggestions?" Dave volunteered after they sat down.

"I can't possibly eat that much," Ellen protested as Dave ordered, but he waived her off. "Just a little of everything. The food here is so superb, you shouldn't miss any of it."

A bottle ("exquisite, and fortunately not too well known," the wine steward said) of champagne appeared.

"To my charming date," Dave said.

The meal was served quietly, unobtrusively, and soon the minutes passed into hours. Ellen was interested in learning about his children and appeared intrigued by his brief career in the minor leagues before he went to law school.

"And," he said, "you must tell me how such an enchanting lady goes to medical school."

Ellen told Dave how she'd thought about becoming a doctor when still in grade school, probably because of the admiration she had for her great uncle, an old-time GP. His stories about some of his most interesting patients hypnotized Ellen; the way he portrayed it, medicine was one genial experience after another. Although the great uncle died when Ellen was twelve, she carried the good feeling right through college. She'd actually started applying to medical school when she met Jeff, and she sacrificed her career to his.

"I got the house and some money after the divorce," Ellen said, looking down at the tablecloth. "You know, things. Stuff. But that didn't hold out much for the future, so without even really considering it very carefully, I decided to apply to medical school." She looked at Dave. "Or more correctly, my friend Jill sent away to a few medical schools for me, and even filled out parts of the applications. And the rest, as they say, is history."

Another sip of the champagne for Ellen and she looked at Dave across the flickering light of the candle on the table. She felt warm and content. For the first time in God-only-knew-how-long there was a sense of well-being.

"Even Roland Brink doesn't bother me now," she said softly.

"Who?"

"An unpleasant surgeon who bullies me around."

"A surgeon?"

"A toast," Ellen said, holding up her champagne, "to Dr. Brink. Because of his stellar example, I've been able to eliminate surgery as a possible future career."

Ellen looked at her watch.

"But I have to get up at 5:00 a.m. - only four hours from now - so I can start my morning surgery rounds with the beloved Dr. Brink." One final sip of the champagne. "I think we'd better go home now."

Clouds were moving in, periodically smudging the moonlight and blotting out the stars. The trip to Bethesda didn't take very long and soon the BMW pulled up to Ellen's house. The entire place was dark save for the front light.

"Thank you for a wonderful evening," Dave said as he escorted Ellen to the door. "I hope I may call you again."

Ellen opened the door, turned on the hall light, then shook Dave's hand, held it for a moment, and leaned over to give Dave a quick kiss on the cheek.

"Thank *you* so much," she said, then gave him a hug.

CHAPTER 7

The weather forecasters got this one just right. Coming up from the south, a mass of wet warm air slid over a mass of cold northern air, and freezing rain began to cover everything, a thick coating on streets, houses, electric lines, trees. Scattered power outages occurred as the lines fell under the weight of the frozen water; cars were damaged sliding off roads; tree limbs crashed into homes.

But Roland Brink started his rounds on time, and expected everyone else to follow suit. On days when he was operating, Brink started his morning rounds at 5:00 a.m. Snow, sleet, ice, hurricanes - it didn't matter. If a student appeared even five minutes late, he or she was excluded from rounds that day.

Brink always wore a freshly starched white coat on rounds, pants well creased, shoes freshly polished.

"Tomorrow I expect you to wear shoes, not boots," Brink said to one of the residents.

"Yes sir, it was just because of the weather today…"

"In the future, then, please leave a pair of shoes here."

The small entourage - Brink, three surgical residents, and three medical students - moved to the Surgical ICU. At 5 a.m. the Unit was tranquil. Nurses sat quietly at their stations outside the patients' rooms, getting up from time to time to put up a new IV solution or to turn a patient slightly to the side. The bellows of the respirators almost accentuated the stillness. The sharp jangle of a telephone briefly disrupted the solitude, but the conversation was quick and it was tranquil again. At this hour the prevailing inertia was that of quiet.

Brink stopped by the first room. The nurse quickly stood up and gave a report on the patient's condition. Following her synopsis, the residents spoke; they'd been by at 4 a.m. and added their comments.

"He should be ready to leave the ICU today," Brink said after the various presentations were finished. He walked into the room. The nurse turned on the overhead switch. A man in his late fifties lay quietly in bed, blinking as the sudden light unexpectedly streamed down. He had been disconnected from the respirator two days earlier and now only had small prongs in the nose delivering oxygen.

"Good morning," Brink said, "how are you?" The surgeon stood by the side of the bed, peering down at the patient.

The patient smiled. It was a weak smile but its intent was clear.

"Much better, thank you," he answered.

Brink leaned over and gently tapped on the abdomen, then listened to his belly with the stethoscope.

"I'm going to start you on some solid food today," the surgeon said. "You've made very rapid progress."

"Thanks to you," the patient answered.

Brink and the patient spoke for a few moments more. The surgeon began to leave.

"Mr. Morse, by the way," Brink said, turning back to the patient, "when the other surgeon did the initial surgery for the perforated colon, you didn't do very well, did you?"

Mr. Morse shook his head. "No," he said.

"Tell me, though," Brink said, "the previous surgeon: did he talk to you, more than I do?"

"Well," Morse drawled, "I suppose so."

"So you were pretty pleased with him then?"

Morse screwed up his face. "Hardly. He botched the surgery. You know that as well as I do."

"But, from all appearances, it looks like *I* didn't bungle it, wouldn't you say?"

"You bet," Morse said.

"And yet, Dr. White over here," Brink said, pointing to Ellen standing in the shadows, "thinks I don't talk to my patients enough."

Morse smiled. "For my money, I don't care. As long as you did a good job."

"Which I did," Brink said quietly, returning the smile.

The team walked across the room to another patient, an elderly woman who had a bile duct cancer. A very difficult tumor, it had been a long operation. It was still touch and go. If the patient survived the immediate post-op period, Brink felt she had a pretty good chance of making it.

The nurse gave an update. Brink studied all the data on the flow sheet, quizzed the nurse on every point, carefully examined the patient, then walked around the bed, checking all the respirator settings and the IVs.

"She's done better since you added more PEEP," the nurse said, pointing to the respirator.

Brink nodded. "Remind me again - when did you call me?"

"About 2 a.m."

Brink nodded again. "And please correct me if I'm wrong, but didn't I call back again at about 3 a.m. to see how she was doing?"

"Yes sir."

The surgeon checked the respirator tubing, then turned to the nurse. "Would you say I've been pretty conscientious about this patient?" Brink asked.

The nurse looked very surprised. "Well, of course, Dr. Brink."

"But I guess that all surgeons keep in such close touch with their patients after major surgery, don't they?"

"Well," the nurse said slowly, forehead wrinkled, "I would have to say no." She paused. "In fact, I would emphatically say 'no.'"

"Do I sometimes micro-manage everything?"

"Well...yes." She stopped. The room was silent except for the bellows of the respirator and a gurgling noise from the tubing.

"Do you think I treat my female patients differently from my male patients?" Brink asked.

"No, of course not."

"Oh," Brink said. "Well, Dr. White over here says I'm a misogynist. Do you think I have a double standard?"

"No sir," the nurse answered quietly, "I don't."

"Thank you so much for helping us out," Brink said. "Dr. White feels that I'm discriminatory. And she thinks I should talk to my patients more." He looked at the residents and the medical students.

"My job," he said, pointing to his chest with that long index finger, "is to help save lives; and when I can't do that, at least make it more comfortable. Dr. White thinks I should be like a psychiatrist. You know, lots of pills and talk."

Brink closed his eyes and rocked back on his heels for a moment. "Have you ever been on the psychiatry ward?" he asked one of the residents.

"Yes sir," she replied, "of course."

"Did you notice how the same patients kept showing up time and again. Talk and pills. But no results."

Brink began to walk out of the ICU, the entourage trailing, as he went on to continue his rounds on the general surgical wards.

"Talk and pills, Dr. White," he said, holding the door open for her and the rest of the group.

* * *

The group continued its rounds until 7:30, moving from ward to ward. Slowly the hospital woke up. The dark in the windows first turned to gray and then, as the sun rose, to pink and finally blue. Brief looks out the patients' rooms showed a world glittering from the ice covering everything. A bitterly cold north wind blew through gleaming dead oak leaves still hanging on to the tree branches. Heavily bundled maintenance workers in the parking lots threw salt on the pavement.

Brink always knew exactly how long to take with every patient; his rounds invariably ended on time, but never before. As soon as rounds were over, he'd head to the Operating Room suite and get ready for his 8:00 a.m. case.

After a curt nod to the medical students and residents, he turned to leave. After rounds, other surgeons might talk to the residents as they went down the hall, but Roland Brink always walked alone. It was still early in the day, but he felt enervated, more of that curious fatigue. Growing older, he reminded himself. His usual brisk gait was slightly slower today and he decided to take the elevator. Brink hated elevators, hated waiting for them, hated stopping at every floor, so he never took them. Except today.

Shaking his head slowly, he walked into the dressing room. Damn the aging process. Staying up all night, calling in, starting early rounds - those things had never bothered him before. But the past few weeks…

He sat down on the couch. For just a minute, he'd stretch out. Just a minute.

At 8:00, he was ready for the first case. Patiently, methodically, he finished his scrubbing, walked into the OR, checked on the patient, chatted briefly with the anesthesiologist, then began the surgery. A straight-forward splenectomy. If some surgeons went in slow motion, Brink went double time: he did his 33 rpm operations at 78 rpm. Cutting, cauterizing, sewing. The spleen came out quickly, neatly. First timers in the OR were always astounded by his skill; old timers took it as a matter of course. Roland Brink set the standard.

His next case was far more complex. An elderly man with a lot of intestinal scarring from a malignancy and radiation needed a variety of diversionary procedures to free up the viable intestine. If Brink failed, the man would need a permanent ileostomy, a pouch on his abdomen.

Brink reviewed the X-rays and CT scans before the procedure. He spoke with the scrub nurse and also discussed the case with the head OR nurse. There were certain precautions he wanted to take to ensure a successful result. He'd try to anticipate every possible problem so he'd be ready for any contingency.

Brink began his meticulous work. The intestinal adhesions proved even more stubborn than he'd expected. Carefully he dissected the scar tissue away from the surrounding fatty omentum. Carefully, deliberately.

He had expected the procedure would take about three hours, but as he reached the two hour mark, it was clear it would take a lot longer. He could feel an aching in his calves, extending up to the thighs. A slight wobbliness in the legs, a rubbery sensation.

What the hell was wrong with him? He'd never felt like this. Brink bent over the open abdomen. Cutting, cauterizing, sewing, ever so carefully, deliberately.

His back began to ache. A slight chill enveloped him. He stepped back for a moment and straightened his shoulders, taking a deep breath.

Carefully, deliberately. An artist in his studio, each brush stroke carefully planned. No errors.

The aching in the legs, the wobbling. The slight chill. The fatigue.

What the hell was wrong with him?

Carefully, deliberately. No place for sloppiness.

"May I have a stool please," he asked.

"A stool?"

"Yes. To sit down."

For a moment, the entire operating room came to a halt. Even the patient's heart seemed to pause for a few moments. Nobody breathed. Dr. Brink asking for a stool.

Brink sat down for a couple of minutes, his hands clasped in front. He could almost feel the fatigue ascending through his back, his neck, his arms, encompassing him.

He stood up, took a clamp, and continued the operation. He was so shaky he could hardly concentrate. All his energy was focused on the abdomen gaping in front of him. Every movement was an effort. Still, he pushed on, cutting, cauterizing, sewing. No room for error. Carefully, deliberately.

At last, as the surgery passed the four hour mark, Brink stapled the abdominal skin and walked out.

"Tell the family I'll be out in a few minutes to talk to them," he said to one of the nurses, taking off the OR gown and snapping off the gloves, pulling the mask down.

Brink headed to the doctor's lounge.

So, he thought, this must be that damned flu that's going around. I keep hearing about it from my colleagues and on the news at night. The evening news, with all the medical "updates." The opium of the people, filling the public full of useless medical information. As if they could understand any of it.

Still, this must be that damned flu.

But of course, he reflected, there's been no sore throat, no coughing. It's a strange kind of flu.

He sat down on the couch, then reached over for a cup of black coffee.

"I'll be over in about fifteen minutes," Brink said into the phone. His next two cases were simple hernia repairs scheduled for the outpatient surgical unit.

Just a short rest he thought, lifting his feet onto the sofa. Just a short rest. He closed his eyes and arched his neck back. It felt good to stretch out.

The deadening fatigue was still there, even as he lay quietly.

The telephone.

"Dr. Brink. This is Marilyn in the Surgi-Center. Will you be coming over soon? The patients are getting a bit anxious."

He looked at his watch. *Good God!* He'd slept for an hour on the couch. Nobody had disturbed him. He'd never slept through anything before.

He shook off the sleepiness, feeling rested, back to normal. Strange, whatever it was.

Brink walked briskly to the outpatient OR suite. He nodded at the nurses, then scrubbed for the surgery. The first one went easily. The second one was also uncomplicated, but by the end of that operation, the fatigue was beginning to creep in again. The wobbliness, the lack of stamina.

His afternoon rounds were very perfunctory. He ran into a couple of colleagues who spoke to him about a variety of medical concerns, but Brink found that all he could think of was finding a place to sit down, of going to sleep.

The surgeon tried to walk as briskly as usual on his way back to his office. It was a struggle but he'd do it. He lumbered up two flights of stairs. He wouldn't stop to rest. Roland Brink had the strength to keep going, even if others might stop.

There were messages galore in the office: call this one, speak to that one; schedule this case, see that consult.

"I must have the flu," he told Marcy. "Tell these people I'll call them tomorrow. Nothing serious."

A pause. "Are you alright?" Marcy asked, her eyes widening.

"Of course I'm alright, goddammit," Brink shouted back.

He got in the Porsche and headed onto Wisconsin Avenue. The ice on the street must have been an inch thick. The curbs were crammed with cars at various angles, some apparently abandoned by their owners. An empty pickup truck on M Street was almost 90° to the oncoming traffic, having slid all the way across the road.

Brink looked at the mess and shook his head. Somebody forgot to tell them to drive competently, he decided. If they don't know how to drive, they have no business out here.

Icicles, ubiquitous icicles - frozen monuments to a winter deity – hung off every surface. The Porsche slipped down the avenue, but Brink brought its errant ways under his control, going slowly when appropriate, turning the car into every spin, braking cautiously, skillfully. He easily avoided any problem.

Perhaps if the world had more people interested in being competent, Brink thought... Perhaps if the world had more Roland Brinks...

The night was brilliant, the stars frozen gleams in the heavens, their beams piercing the dark veil of the cloudless sky. Leafless trees swayed in the cold wind.

Brink headed over Chain Bridge and into McLean, his attention riveted on the glacial blacktop in front of him.

The Porsche skated into the circular driveway, turning slightly off the pavement onto the edge of the grass. Brink slid out of the car towards the front door, and fumbled with the keys. They dropped from his hands onto the glazed surface beneath, and the surgeon got down on hands and knees to feel for them. His hands were cold, his breath frozen. He felt stuck to the ice and only with great effort did he pull himself up. His right hand shook as he inserted the key into the lock.

Taking off his coat and shoes, he started to head to the basement, then, changing his mind, walked over to the bar. The Johnny Walker had never felt so good going down. Stretching out on the white couch to take a few more sips, he reached for the Washington Post and began to read the front page. A couple more swallows and he set the paper down.

He reached under the adjacent table and flipped a switch to the hidden computer tower. The small screen soon lit up, and several moments later, the chessboard appeared.

Brink had been thinking about his next move for the past three days. He reached over to the real chessboard and moved the bishop five diagonal spaces, then repeated the move on the computer screen. He pushed the 'Enter' button.

Several seconds later, the computer program responded, moving a knight from the back row.

Brink saved the change, then turned off the computer. He'd been considering his move for several days; the computer took several seconds.

He picked up the newspaper again, but after only a couple of minutes, set it down. Too tired to read. For now, he'd take a hot shower, then go to bed. He took one last look at the real chessboard. Each piece was in its assigned place, pawns in the struggle between Brink and the adversary hidden in the computer tower.

Brink got up.

Except for a little creaking of the floor under his feet and the sound of the forced hot air coming in through the duct work, the house was silent as he climbed the few stairs to his bedroom.

The hot water felt good – had it ever felt this good? – as it cascaded over him, but within a couple of minutes it had sapped his remaining vestige of strength. Great billows of steam over the top of the shower fogged up the bathroom. With enormous effort – more effort than he could ever remember – he washed himself.

When he reached the axilla – the armpit – and felt a stony hard mass, the size of a marble, all at once he knew. Now he knew why the fatigue – the overwhelming, overpowering fatigue. There was only one disease that gave a hard unforgiving mass like that.

But he didn't have the strength to deal with that now. All he could think of was the bed. He quickly finished the shower and dried off, then – alone in the large house in McLean – he put on his silk pajamas and stumbled into the bed. Never had the bed felt so good as he stretched out, pulled the covers up, and closed his eyes.

Tomorrow would be time enough to deal with the mass.

CHAPTER 8

The oblique rays of the late afternoon sun highlighted the dirt on the front windows of the Georgetown townhouse.

"Do you think he'll ask you out again?" Jill asked, as she got up, pulling the shade down to mute the glare.

Ellen shrugged her shoulders. "Don't know. I don't think I was a very exciting date. I'd been up most of the night before and kept yawning."

"But he seemed interested?"

Ellen looked at her closest friend. Jill hadn't aged as gracefully as Ellen; she'd put on a lot of weight and only wore big dresses without any middle, like decorated sackcloths. Even in the dead of winter, she always wore a sleeveless dress, and the flesh on her upper arms jiggled when she moved. Forever starting a diet, Jill had a basement full of unused exercise equipment, souvenirs of a thousand resolves.

Well, the covering might be different, but underneath it was the same. Jill, who still thought The Three Stooges were funny and who would give everything she owned to Ellen if she asked.

"I'm too old anyway," Ellen said.

"Too old? For what?"

"I have too many obligations to start thinking about a relationship. Medical school takes almost everything out of me and whatever I have left is for my kids, especially Brent. Deb's old enough to manage on her own, but Brent still needs a mother to check his homework, listen to his problems, just to be around."

"So, if Dave calls you up and asks you out…?"

Ellen laughed. "I'll say yes in an instant." She took a short breath and let it out slowly. "He seems very smart, well read, thoughtful. And it sure doesn't hurt that he's so attractive."

"And he's not married."

"He said he only recently got divorced, which is why it was easy to move to Washington. No strings."

Ellen closed her eyes. "It might be nice," she said quietly.

"Let me get you some tea," Jill said, walking into the kitchen. "A Christmas present, a new blend from Sri Lanka."

Ellen looked out the large picture window to the back yard. A chickadee nervously took a seed from the feeder, then flew off. Moments later, it reappeared - or was it another look-alike? Another fidgety beakful of seed and it zigzagged away.

Jill hadn't said anything about it, but Ellen had seen right away that the picture of the four of them – Jill, her husband Rick, Ellen, and Jeff, on vacation in the West Indies six or seven years ago – had been removed. In its place was a photo of Rick with a huge grin, almost hugging his new Mercedes sportscar. Ellen thought he looked more than just happy; he looked ecstatic.

Ecstatic like one of those unbelievably smiley guys posing next to some huge fish he'd just caught.

Ellen could hear Jill working with the teapot in the kitchen. She looked around at the old Georgetown home, with its ten foot ceilings, floor to ceiling windows, plaster crown moldings. The oak floor was warped in places, the oriental rugs sitting unevenly in the dining and living rooms. The overstuffed sofa and chairs seemed at variance with the general ambiance yet somehow seemed to fit in.

They'd all had such a good time in the West Indies. Jeff and Rick went off to play golf while Ellen and Jill either played tennis or swam. There was plenty of beer and plenty of food and they never stopped laughing.

A couple of years after that, Jeff got into some trouble at his law firm. Nothing really serious, nothing really damaging to his career, but an embarrassing problem. Ellen was upset by the whole business, but nothing in her relationship changed: Jeff was her husband and she'd be there for him. Ellen prepared all his favorites foods and even watched Sunday football games with him. She couldn't imagine it any other way; Jeff was the most important person in her life.

But Jeff seemed to change, becoming morose, uncommunicative.

And so, with Rick solidly entrenched in middle age, he traded his old car in for a new Mercedes. And in time, Jeff traded in Ellen for a younger woman. Hmmph.

Jill returned with the tea.

"Very good," Ellen muttered.

Jill leaned on her elbows on the dining room table and stared at her friend. Ellen took a few more sips, the steam fogging her glasses.

"Well," Jill said, "what is it?"

"What is what?"

Jill put her chin on her palms.

"It must be my recent date," Ellen said.

Jill said nothing.

"You think there's more?" Ellen asked.

Jill shrugged her shoulders.

Ellen looked out at the bird feeder again. Some kind of woodpecker had taken over and was making menacing pokes at the chickadee as it tried to grab a seed.

"I think I made a mistake going to medical school," Ellen said. "More and more, I don't think I'm suited to be a doctor."

Jill poured more tea.

"I've been watching the doctors around me," Ellen said, "and they just don't seem the way doctors used to be, or ought to be."

"Meaning?"

"When I was pregnant," Ellen said, "I remember getting a sense of warm fuzzies from my obstetrician. I just *knew* everything was okay because he said so. Even when I was in labor, just having my OB there made me feel so much better. He was a *doctor* – you know what I mean? Not just a technician. In fact, when Deb was born, I never even had a sonogram."

The woodpecker was gone. Some little reddish-brown bird she didn't recognize had taken up a brief residence at the feeder.

Ellen shook her head. "When I was working as a nursing assistant on the OB service last summer, the doctors barely even talked to the expectant mothers. The nurses said a few words, the doctor asked a couple of questions, then they did a sonogram."

"Weren't those clinic doctors?"

"Well, yes, but are those women entitled to any less humanity than the fancy folks?"

"No, I didn't mean it that way. I meant, is it possible that they were still in training and hadn't learned the 'people skills.'"

"I hope you're right, but I doubt it. Just look at Brink." She paused. "Brink," she said again softly.

"Aha, now we get to the bottom of the issue."

"What? Brink?"

Jill nodded.

"I'll tell you," Ellen said, "he's just an extraordinarily well trained technician. But he sure is no doctor."

"You'll be different."

"I hope you're right, but the process is so overwhelming, so dehumanizing, that I worry about myself too. A lot of med students started out with noble ideas and the process just crushes them. You study, study, study. Two and three a.m., memorizing where this nerve goes, how this protein is formed, why this germ does what it does. White coats, fancy medical jargon. And all the while, the patient lies in bed and wonders what the hell is going on. Most seem intimidated, afraid to ask questions, and when they do, all they get is a quick answer, a brush off."

"Can't you be different? You can only win one battle at a time."

"Maybe." Ellen looked away. "But this morning, I was talking to an elderly man who's dying from some type of liver disease." She turned back towards Jill. "Lying there in the fancy hospital bed with all the up and down and sideways buttons, he had this look in his eyes that was almost pleading with me to be his friend. I sat down and listened to his questions. I really wanted to answer them as best I could. At one point, he reached and grabbed my hand for a moment. Just then, my beeper went off and I had to leave to go to a conference. I excused myself before I'd really had a chance to talk to him." Ellen's face seemed to drop as she talked, almost sagging. Her hands, usually in constant staccato motion when she spoke, lay quietly at her sides.

"Up and down and sideways," she said again, "like a Three Stooges comedy, but with a real human being."

The bird feeder was empty.

"You know what?" Ellen said after a while. "When I went back after the conference to talk to him, he'd been taken downstairs for a CT scan. Hmmph."

"You can still go back."

"Of course, but I'm so busy myself. I still have a fifteen year old who needs me to accompany him to the mall to buy overpriced sneakers, and.... I've got all my other ward and educational commitments."

"And maybe Dave?"

"You said it, not me."

* * *

Ellen sat at the red light, trying not to look into every BMW that passed.

Trying not to think of Dave was like sitting in the corner not thinking of elephants.

She reached over and fiddled with the radio dial. Suddenly, the Chopin 'Revolutionary Etude' teemed out of the car radio, great scales heaving up and down, notes clattering from the speakers. Properly played, each note found its assigned spot, the artist's technique subordinated to the music even as it dominated it; but improperly played, the sounds would trip and stumble over each other – the orderly revolution became chaotic.

Ellen reached over to lower the volume. It had been this piece that had defeated Deb. She'd quit the piano, unwilling to continue the struggle for mastery. Too hard, she'd said. Too much effort.

And now the Chickering sat in the living room, more occupied with gathering dust than with Chopin.

Too hard. Too much effort.

CHAPTER 9

George Tucker scratched his head and looked at his daily schedule again, hoping that he'd misread it or that it had somehow miraculously changed. No such luck. He took a couple more gulps from his mug, then set it down in a clear space he'd made on his desk. Today he'd work harder not to spill the coffee.

Another killer day. He looked at the roster: McKenna, Wilson, Rosenberg, Stanford. Each of his first four patients had terminal cancer. Each one was different, each malignancy ravaging its unwilling host in a different way, each causing emotional and physical pain to the patient, the family. Each of them turned to George Tucker for support and comfort, for compassion. And for hope.

Each of these patients had come to him with the diagnosis of cancer. Each had heard about the brutalities of treatment - overwhelming nausea, hair loss, weight loss. Each knew they didn't want *that* kind of therapy. But in the end, each had submitted to it because it was all there was left. Only surgery and chemotherapy and radiation, and hope and prayer, stood between them and the other side.

Some had trusted completely in Dr. Tucker, casting their lots with him right from the start. Others had tried the alternative therapies, the "cures." They'd been through macrobiotic diets, camphor injections, megavitamins, herbal treatments.... the list went on and on.

But in the end, they turned back to the slightly stooped middle-aged oncologist with the thick black glasses, and the moustache that was almost centered; the man who could get lost going to his own house but never forgot the minutest detail of any patient's history. The man who, as a boy, was always the last one picked when the kids chose up sides, now was chosen first by his patients.

George Tucker was no Pollyanna; he offered them realism with hope. When the spiritualists and naturopaths had abandoned their patients to go off to "cure" others, Tucker was still there. He'd try to help them deal with their impending loss - the loss of life, their most precious gift. He'd help the family prepare for the future. He'd do his best, not always successfully, to try and make the patient's death comfortable. "Thank God he didn't suffer," the family would say at the funeral.

And, he would say to himself, thank God *she* didn't suffer either. My Cathy; thank God she went quickly. And that awful void, that overwhelming hollowness, would fill his chest. My beautiful Cathy, he'd repeat. How did I ever deserve one like you? And if the mourners at patients' funerals saw the tears in his eyes, they'd think it was for their loved one.

George Tucker saw these saddened people and his heart ached for them too.

Of course, there were also the successes. The colon cancers, the melanomas, the breast cancers, the prostate cancers. Some of these people were cured, others were in prolonged remission. After their emotional wrenchings and personal agonizing, they resumed their lives again, and the mundane once again assumed the dominant place in their lives. Instead of worrying about their next chemotherapy or the major surgery, or the loss of their lives, they worried again about repairing the storm windows or fixing the dent in the fender or deciding what to buy everyone for Christmas. These were the people George Tucker would pass in the mall or see at the supermarket; they'd come over to shake his hand and make some pleasantries. Sometimes they'd have their kids in tow, or their spouse. They'd smile and chat, then leave and get on with their lives.

But today, deep in the middle of the long temperate winter, the sun had not yet risen in the east. Tucker looked around on his cluttered desk. *The coffee had disappeared*!

His office was small. Although there were two chairs opposite the desk, they had papers and charts stacked on them. Books and magazines were stuffed sideways in the bookcases, and scraps of paper were taped to the wall, the lampshade - anywhere Tucker could find a spot.

The coffee was finally relocated under a chest Xray. It had been bitter at the start, now it was also cold. I've got to change the coffee filter, once and for all, Tucker reminded himself.

He looked at the schedule once again: McKenna, Wilson, Rosenberg, Stanford. All nearing the end. Would he have the strength to go through another day like this? Where was the separation from his patients? Why couldn't he see them, comfort them, and then forget them? Why couldn't he leave them behind?

And when they died, he knew their places would be taken by a new group of patients. New patients and families, just as frightened of the future as those who'd gone before.

More than once, he'd thought about quitting medicine altogether. Or maybe he'd go work for a pharmaceutical company. But in the end he knew he'd always stay a doctor. A healer - if not always physically, at least emotionally.

One more sip of the coffee; cold and bitter. He made a face. Got to get new filters. No excuses this time. He wrote down "coffee filters" on a scrap of paper and taped it to the side of the X-ray view box.

The oncologist began the daily task of filling out forms. Paperwork, paperwork, paperwork. He checked boxes, signed his name, checked more boxes, signed his name again, checked still more boxes. Forms, forms, forms. Like the Sorcerer's Apprentice, as soon as he finished one, two more would appear. He explained why this patient needed a commode, why that patient needed a handicapped access sticker, why a generic wasn't an appropriate substitution for another patient.

I really must have another cup of coffee he decided. He looked at the used filter, probably in its fourth or fifth incarnation. It just wouldn't do. Maybe under the sink.... He got down on hands and knees and rooted around in the cabinet. A tin of brown shoe polish, a spare can of shaving cream and a razor, an owner's manual for a television. How did *that* get in there? Better not throw it out; it must have been put there for a reason. Ah! A box of ancient Melitta Filters.

The filters were slightly dusty and large enough for a church picnic coffeepot, but there was real promise here. A few snips of the scissors and he had the solution. Now he'd have palatable coffee.

For a moment, as the small pot began to make chugging sounds, he sat in his desk chair, closed his eyes, and leaned back. At least until two years ago, he'd always had Cathy at the end of the day. Just coming home and being with her, even in the same room. The slightly dumpy, sagging middle-aged man, and his beautiful Cathy. She'd hug him, make him feel like it was all worthwhile. If he came home late...she'd be there. If he came home later.... there she was, waiting for him, smiling, hugging, loving him. The balm that helped soothe some of the daily agonies of taking care of the cancer patients. She'd always quiz him: what happened today? Did you see anybody interesting today? But George was emotionally spent. All he wanted was to be with her, giving her a hug, looking at the paper. Sometimes he'd sit quietly with her, reading his medical journals, until it was too late to stay up any longer.

And then she died. Just like that. He'd said goodbye to her in the morning, just like he had thousands of times before. Two hours later she ruptured a cerebral aneurysm. No warning. She was gone.

George had redoubled his efforts at work, taking on more and more responsibilities, looking for some other meaning in his life, life without his Cathy.

The coffee pot was steaming away. He stepped over the charts on the floor and poured himself another cup. George stared into the black liquid, its steam briefly fogging his glasses. For a moment, a brief second, Cathy seemed to be with him. Why, he had but to wipe off his glasses, look over and she'd be there, on the chair, reading.

He frowned as he took his first sip. Today he'd be spending part of the afternoon with his two medical students. What were their names anyhow? Tim and Tom? Stu and Sam? Biff and Boff? He couldn't remember. They'd see some of his patients with him, and do some preliminary evaluations on his hospital consultations.

What dolts. These were absolutely the two worst students he'd ever had.

All they could think of was leaving at 5 o'clock and getting out into the real world to make money.

No, 'dolts' wasn't the right word for it. They were actually quite bright, but they saw medicine strictly as a business, not a calling.

The sun crept over the top of a nearby building, its sharp rays momentarily blinding him. A change of the seat angle and he regained his eyes. Looking on the desk for a clear space, he set the half finished coffee down. It was near the right corner, he made a mental note.

George filled out some additional forms then decided to make some early morning calls. It was nearly 8:00 a.m., not too early.

"Mr. Vincent, this is Dr. Tucker returning your call from yesterday."

"Thanks so much for calling," Vincent said. "One of my friends read in an Italian publication about a T cell stimulant factor from a rare plant, which apparently has had fabulous results treating lung cancer patients. Some clinic in a small Italian town, I understand. I'm sure you're familiar with it."

"Actually," Tucker said slowly, "I'm not."

"Well, they treated twenty lung cancer patients with this material and apparently everyone got better. It sounds very promising. Don't you think my wife should try it?"

Tucker shook his head slowly. He wanted to tell Mr. Vincent about krebiozen and laetrile and other "miracle cures" that had come to naught. He wanted to "blow him off." Forget it, Mr. Vincent, it's rubbish.

But Mr. Vincent's wife was dying. How could he just tell him to forget it?

Fraudulent claim or no, the man was grasping at something. Anything.

"Mr. Vincent, I wish I could tell you I've heard of this material, but I haven't. But I have heard of dozens of other wonder cures that have come to nothing." He paused. "Believe me," he said, "I can understand your concerns. I wish there were something I could do to offer you more hope. But I'm very skeptical of this new miracle."

"But, couldn't you at least look into it for us?"

Like he'd looked into so many other cures and miracles. He'd already given so much to the Vincents, calling them at all hours, visiting them at home, speaking to relatives. And now they wanted him once more.

"You know, Dr. Tucker, I'd take her to Italy to get this treatment if you thought it might help her. I'm not a wealthy man, but I'd pay anything to fly her anywhere to get help."

"Of course you would," Tucker said. He'd seen their home in Silver Spring, a modest cape. They weren't affluent. Mr. Vincent would need all his resources to live on after his wife's death, but he was willing to impoverish his own future to go to Italy for the miracle cure: The T cell factor substance or whatever the hell it was called.

"Mr. Vincent," Tucker said. "I'll make a few calls and look into it. I'll get back to you tonight."

He'd call his researcher friend at the NIH tonight and see what he could learn.

"This is Dr. Tucker," he said to the next patient.

"My feet are still numb. Is there anything I can do?"

"You know, it's from the vincristine. Unfortunately, we see that in a lot of people who take it. How much does it bother you?"

"It's not too bad, but sometimes when I stand in high heels for a while, my feet really feel funny and I have to sit down."

Tucker's right hand homed in unerringly to an itch on his leg as he permitted himself a small smile. Last year, the calls were about life and death, the acute lymphocytic leukemia having taken over her bone marrow, her liver, her spleen. She was fighting serious bacterial and fungal infections, her mouth red and raw and too sore to swallow, getting food intravenously. More and more poisons were pumped into her, trying to kill the malevolent cells intent on destroying her. She'd been through hell.

And now she was worried about some numbness in the feet when she stood too long in high heels.

"I know how unpleasant that can be," he said. "It may talk another year to reach maximum improvement. How about trying a little Elavil; that can sometimes help."

"But that's for depression. I'm not depressed."

"In the dose I'm giving you, it's useful for nerve pain."

"You're sure you don't think it's all in my head?"

I saved your life, Tucker thought, brought you back from the dead, and now you question my motives?

"I promise you, it's for nerve pain. Have I ever been dishonest with you?"

"Oh no, I didn't mean it that way. It's just that...."

Tucker had no sooner effectively dealt with the itch on his leg when another appeared de novo on his forehead.

The oncologist finished up a few more calls, all the while watching the clock, waiting for his patients to start coming in: McKenna, Wilson, Rosenberg, Stanford.

He thought he heard a quiet knock on the waiting room door. He put down his papers and listened again. A series of knocks. He stood up, narrowly missing the half filled coffee cup on the right side of the desk, and headed to the waiting room.

Probably the first patient, arriving early. Tucker had forgotten to unlock the waiting room door when he came in. He leaned over a chair to reach the light switch, then opened the door.

"Roland," he said to the tall slim figure in front of him. "Come in. To what do I owe this honor?"

Roland Brink walked with the oncologist to his office. Tucker cleared a space for him on one of the chairs. Brink surveyed the small overcrowded office for a moment, then turned to Tucker.

"I've got cancer," Brink said quietly.

"Pardon?"

"I don't know what type," the surgeon said, "but I found an axillary lump last night, hard as stone. I've been feeling very weak recently and I assume it's from this malignancy."

Over the years, Tucker had used Brink for many surgical procedures, had spoken to him hundreds of times, seen him at meetings, even occasionally lunched with him, but as the oncologist looked across the desk at the surgeon's impassive face, he felt as if he'd just met him for the first time. The man on the other side was a stranger.

Tucker took out a sheet of paper and carefully wrote Brink's name across the top, then reached across the desk to get a manila folder, knocking over the almost empty coffee cup with his arm. He smiled weakly as he wiped up the few drops from the desk; he tried to erase the dark stain from the paper he'd just set out, then crumpled it up and started a fresh sheet, once again writing Brink's name across the top.

The surgeon watched, saying nothing.

At last the oncologist was ready, and began asking the surgeon a variety of questions; after a few minutes, he led him to a large examining room. Unlike his office, where patients seldom came, this room was neat. A small metal desk, bolted to the wall, was next to the door; two small wooden armchairs were adjacent. An examining table was against the opposite wall, a stethoscope hanging to its left. In a cabinet with a glass door were a variety of medicine bottles on one shelf, some pamphlets on a second, and assorted medical instruments on a third. A small screen in front of a dressing area completed the room. Several pictures that looked like refugees from a church bazaar sale graced the walls.

The surgeon got undressed and sat on the examining table. A brief examination confirmed that the mass was as hard as stone. Little doubt that it was malignant.

The oncologist looked at his new patient. Muscular, face and body taut, no hair out of place, quietly awaiting instructions. The picture of what a doctor should be: handsome, physically elegant, and − except for now on the examining table − immaculately dressed.

Cathy had never liked him.

"Put on your clothes and come back to my office."

Tucker briefly scribbled something on a piece of paper, then spent a moment trying to straighten up the office.

"We'll need a biopsy to start," Tucker said when Brink had come in and resumed his position on the chair. Flawlessly dressed with silk tie carefully knotted, gold Rolex on the left wrist, hair perfectly combed, the surgeon's demeanor was as impassive as his dress.

"After that," Tucker went on, "we'll get a CT scan of the abdomen." He took out an X-ray requisition form. "But, let's start with a few blood tests and a chest X-ray." He scrawled a few notes, then looked up. "Roland, I'm not sure what this is, but it might be a very difficult..."

Brink held up his hand. "George," he said, "I want to find out what it is and get it taken care of. If you can cure me, terrific. If not, do your best and I'll be a good patient."

Tucker unconsciously looked down at his somewhat bulging middle, the white shirt with buttons slightly straining, then brought his gaze back through his thick glasses at the patient. He resumed his writing.

"When can you get the biopsy?" Brink asked.

"Today, I guess. Whom do you like?"

A faint smile on the surgeon's lips.

"Marconi," he said. "He's as good as any."

"Except for you," Tucker heard himself saying.

"Except for me."

CHAPTER 10

Dr. Andrew Graham seemed to have a pleasant personality and way with people. At least that's what Ellen decided after her first afternoon rounds with him. And, Graham worked quickly; he only spent perhaps five to seven minutes with each patient, so rounds were over pretty quickly. Not like those interminable rounds with Brink. Of course, Brink probed and questioned and got to know the patients far better. And, Ellen grudgingly had to admit, although she detested him and his style, she learned a lot more from Brink. Overall though, what a relief to be away from that man.

Everybody had seemed surprised to show up on rounds that morning and be told - without any warning - that Dr. Brink would no longer be "on service." The medical students' consensus was that his intemperate behavior had finally caught up with him. Ellen was glad she'd spoken out.

Still, no one was really quite sure why Brink wouldn't be going around with them any longer.

But Ellen had another agenda, one far more personal and immediate. She looked at the watch. Eight hours to go....

It was so odd, feeling this way, like some high school girl waiting for a date. But Dave had called her last night and invited her to dinner. Ellen wanted to be cool, matter-of-fact. She wanted to be.... what was the word?.... mature. But here she was, waiting, looking at her watch, feeling her heart pounding a bit faster.

She hadn't the time to get her hair done up nicely, but she did get up especially early this morning to get it ready. Deb, who found the whole thing mildly amusing, agreed to help her with her makeup. After volunteering to lend her mother a dress, Ellen decided it was too short, that she didn't really have the legs to carry it off. Still it had been a tempting offer, but in the end Ellen decided to go with a slightly tired but still serviceable dress.

But that was still eight hours from now....

With her white coat down to her hips, stethoscope in the left hand pocket, a passel of pens, flashlights, and note cards in her breast pocket, Ellen felt like a *real doctor*. She had all the accoutrements of the profession; now all she lacked was the knowledge, skill, and experience.

The Chief Surgical Resident was doing the first OR case this morning, and Ellen would assist, in her perpetual role of retractor holder.

"Have you practiced your knots?" the Chief Resident asked.

Had she practiced her knots? Anywhere, anytime, anyplace....whenever no one else was looking, on door knobs, on newel posts, even on a small wooden dowel she kept in one of her pockets. Ellen practiced square knots, feeling like a hybrid between a boy scout and a neurosurgeon. Over, under, around, through.

"Yes, Dr. Thornton," Ellen laughed, flushing slightly. "I've practiced my knots."

"Good," the Chief Resident said. "And, please call me Amanda."

The case went smoothly, a simple ventral hernia repair. Ellen held retractors and got to try a few knots.

"Well done," Thornton said, bending over to staple the skin closed.

"I was thinking how clumsy I was," Ellen said.

Thornton winked. "Not as easy as the door knobs?"

"How did *you* know?"

The Chief Resident smiled. "I was a student not so long ago."

"Thanks for your help," Thornton said when they were finished. Ellen left the OR, walking a bit taller, smiling. She'd felt useful and appreciated. Even if Amanda's hands weren't as quick as Brink's, well....

No, she told herself, catching a frown. I don't have to deal with him any more. He's out of the picture.

And, looking at her watch, only six hours....

Ellen made the rounds to see her patients. Each seemed glad to see her, each in a different way. Some were serious, others affable, some slightly silly, some frightened, some confident. How fascinating to be a doctor and see all these different people.

Hard to believe only yesterday she'd been complaining to Jill. What was she thinking? Ellen was glad she'd decided on medicine. She, Ellen White, would be a 'healer.' Was that word too hackneyed?

"Sit down, dearie," said an elderly lady who had an oversized head covered with too much rouge and lipstick, after Ellen introduced herself.

Ellen did as she was told. The patient in the next bed reached up and pulled the curtain closed. The elderly lady looked Ellen over, frowning slightly on reaching the blue denim skirt.

"How are you feeling today?" Ellen asked the woman.

The old lady looked at the skirt again, then the lower legs. Ellen shifted a bit in the chair. Looking up, the patient surveyed the medical student's face, then tilted her head slightly. A large smile slowly deformed her lips upward, showing red lipstick stains on her yellowed teeth. Her forehead crinkled down, trying to meet up with the corners of her mouth, new wrinkles appearing across her nose.

"What did you do before you were a doctor?" the old lady asked.

"Medical student," Ellen corrected. "I was a mother and a wife. I used to volunteer at the church and sometimes at the library."

"You know, dearie, I used to work at the church. I did some secretarial work for the minister. Reverend Evans, he was my favorite, but Reverend Monfort was very nice too. I'd bring them their coffee and call the parishioners. What did you do?"

"I used to work with homeless women at a shelter supported by the church. Battered women, abused children. It was sometimes pretty trying."

"Things certainly have changed, dearie." The oversized smile again on the oversized head. "People are so violent these days. You can't pick up the paper without reading about these things. When I worked for the church, we didn't have this kind of problem. Men didn't beat up women back then, or at least not very often." She frowned. "It's terrible nowadays."

Ellen looked at her feet, then back at the old lady, who now produced a smile that tried to consume her face. Lips, red rouge, red and yellow teeth. Oversized head.

"Women didn't become doctors in those days," she went on through the smile. "They were home where they should be, with their husbands and children. A woman's place is in the home, don't you think? If more women were there, we wouldn't have so much violence."

The smile stayed as big as ever, but the old lady tilted her head forward, so that her crinkled eyes, crusted with rouge, were focused on Ellen.

"Women today just want to have affairs. Some of them get AIDS, you know, and they deserve it. They don't care. They just want to have a good time."

The old lady lifted her head up, the smile fading, chin jutting forward.

"Oh not you, of course, *dearie*. I'm sure *you're* different."

Ellen looked away, suddenly interested in the light fixture.

The old lady batted her eyelids, the smile returning, slowly… slowly expanding.

"I can remember what the Reverend Evans used to say about just this thing." She leaned forward, staring at Ellen, who, under the pressure of the gaze, brought her eyes over for a moment, then looked away again.

"One day," the old lady went on, "Reverend Evans came in, wagging his finger at me. That's how I knew he was going to say something important. Well, it was a lovely spring morning and, as I was saying, Reverend Evans wagged his finger and...."

Ellen stood up.

"I'm sure he was a fine man," she said, "but I really have to complete my rounds now."

"Please come back when you have more time," the old lady said, her voice trailing Ellen out the door. "Women are in such a hurry these days. When I was younger..."

Ellen went to the chart rack, suddenly realizing she hadn't examined the old lady, let alone ask her about her problems.

"She's a charmer," one of the nurses volunteered.

"Unredeemable," Ellen said. "I've just met her and I detest her already."

"Don't," the nurse said. "She's a sad old woman, sick and alone."

Ellen looked at the nurse, a tidy woman in her mid thirties. For a moment, the nurse looked back at her, then turned and began taking some medications out of a cabinet.

"Thanks," Ellen said. "There's more to being a doctor than tying surgical knots."

She looked at her watch. A little over four hours.

"See?" said her next patient, another older woman. "I got the pictures I promised. They're right here in the drawer."

The woman leaned over. Her room was filled with family pictures, get well cards, balloons. There were flowers everywhere - the window sill, the nightstand, even on the floor.

"These are yours?" Ellen held the pictures.

"My first grandchildren. Twins. Can you imagine!"

"They're beautiful," Ellen said, looking at the beaming grandmother's smile. "And I can see in their eyes - they're very smart."

"Of course," the grandmother said. "The pediatrician said they're far ahead of the usual children. They're bright, maybe even brilliant!"

Ellen nodded.

The older woman laughed. "Isn't that what a grandmother's supposed to say?"

Ellen smiled.

"Actually they're only six months old, and not even reading Tolstoy yet. But terrific at wetting diapers." She laughed again.

Ellen hugged her.

"Thanks," she said, her eye wetting a bit. "You're wonderful!"

"What did I do?" Grandma asked.

"Made me glad again that I've decided to become a doctor."

Ellen sang quietly to herself as she walked down the hall a few minutes later.

"Hey," an old man yelled out as she walked by his room.

Ellen stuck her head in. "Do you need something?"

"Yes," in a gravelly voice. "Change this bedpan for me."

"I'll get a nurse," she said softly, stepping away.

"Hey nursie," the gravelly voice yelled after her. "I thought I told you to change my bedpan."

Ellen kept on walking, suddenly remembering the old man with the liver disease, the one she'd never had enough time to talk to. She looked at her watch. Now, at last, there was time to speak with him, just to sit and talk. To hold his hand, as it were. No machines, no technology. To be a healer in the real sense of the word. She began to hum to herself again.

Her steps took her up two flights and across a bridge. She walked over to the man's room and looked in. Empty.

She went to the nursing station. "Where has Mr. Milton been transferred to?"

"Who?"

"The man in room 453."

"Oh him, "the secretary said. "He died this morning."

CHAPTER 11

For a fraction of a second, the man kept his hand on the handle without opening the door. Then he pushed it and walked in.

"I'm Dr. Brink," he announced to the receptionist.

The waiting room was empty. Brink sat down and picked up a magazine. Flipping through the pages without looking, he periodically gazed around the room. On the far wall was a rack with plastic slots, each filled with a pamphlet about a different kind of cancer. Support group information filled a nearby tabletop. The nondescript furnishings included chairs covered with a tweedy gray fabric and a steel gray rug. On one wall was a print of a mountain, on another a sailboat.

The telephone rang often, keeping the secretary busy. From time to time, a nurse appeared behind the desk.

An oldish woman walked out, supported by an equally elderly man. She blinked as a dart of cold winter sunlight hit her eyes through the one small window in the waiting room. Her pace was slow, each step carefully planned. She seemed to need the man's support, but still tried to make it on her own. The sallow face with wispy hair somehow seemed to echo the flesh hanging loosely off her thin frame. She continued her slow gait, even as the man hurried over to get her coat and hold it for her.

"Next Wednesday, same time?" the secretary said.

The couple nodded.

Brink continued scanning the magazine, scarcely looking up, hardly hearing the secretary's "have a nice day" as the elderly couple left.

"Coffee? Dr. Brink. Dr. Tucker's running a bit late."

Brink shook his head no, flipping the pages, one after another.

More telephone calls, more page turning. More patients coming out.

"Sorry to be so late Roland," Tucker said by way of greeting.

Brink waved him off. "No problem," he mumbled.

The surgeon followed the oncologist into his office. His desktop appeared less cluttered than it had been a few days before, but a new stack of X-rays had taken over one of the chairs. Tucker shuffled various papers around for a few moments, looking up once or twice at Brink. He knocked over a picture of Cathy, hurriedly setting it upright.

"Roland," he said at last, "I'm not quite sure how to approach this with you, but we've got trouble."

The surgeon sat quietly, not moving.

Tucker adjusted the knot on his tie, then flicked off some lint on the sleeve. He scratched his head. Taking a quick sip of coffee, he leaned forward over the desk, peering through the dark glasses. "You've got a lot of disease," he said slowly. "Far more than I had expected clinically."

Roland sat virtually motionless.

"You've got a diffuse large cell lymphoma."

"What does that mean in English? It's a long time since I was in medical school."

"Well, they weren't using that terminology when you were a student anyway. Basically, we divide the lymphomas into three types, low, medium, and high grade. We do a regular histologic analysis, then cell subtyping to see if they're B or T cells."

"And mine?"

"I pulled a few strings and got the guys at the Armed Forces Institute of Pathology to look at the lymph node slides quickly; and I showed them to a friend at the NIH. They both agree."

"That it's this..."

"Diffuse large cell lymphoma."

Roland nodded. "What does that mean for me?"

Tucker's eyes drifted off for a moment to a picture on the wall. A much younger version of the oncologist was standing with his arm around the waist of a young woman, in front of a swimming pool. They were laughing.

"It means," Tucker said, bringing his gaze back to the patient, "that the disease is pretty widespread. Not only in the axilla, where you found it, but in the last few days, you've had it in the inguinal nodes as well. The CT scan shows a lot of retroperitoneal disease and splenic and liver involvement." The oncologist stopped, leaned back for a second, then moved forward, taking another sip of coffee.

"The bone marrow also shows some disease," he went on, "which is a little unusual for this type of lymphoma."

"What are my chances?"

"Well, that depends on a lot of variables. Will you go into remission on the first course?; can you tolerate full doses of chemotherapy?; will you...."

Brink held up his hand.

"Please, George," he said, for the first time looking away from Tucker, if only for a fraction of a second. "Just tell me. What are my chances?"

The oncologist got up and walked over to a file cabinet. He rummaged around for a moment, then pulled out a reprint on "Lymphomas," setting it down in front of Brink. The surgeon watched Tucker's every moment, never looking down at the reprint.

"My chances, George?" he said again.

"I'd say 50-60% chance of a complete remission, and another 50% chance of a cure if you go into remission."

"Bottom line, then -- about a 25%-30% chance of a cure."

"Something like that. But I have to tell you, the pathologists thought there was something a little funny about the cellular histology. It may not be a clear-cut large cell lymphoma."

"Meaning?"

"Meaning that I'm not quite sure whether the usual odds apply to you. Maybe you'll do better. Or worse. I really can't tell."

For a moment, neither man said anything. Tucker looked around the room, then fixed his eyes on the telephone. It remained silent. Another piece of lint was flicked off his sleeve.

"Can I work during the therapy?" the surgeon asked, breaking the silence.

"Well, it's going to be pretty arduous. We've gotten more aggressive in the past few years, leading to slightly better survival, but with increased toxicity. So there may be times you may not feel like working."

"But if I feel up to it?"

"Yes. But, if your white count is very low, for example, I'd probably like to keep you away from sick patients who might have resistant organisms."

Roland nodded.

"I've spoken to a number of folks about you," Tucker said. "I think we'll start you on CHOP therapy with Bleomycin and maybe methotrexate."

"CHOP?"

"An acronym for cyclophosphamide, doxorubicin, vincristine, and prednisone."

"Doxorubicin? The stuff we used to call 'the red death' in medical school?"

George nodded.

"Let me tell you about how we'll administer the drug and what the side effects might be. With any luck, we can avoid a lot of the problems, but probably not all of them."

Roland leaned forward. "George, I came to see you because you are the best oncologist. I will leave everything up to you. The side effects? I'll deal with them when they come up. I have enough things to occupy me now without worrying about that. That's your job."

George leaned back and closed his eyes, tapping his fingers against one another.

"Roland, I have to be frank with you. I've known you for many years, but you're a very private person, so I don't know you very well. I need to tell you: you're going to get very sick with this therapy."

"I'm prepared for that."

"No, Roland, let me finish. You're not only going to be sick, but there will certainly be times when you won't be able to care for yourself very well. Do you have any family or friends who could help you?"

"No."

"You live alone?"

"Yes."

"You're not being very helpful."

"George, I'm the one with the lymphoma. You treat the cancer. I'll take care of myself."

"I don't really think you..."

"I do."

"Don't you have *any* family?"

The surgeon's blue eyes continued burning through the lenses.

"My mother lives in New Jersey and I have a brother in New York. I hardly keep up with them. We're pretty much estranged. They'll be of no use to me."

"Don't you at least want to tell your mother? Sometimes at times of illness...."

"No, but I appreciate your interest. Now tell me, when do we start?"

"Friday, if that's okay with you. I like to give therapy on Fridays because that way, you have the weekend to be sick."

"I have a case scheduled Friday morning. I'll come over after that."

"You probably won't feel much like working the rest of the day. Maybe you should take the whole day off."

"I'll start my rounds early to be sure I have everything in order."

"Do you feel strong enough to operate on Friday?"

"I wouldn't operate if I weren't competent to do so," Roland answered, lips barely moving.

George shook his head. "I've been doing this for well over twenty years and I've never seen a patient like you."

"Is that a compliment or an insult?"

"I'm not sure. I'll let you know Friday."

George got up and, coming around the desk, embraced the surgeon's hands, slowly shaking them up and down.

"I promise you, Roland," he said, "I'll do the very best I can." His voice was low, almost cracking.

"Of course you will," Brink said, his voice strong. "I'd expect nothing less."

CHAPTER 12

Snow swirled down Columbia Avenue, NW, and the walkers pulled the coats tighter around their necks. Everywhere shards of light sprang from windows and neon signs and streetlights, penetrating the early evening darkness. Although there had been scattered reports of crocuses in bloom, tonight, at least, it was still the north wind's domain, holding court, keeping the warmth at bay.

But the wind couldn't keep the warmth out of the hearts of the Lenten revelers, and couldn't temper the warmth inside each building. Adams-Morgan, heart of the immigrant community, was turning out this Mardi Gras night to celebrate.

Dave pushed the door open and Ellen walked in.

"Welcome to La Selva," the man at the counter said.

"This is one of my favorite Peruvian restaurants," Dave said after they were seated.

"But you've only been here for a few weeks, "Ellen said slipping her coat onto the back of the chair. "I've lived here for twenty years and you already know my town better than I do. How can that be?"

Dave winked.

"A pisco sour?" he asked.

"What?"

"It's the Peruvian national drink, a kind of cocktail made from a clear grape-liquor."

"Sure," Ellen said over the noise. The restaurant was filled, people talking, waiters running. Music was blaring from speakers, making it hard to hear some of the conversation.

Applause, and a band walked up to a makeshift stage. A man was holding some kind of woodwind instrument, and two others had guitars. One guitar looked pretty conventional, but the other was tiny. The man who had greeted them at the door jumped onto the stage and said something in Spanish that Ellen couldn't understand. Cheering. "And now," he followed in English, "I want to present 'Los Muchachos de las Montañas." More cheers.

"They're a group from the Andes Mountains, and these are special kinds of instruments they use," Dave said.

"What?" Ellen yelled.

Dave repeated it, bringing his mouth up to Ellen's ear. He held his face there for a few seconds after he finished speaking.

The Mountain Boys began to play their songs, the woodwind pipe blowing out an ethereal reedy melody, the big and little guitars accompanying, while the threesome sang.

Ellen took a sip of her pisco sour.

From time to time, the front door opened to allow new patrons in, bringing with it a reminder of the nearby winter as cold air poured into the restaurant.

"Close the door!" somebody would yell in English or Spanish, and soon the restaurant would warm up again. The warmth of the crowd helped the wheezy old heating system. Tables were crowded in everywhere, wooden affairs with simple straight-backed chairs. Some type of woven fabric covered each table, with candles in the middle of each. Waiters tried to weave between the tables, usually not meeting with much success. A crowd in the far corner under a poster of Macchu Pichu began to laugh.

The pisco sour felt good going down and suffused Ellen with a sense of warmth - internal warmth - and contentment. She was glad she'd bought new clothes for the occasion, even if had she practically driven the saleslady crazy this afternoon with her alteration demands. Her hair had never looked better - even Tony the hairdresser had stopped complaining about politics and taxes and his mother-in-law long enough to do Ellen's hair up right.

Ellen watched the Mountain Boys, but felt Dave's gaze, and turned to see him watching her.

"A toast to a beautiful lady," he said softly, and Ellen had no trouble hearing that over the crowd and the singing. The music mesmerized her, and she closed her eyes and leaned back slightly in the chair, feeling the warmth of the night, surrounded by the Andean music. She put her hand on the table. Dave put his hand on top of hers.

With Dave's assistance, she ordered dinner, but the pisco sour felt good and she was in no rush for the meal to come. She would try the ceviche, followed by rocoto relleno ("What's that?" Ellen asked. Dave shrugged).

A diminutive ancient lady walked in, paying no attention to the "Close the Door" cries. A scarf covered her head, and she carried a small armful of roses, winding her way among the tables. "Roses?" she asked each patron, never seeming disturbed by their lack of attention. "Roses?"

The crowd erupted with laughter as one of the guitarists yelled out something in Spanish. Someone in the audience shouted back and everyone started laughing and applauding – even the English speakers, having no idea what was going on, joined in the overall fracas, laughing and applauding

"A rose here," Dave called over the noise, giving the ancient woman two dollars as she walked by. She handed him the rose, nodded, and then left for other tables. "Roses?"

The Mountain Boys left the makeshift stage to get something to eat.

"How did you learn about this restaurant?" Ellen asked again.

Dave smiled. "When I used to come to Washington on business, I would come here with some of the other lawyers in my firm."

"Did you come often?"

"Once a month."

"What did your wife do when you were here?"

"Before my divorce?" Dave answered quickly.

Ellen nodded.

"She'd stay in Denver."

"Did she ever come here with you?"

Dave nodded. "Yes, a few times I think."

"Why did you get divorced?"

Dave looked up at the empty stage.

"We just couldn't agree on too many things," Dave said.

"Am I being too nosey?"

"Not at all." Dave raised his hand to signal the waiter. "Another pisco sour," he called out. "Sure is cold out there," he said. "These sours help keep out the cold."

The Mountain Boys were back on the stage again, and now they went to the tables to get the patrons to sing along.

The ceviche arrived.

"I've never tasted anything so good," Ellen said.

"The pisco sour stimulates the appetite, no?" Dave said, calling to the waiter for another round. One of the Mountain Boys came over to Dave and had him sing a short chorus of "The Saints Go Marching In."

"Very Peruvian," he laughed when he was done, clasping Ellen's hand tighter. The clock on the wall said 9:00, but it seemed as if the evening hadn't even started. The crowd was just beginning to get unwound from a long day at work, and was starting to really warm up to the evening. Ellen knew it'd be a long evening. She put her morning rounds out of her mind. That was a worry for another time.

God, how awful she'd feel when the alarm went off at 5:00. But, for now...

CHAPTER 13

"And how are we today?" the nurse asked.

Roland Brink looked up from the chair. "I wouldn't have the remotest idea how you are, but I'm fine, thank you."

There was a prolonged silence as the nurse looked around the room, everywhere it seemed but at the patient. After fumbling in a small drawer, she went to a closet, which was gone through carefully, taking out IV equipment and other medical supplies.

Brink sat upright in the chair-sofa, a renegade from the blood donor suite. A patch of black plastic tape covered a rip in the yellow vinyl fabric. The chemotherapy room itself was appointed with a dark brown rug and matching drapes, photos of mountain scenes, and a couple of standing lamps. On an end table was a small radio; a clock on the wall, the brass pendulum moving back and forth through a window that said 'Regulator,' quietly ticked the passage of time. The solitary window on one wall opened onto a vista of the Whitehurst Freeway atop Georgetown. Roland's eyes focused at some distant vanishing point on the horizon, the cars speeding well below his vision.

Following a request, Brink lay back in the chair. The nurse placed a tourniquet on the forearm, found a large vein, wiped the skin with alcohol, and inserted the intravenous catheter. Carefully she taped the plastic tip to a stabilizing arm board. Roland continued to look into the distance, never once watching the nurse.

After checking the tubing, the intravenous fluid began to run in. Wordlessly the nurse left the room. The surgeon closed his eyes and lay back on the chair. A song on the radio ended and the announcer came on with a few ads, then a plug for "Easy Listening Radio," followed by more music. Cars went through their paces on the Freeway below, but the surgeon didn't see them.

"Sorry to keep you so long," George Tucker said, walking in. He pulled up a chair and sat next to Brink, who rose to a sitting position. Tucker put out his hand, waving him back to the reclining position.

"Did you operate this morning?" he asked.

A thin smile briefly twitched across the surgeon's lips. "Yes," he said, "but it was only a gallbladder. Nothing too complicated."

"How're you feeling overall?"

A shrug. "Somewhat weak, but I took your advice and tried to eat more. Still, I think I've lost a few more pounds, but otherwise I feel okay."

"What are your plans for the weekend?"

"As per your orders, I'm going home and will rest. I'm a good patient."

"Scared?"

The surgeon pinched his lips together and closed his eyes for a few moments. In the distance was the faint roar of a jet in its final approach to National Airport, getting ready to scrape the waves before landing.

"Scared?" Brink answered. "It doesn't matter, does it? Being afraid isn't going to change my outcome one bit, so I'm not dwelling on it. I have every confidence that you'll do the appropriate worrying for me."

The airplane disappeared from view.

"I'm planning on giving you three courses of the chemo," Tucker said. "Today I'll give you the cyclophosphamide, daunomycin and vincristine intravenously. You'll take the prednisone pills at home for five days. In eight days, assuming everything all is okay, I'll have you come back for a shot of IV bleomycin. The most recent data suggest this may help eliminate some residual foci in the brain." Tucker looked out the window for a moment as another plane began its final descent. "You've got a lot of disease, Roland, and we need to be as aggressive as possible. I'm toying with the idea of perhaps giving you methotrexate in two weeks, but I'll check with a few folks at the NIH before I do that. Of course," he paused, "I'll also want your input."

"My input? George, I'm a surgeon. I wouldn't know how to give a qualified opinion, just like I wouldn't expect you to tell me how to do a diverting colostomy."

"I'm not sure they're the same things, Roland. I really believe patient input is important."

Roland gave his brief thin smile again. "How about if we agree to disagree on that," he said. "Part of the problem with medicine today is too many patients wanting too much information they're not equipped to deal with. They think they're entitled to participate in their care, getting multiple opinions, accessing information on the Internet. Can you imagine? These untrained amateurs are going to help *me* decide what to do for them." He sneered. "What bullshit."

"But it's their lives, Roland. Don't you think…"

"No I don't. If they want philosophy, I know this guy who can quote Plato. But if they want a good surgeon, they can come to me."

Tucker managed to shrug and scratch his head at the same time.

"And," Brink went on, "if they want a good oncologist, they can come to you. Just like I have."

"Okay," Tucker said. "Let's agree to disagree. But," he wagged his index finger, "if you ever need me Roland, I'll be here."

"Noted."

"Alright, my nurse will be in to give you the chemo. Would you like me to change the radio station and turn the lights down?"

Brink smiled, a real smile. "C'mon George, just give me the damned chemo."

Tucker laughed. "Please stick around for at least two hours afterwards. If you're okay, you can go home then, but remember – no driving."

"I remember. I'll take a cab."

"A *cab?* Nobody would drive you home?"

"I didn't ask anyone."

"Holy Christ!" Tucker said. "You are one stubborn S.O.B." He shook his head from side to side. "Look, *I* will drive you home."

Tucker went out, muttering.

The nurse came in, checked the IV, and rolled up Brink's sleeve a little further. She saw the tiny skull and crossbones tattoo on the upper arm, but said nothing. The Ativan and Zofran began to run in, trying to reduce the chemotherapy-induced nausea and vomiting.

"It'll take about fifteen minutes," she said, "then I'll give you the chemo. This combination helps prevent vomiting in most people."

The anti-emetics injected, the nurse left the room. Brink stared out the window, bringing his horizon down to the cars on the Whitehurst and looking out to the planes descending. He began to float slightly as the medicines carried out their assignment. The vinyl chair felt softer; the cars on the Whitehurst grew fuzzy; the distant airplanes left his focus entirely. The nurse came back and pulled a thin blanket up over her patient. From time to time, Brink opened his eyes long enough to look at the clock on the wall. The surgeon nodded in and out of sleep, the uncompromising pendulum steadily marking off fifteen minutes.

"This is the daunomycin," the nurse said, startling Roland who abruptly opened his eyes and shivered for a moment.

"I'll infuse it over five minutes," the nurse continued. "Please tell me if it causes any burning."

Brink nodded.

The nurse adjusted the rate of the IV, carefully measuring the drops against the second hand on her watch, never once looking at the clock on the wall. "You may feel some flushing of the face," she said, "and don't be surprised when your urine turns red for the next couple of days."

Brink tried keeping his eyes open to watch her draw up the medicine. After checking both the bottle and the syringe three times, she readjusted the IV and began the process of injection. Almost motionless, she slowly pushed the red liquid into the tubing, entirely by hand.

When it was finished she left. Roland dozed, occasionally opening his eyes to look around, but quickly fading out again.

The nurse returned a few minutes later, drawing up the cyclophosphamide with equal care, mixing it in about 150 cc. of a special diluent, then running the medication in over half an hour.

Finally, the vincristine was drawn up and administered by very rapid intravenous injection. It was about an hour in toto to give the three chemotherapeutic agents.

"Do you have your prescription for the prednisone?" she asked.

"Yes," Roland said, beginning to awaken a bit.

"You take 100 mg. daily for five days."

"Dr. Tucker already told me."

The nurse pulled the IV tubing out and took out a bandage with a picture of Snoopy on it. For a moment she looked at the it, then at the surgeon; she put Snoopy back in her pocket and took out a plain bandage instead, applying it over the former IV site.

"I'll see you next Saturday," she said, "for the bleomycin injection."

Brink nodded.

The nurse began to walk out, then as she reached the door, she turned around and looked at the figure lying on the recumbent chair.

"Good luck," she said softly, then left.

When George Tucker looked in one hour later, the surgeon seemed to be resting quietly, so he left him alone. He reappeared in thirty minutes.

"How are you, Roland?"

"A bit nauseated, but otherwise not too bad."

"Are you ready to leave?"

Brink nodded yes.

Tucker brought his Ford around to the front of the building, then ran inside to help the surgeon. Although unsteady, Brink clearly was working at walking straight and fast.

Traffic in Georgetown moved very slowly with Tucker dividing his time between grumbling about the incompetent drivers and fiddling with the radio station. In time, they reached the Key Bridge, headed over the Potomac, and into Virginia towards McLean. The sun was setting, its rays momentarily blinding Tucker. There was little conversation, except for Brink periodically giving directions.

The white concrete and glass house was dark. Tucker drove his car around to the front of the driveway.

"Can I come in and give you a hand?" Tucker asked.

"No thanks."

Brink got out of the car and started up the path to the front door, fumbling for the keys. Tucker waited until the key was actually in the lock.

The surgeon opened the front door, then looked at the driveway.

The oncologist was beginning to back out.

"Thank you George," Brink said quietly, followed by a staccato wave of the right hand.

CHAPTER 14

Seeing her reflection in a window, Ellen tried standing up straighter, but after a moment she slouched down again. Having been awake almost all night, it was just too much effort. She was slowly sinking towards the center of the earth, shoulders drooping, dulled eyelids pulled down, hair swinging aimlessly in front with each thick step. Her white coat, couture of the profession, its pockets filled as always with shreds of paper, lab slips, notebooks, pens, and the stethoscope, hung limply, its crisp whiteness and starched creases having long since yielded to the grime of the daily routines.

So, Ellen thought, this is medicine, the profession I chose for myself at midlife. Maybe a tabloid would take an interest in her story: "*Used Model To Save Lives*" the headline would yell.

Of course it hadn't always been so. When she lived in New York City and worked for a Madison Avenue ad agency – a disposable gopher with a Vassar degree – she'd had different plans for the future. A successful business career maybe. Until she'd met Jeff, that is, a young Columbia Law Student, socially awkward, poorly dressed, but full of spirit and ideas, with big plans for the future. They'd gone to the Metropolitan Museum, the opera, walked down Fifth Avenue peering into Tiffany's, eating ice cream at Rumplemeyer's, falling in love, and planning their life together. Jeff made law review, was offered a job in Washington, proposed to Ellen, and they moved to a small apartment on upper Connecticut Avenue populated by grandmotherly types and small dogs.

Washington was different from New York and Ellen couldn't get the kind of job she wanted, not yet anyway. She took a job in a jewelry store downtown, but knew it was just a matter of time until the right opportunity opened up. But not yet... Jeff was working 14 to 16 hours a day at the law firm, determined to make his mark, and Ellen waited for her chance. Then she got pregnant with Deb and five years later Brent, all the while Jeff worked harder, became a better dresser, traveled all over the U.S., made partner, earned more money. They moved into the suburbs to a big house, sent the kids to private schools. Ellen drove carpools to soccer, basketball, religious school. When she wasn't carting one or another child around, helping with math homework or term papers, or bugging Deb to practice Chopin or Bach on the Chickering, she worked with the homeless, helped at bookfairs, took jobs with the PTA, learned to arrange flowers. And all the while Ellen waited for Jeff, who'd told her he was getting ready to slow down, spend more time with her.

And she waited.

Going to medical school certainly wasn't in her plans, but when Jeff came home one night and announced he was moving out and wanted a divorce, it was Jill – who else? – who'd jumped in and told Ellen to get a life of her own.

"Used Model to Save Lives."

Ellen looked at her watch. Still two hours before the 8 o'clock case. She'd grab a cup of coffee and head to rounds. She straightened up, stood tall, showing her mettle to the center of the earth, fighting back – take *that*, Isaac Newton! Somehow she'd get through the day.

She'd get through the day. Tired. She was so tired all the time. Instead of dreaming about Caribbean cruises, parties with friends, and beautiful clothes, any available space in Ellen's brain was possessed by visions of hot showers, mattresses, and pillows.

After Dr. Graham hurried through obligatory morning rounds, Ellen went around with some of the residents, then scrubbed for the OR. The case was shorter than she'd expected and Ellen spent all her time holding retractors. The nondescript surgeon hardly spoke. When it was over, Ellen had learned nothing except, she told herself, that she certainly didn't want to be a surgeon. Arrogant unpleasant people like Brink, and vanilla wafers like this guy had cured her of ever wanting to use a scalpel.

She could have used the time better sleeping. There was no reason a bright woman had to hold retractors when somebody of lesser stature could've done the same thing. Ellen was too smart to... whoops! She stopped. Don't want to start sounding like Brink.

Still.... that bed would have....

"Going to the appendicitis lecture?" a fellow student interrupted her thoughts. Ellen had forgotten, but now dutifully lumbered to the lecture hall in a remote part of the hospital campus in an ancient building she'd never been in. After actually finding the lecture hall, she then spent most of her time in the darkened room either sleeping or dreaming about Dave. The ceviche had been wonderful and although she'd never quite figured out what the rocoto relleno was, with all that pisco sour in her, she didn't care. She and Dave had held hands; she'd felt soft, perhaps enticing, maybe even seductive?

The lecture continued. When she actually was awake, she kept checking her watch. Brent was taking his French exam right now; she was worried about him. His schoolwork was slipping, and she wasn't home enough to help out. Her son needed her. Should she drop out of medical school? What then?

Could Ellen be a quitter?

Would anybody notice if she ducked out early and went home to take a nap? A formal nap, a comfortable nap, that is. Not only was the prehistoric lecture hall seat a treasure trove of old springs, but there was an elephantine piece of dried bubble gum stuck to the seat in front of her and she kept hitting it with her knee. Leave early? After all, she wasn't exactly a kid and she *had* been up all night. Every sick patient in Washington, it seemed, had found their way to the Cleveland Park ER. Gunshot wounds, intestinal obstructions, red hot gallbladders, perforated ulcers, all landed in the ER, and Ellen got to meet every one. The clock ticked away the hours of the night, as Ellen took histories, started IVs, checked labs, discussed the case with the residents, called attending physicians, talked to families. And drank coffee and took Tylenol.

Ellen switched her lecture hall seat only to discover there was an unpublicized epidemic of seats with springs sticking out. No matter how she sat, each seat was uncomfortable. At last she pushed her notebook under her. After moving it a few times, she finally chanced on the most reasonable position.

Twisting left and right on the notebook on the chair, she sure didn't feel soft or enticing or seductive right now. She just felt uncomfortable.

At last the lecture was over and she headed to the surgical wards.

"Ellen, why don't you go home early. You were up all night."

Her benefactor was one of the Senior Surgical Residents, a man in his early thirties, who'd been there, done that. He knew how she felt. Except, of course, she was 45 and he was still almost a kid.

"Thanks," she said, wanting to give him a hug.

"Used Model Goes to Bed."

* * *

Ellen stood at the garage door for several seconds, listening.

Music from the Chickering. A Bach fugue.

It had to be Deb. She used to play this piece. Back then it moved smoothly, each note clearly articulated, each voice entering on time.

Now it stumbled along, hesitant, unsure. Deb hadn't been near the piano – hadn't even touched it – for several years.

As soon as Ellen opened the door, the Chickering fell silent. By the time Ellen reached the den, Deb was lying on the coach, reading a book. Ellen started to say something about the piano, then changed her mind. The two greeted each other and briefly spoke about several things.

Brent was home, wanting to talk to Ellen. She resisted the urge to ask how long Deb had been at the piano, and Brent volunteered nothing. Ellen did her best to pay attention as Brent reviewed all the day's school activities, classes, tests, teachers, hurts, intrigues. Sometimes she tuned out for a few moments, reliving her own teenage years through his stories. It was boy now, girl then, different towns, different friends – none of that mattered. The broad brush strokes were the same. At last Brent was finished. Ellen was proud of herself. She hadn't even nodded off once.

"Oh yeah, Mrs. Sorrel called," Brent said as Ellen headed upstairs to the bed. "Don't forget you're going to meet her for dinner."

Jill. Ellen *had* forgotten. She set the alarm clock for 6:00 p.m. and crawled under the covers. Never in the history of humanity had a bed felt so wonderful. And such good springs! I only hope I don't dream of retractors. Better to think about Dave. It had been a wonderful evening, even if it was cut short rather abruptly when Dave, looking at his watch, had abruptly ended the meal and driven Ellen home. "I almost forgot about an appointment," he'd said mysteriously. An appointment at 2 a.m.? It had certainly cut short the wonderful feeling but, well, it probably was legitimate. But Dave hadn't said anything about another date.

Ellen drifted off to sleep, trying to get some rest before meeting Jill for dinner, and trying to decide whether to dream about Dave.

* * *

"You look exhausted," Jill said. She was wearing a sleeveless blue sackcloth. Ellen had on a sweater over a turtleneck.

"How's Rick?" Ellen asked, peering over the top of her teacup. "I haven't seen him in a while."

"You're changing the subject," Jill said, "but he's fine, and still doing God's work."

Ellen lifted an eyebrow. "God's work?"

"Yes, he's still litigating for all those affluent rogues who want more. And to show he has a good soul, he sometimes does it on a contingency basis."

Ellen laughed.

"Oh, you *do* know how to laugh," Jill said.

Ellen sighed. "It hasn't been easy lately." She broke off the end of the croissant, then buttered it carefully. She stirred the tea slowly and squeezed in a few drops of lemon, squirting herself in the face. From the CD player, Dave Brubeck seemed to soften everything.

"I never pretended to understand men," Ellen said, "but I always found them, how shall I put it, agreeable to be around."

"Dave?"

"Yes. The more I think about it, the stranger it seems. At first, I had such a wonderful evening, I figured it was just a fluke. But now it's three days and I haven't heard a word."

"You really like this guy."

"He's so charming and seems so genuine, so courtly, almost old-world, that I almost allowed myself to dream. I felt so alive for the first time in...I can't remember. And then he dropped me. Poof! I had no plans for anything enduring, you know, but it was nice while it lasted. Hmmph."

"Hey. It's not over. He's probably real busy but I bet you hear from him soon."

"Maybe. I just think I don't understand men. Did you know I just learned my former husband is living in Virginia with a woman fifteen years his junior. And then there's that misfit surgeon, Brink, who insults and abuses me, holds me up to ridicule, treats me like dirt."

"Hey again. That's should all be past tense."

"Alright then, he treated me like *dirt*." She practically spat the word out, this time accompanied by a full blown sneer.

"Look," Jill said, "you're too busy wallowing in self-pity to see how successful you are. Take the long view. You're at the top of your medical school class. You can't help but succeed."

Ellen looked away from her friend, tracing the outlines of a picture on the wall with her eyes. Can't help but succeed?

"And," Jill said, "you must be very proud of how Brent is turning out."

"Brent? I've let him down. He... no, don't shush me, Jill. I haven't been there for my own kid. I can't make up for Jeff's absence – Brent spends one day every other weekend with his father and that's all. They do 'men stuff,' going bowling, to ballgames, but not the day-to-day interactions that really matter. And I'm not picking up that slack."

She tapped the tabletop a few times slowly with a half-open fist. "Jeff White & Son," she said. Then, "I wonder if Chickering went bowling with his Sons."

"What?"

Ellen shook her head. "I heard Deb playing the piano," she said.

"I'd guessed she would."

"How could you ....?"

Jill smiled. "Deb was over here last week and we got to talking. She told me she really missed the piano, that a part of her was tied up in the instrument." Jill sipped the tea, then reached over and poured some milk into the cup. "Deb feels like she let herself down when she stopped playing."

Ellen nodded. "I've always had the sense she felt like a quitter. It got too hard and, rather than working harder, she gave up." She finished the last swallow of tea. "Deb's goals were unrealistic. She didn't have to be another Liszt."

The telephone rang and Jill picked it up in the next room, returning in a minute with a message.

"That was Brent. Somebody from your surgery team wants you to call them."

Ellen squeezed her lips together and frowned. She picked up the phone and called the number, listening carefully and nodding. She hung up.

Wordlessly she sat down at the table, the lines in her face deepening by the moment, the eyes narrowing, nostrils flaring. The color fled her face, even as the veins on her forehead were purpling more, neck muscles straining.

The jaw was clenched. She reached over and, picking up the salt shaker, squeezed it and got ready to hurl it at the wall.

"Damn!" she spat out quietly. Then, "Damn!" in a loud voice, almost a scream. "Damn, damn, damn!" Her forearm quivering, she set the salt shaker down. "Why me? What did I do to deserve this?"

"What happened?" Jill asked..

"They want me to come in to scrub on a case. There are a ton of emergencies and they need bodies. Didn't I pay my dues last night?" She banged the table with her fist. "Jill," she said, suddenly sobbing. "I'm so tired. I worked all night. All night, do you understand, so I could become a doctor. And for what?" Another crash of her fist on the table. "So I could ignore my child, be disappointed by my recent date, scorned by a misogynist surgeon, thrown away like so much garbage by a faithless husband. Jill, I'm so tired of it all." Her sobs increased as she put her head down on her folded arms across the table. "So tired."

Jill came over and put her arms around her friend, saying nothing.

Ellen whimpered quietly. After a minute she lifted her head from her arms and looked out the window into the darkness, eyes focused blankly. She dabbed a few tears on her cheeks, then her eyes. "Well," she said, hugging her friend back, "next time I won't tell them how to find me." She wiped the eyes again. "I don't have to go in for another fifteen minutes, so maybe we can finish our little party."

Ellen laughed. "Our party," she repeated.

"When do you finish the surgery rotation?" Jill asked.

"Next week."

"What're you taking next? Maybe you'll have more time for Brent once you get away from all those surgeons."

Ellen sniffled and took a bite of her croissant. "I hope you're right," she said. "I hope there'll be more time on my next rotation. I'm doing an elective in oncology."

"Cancer patients? That should be cheery, really help improve your mood."

"I took oncology because everybody says I'll learn a lot from the preceptor, who's supposed to be a terrific teacher. Guy named George Tucker."

"Maybe he'll restore some of your faith in doctors," Jill said, pouring more tea into Ellen's cup. "And men."

CHAPTER 15

Roland Brink got up at 4:30 a.m. He showered and shaved like always. Even though he'd decided to give up the teaching rounds – at least not this month or until he was medically more stable – he still planned on carrying on as usual. He was, after all, Roland Brink. The weekend of enforced inactivity had been too much, so he'd gone in yesterday, Sunday, to make rounds on his patients.

He had a full day scheduled. Rounds in the early morning, surgery until early afternoon, then office hours. At some point he'd have to slow down, at least temporarily, as the chemotherapy began to "do its thing," but for now he would keep right on going. He'd never had any patience for those people who gave in so readily to illness.

Brink swung the Porsche out of the driveway onto the dark road, passing houses with their lights off but alarm signals visible in the doorways, and turned on the radio. After the third impossibly-cheery ad, Brink changed the station, just in time to pick up more ads.

No, Roland Brink decided as he silenced the radio, I'm more than just a fighter, I'm a realist. I have little use for those who used illness as an excuse to avoid life's responsibilities. Courage? Hardly. I'm just doing what everybody should do.

The Porsche crossed the Potomac. It was still dark; scattered car headlights gleamed through tree silhouettes off M Street. A cold northwest wind, unusually bitter for early March, stirred up choppy wavelets just visible in the light at the boathouse dock. In the distance the Washington Monument was brilliantly singled out from the surrounding black. The Porsche turned into Georgetown, its streets empty at this hour, except for a few homeless people hidden under blankets in doorways.

As usual, Brink was the first doctor in the parking lot. The brittle wind pierced him as he walked to the doctor's lobby. And, as usual, he wasn't wearing an overcoat.

After a quick cup of coffee, he headed to the wards. He walked up the stairs although it began to get very difficult by the fourth floor. Making a fist and sweating slightly, he put one foot after the other and continued up to the sixth floor. Short of breath, he kept going.

Roland Brink knew he had more than fortitude; he had character.

With only a couple of patients in the hospital, rounds were over more quickly than usual, so he went to the doctor's lounge and leafed through a couple of surgical journals.

A second cup of coffee would taste good – extra strong.

As eight o'clock approached he began his walk to the Operating Room. The first case was pretty routine – a splenectomy in a lady with a clotting disorder. Then there was a case he'd do jointly with a gynecologist, an ovarian cancer with lots of bowel adhesions. Finally, tumor debulking of a sarcoma of the leg – tedious but simple enough.

Scrubbing at the sink outside OR Room #1, he reviewed the details of the first case. He'd need to be very careful, not only to get the spleen out but to look for accessory splenic tissue.

The case went quickly... fast even for Roland Brink.

He was just as glad, he decided, since he felt just a bit nauseated and had some leg muscle fatigue. A few minutes rest would help.

Brink readied himself for the second case. He'd be working with Bob Lansing, the Chief of Gynecologic Oncology. Competent enough, he supposed, but still a gynecologist, not really trained in the finer subtleties of surgery. These gynecologists all lived under the delusion that they were surgeons. Brink would keep an eye out, all the while he was freeing up some of the bowel from the ovarian cancer.

Lansing was standing over the patient's draped abdomen, saying something to one of the nurses. Everyone laughed, but the laughter stopped abruptly as Brink entered the room. The surgeon took his place opposite the gynecologist, surveying the operating room with a slow left to right movement of the head.

The gynecologist made the initial incision. Thick tumor covered the exposed peritoneum, but Lansing moved to the pelvis to mobilize and then remove the uterus and ovaries. One normal ovary was easily removed, but the diseased malignant ovary had grown into the surrounding tissue, far from its normal hegemonic domain, choking and strangling everything in its reach. Brink watched over the top of his mask, hands folded in front of him. The mechanical sound of the respirator's bellows cut through the electric hum of the spotlight.

Having removed the ovary as best he could, Lansing pulled his hands back and said something quietly to Brink. The surgeon bent his head slightly forward and began his part. The tumoriferous omentum was mobilized and the bowel rotated up and away, revealing a large mass of matted tumor. As

Brink began to cut, he was so skillful that, although Lansing typically would have helped other surgeons at this point, in this instance the gynecologist simply observed. Brink's hand were everywhere at once. Lansing stood quietly, watching. The anesthesiologist at the head of the table, separated from the open wound by a green cloth, seemed to nod off, suddenly awakening every few minutes to check the vital signs and scribble a few notes on a clipboard.

At first, Brink thought he must have pulled a muscle in his back. The twinge wasn't very noticeable and the surgeon shifted his weight a bit. Things seemed to get better. For about two minutes.

The twinge got stronger and he could feel it becoming more intense, now spreading down his back, now coming around to the side. It throbbed slightly, but kept growing, becoming stronger.

Brink shifted from left to right, trying to straighten up. With each wave of pain, his forehead began to bead up with more sweat. The surgeon felt his pulse speeding up, and he began to breathe more rapidly.

He leaned over the open abdomen and continued to cauterize, to cut, to mobilize intestine.

The pain continued to grow.

Brink cut and cauterized faster.

His pulse got faster, the breathing shallower. Never before had the surgeon noticed how hot the overhead lights were. The sweat beaded up faster on his forehead, prickling under his gown, dripping down his chest.

And the pain grew.

"Are you alright Roland?" the gynecologist asked.

"Of course I am," he snapped.

Faster, faster, he cut.

And then it happened. He hit an artery and blood began to spurt up out of the abdomen, onto Roland's gown, onto the gynecologist's gown, onto the floor.

Roland Brink never cut arteries by mistake.

The blood squirted and pumped, and it was impossible to see where the cut had been made; the operating field was too bloody.

Brink bent over to his left. Anything to try and relieve the pain. He reached into the abdomen to find the pumper. His hands almost flailing, he pushed bowel to the left and the right to find the artery. No longer able to stand erect, he leaned over the abdomen hunting desperately for the vessel.

All at once, the artery stopped bleeding, and the suction quickly cleared the blood. The gynecologist had found the bleeder and clamped it off.

"I don't feel well," Brink said, gasping. "You close up."

He walked out of the OR, leaning forward and to his left. A nurse helped him remove the bloodied gown. All the OR personnel stopped what they were doing and watched him. A patient on a stretcher passing through squinted at the surgeon. One of the nurses ran over to prop him up.

"Can I help you, Dr. Brink?"

The surgeon wriggled free. "No," he said hoarsely, "I'm fine."

He walked over to the doctor's lounge and lay down on the couch for a moment. The pain was beginning to move around the side towards the front.

Another surgeon came over to offer assistance.

"I'm fine," Brink said, but the other surgeon was not so easily put off. A wheelchair appeared and Brink was rolled towards the Emergency Room. One corridor lead to another, then to an elevator. Brink sat hunched over in the wheelchair, the small entourage watching as the elevator lights ticked off the floors.

Arriving in the ER, curled into the fetal position, pallid, sweating, breathing rapidly, Brink barely felt them start the IV, hardly felt the needle withdrawing blood, didn't even note the EKG monitor beeping, didn't hear the nurse washing her hands. He was so focused on the intense pain, he didn't see the entire ER staff peering in behind the curtain, talking quietly among themselves and pointing at him. Moaning softly he didn't even realize the nurse was giving him an injection of Demerol.

The pain began to move down towards the groin and, under the influence of the narcotic, went from agonizing to merely severe. Sweat still poured off his forehead, and dribbled down his chest, mixing with the blood on his green OR suit. Brink remained in his curled up attitude, except once to cast a glance at the crowds by the curtain. One look from the surgeon and they dispersed. A nurse wiped off his forehead and gave additional Demerol.

And then, all at once, the kidney stone passed from the ureter into the bladder. The intense pain stopped. It didn't just slowly melt away, it disappeared. Brink suddenly could feel the powerful numbing effect of the narcotic, now no longer occupied with deadening the pain.

He fell asleep.

"You better?" George Tucker asked about an hour later when he arrived.

Brink opened his eyes and nodded weakly.

"Are you alert enough to understand me?"

Another nod, this time with his eyes closed.

"You have a lot of lymphoma, and that chemo really killed off a huge mass of tumor. So, even with you on the allopurinol, the load must have been too great and all that extra uric acid from the dying tumor precipitated in the kidney. Your first kidney stone. Do you understand?"

But Brink was snoring now. A nurse came over and first adjusted the rate of the IV, then the knot on Tucker's tie.

"The back piece of the tie really shouldn't be lower than the front part," she said, smiling.

'Thanks," the oncologist said. "You know, I really should've used a mirror when I tied it this morning."

"And every other morning too," she said, but too low for Tucker to hear. She smiled again, then leaned over and adjusted the collar on his white coat.

Tucker examined his patient again, then shook his head. "I can't believe he tried to operate today," Tucker said, leaving the ER cubicle. He'd call a urologist to see his patient, but for now, at last, Tucker would lay down the law: no heroics. No work, period, until things had stabilized.

"He can go home when he's fully awake," Tucker said to the head nurse as he walked out, shaking his head. "That's one tough dude."

The nurse muttered something back which Tucker didn't catch. From the tone of her voice, he decided it was just as well.

CHAPTER 16

"Fired," George Tucker said. "I've been fired."

Ellen White stood at the open door, briefly surveying the oncologist's office. The desk was stacked higher than usual with papers, charts, journals, X-ray folders.

"Pardon me?" Ellen said.

Tucker was staring at a letter. He turned it over, then looked in the now-empty envelope. He closed his eyes and slowly shook his head back and forth.

Ellen stepped into the room and coughed quietly. Tucker opened his eyes.

"Please sit down," Tucker said, nodding towards an available chair. Ellen looked down at the chair with its charts and papers on the seat.

"Just put that stuff over here," Tucker said, pointing to an already filled area on the desk.

"Are *you* the new medical student?" he asked, looking over the top of his glasses.

Ellen nodded, as she moved papers onto a precarious spot on the desk.

"I hadn't expected anyone quite so..." Tucker let the words trail off.

"So mature?"

"Yes, thank you." He scratched his head. "Mature. Precisely."

"I started medical school late."

Tucker nodded again. For a moment, he stared at nothing, then looked again at the letter.

He stood up and extended his hand, nearly knocking over some charts in the process.

"George Tucker," he said.

Ellen returned the handshake, then sat down carefully on the now-cleared seat.

"Where do the patients sit?" she asked.

Tucker, now seated and staring at the letter again, looked up.

"I don't usually see patients in here," he said. "I see them in the examining room."

He put the letter down.

"I was fired," he said slowly, "and that's why I seem distracted. It happens to all doctors, but it's never easy. In this particular case, I've been looking after this woman for at least five years after treating her for thyroid cancer.

She's done well. Now I get this note. Please have her records transferred to Dr. So-and-So. No explanation. No 'thank you for your past services.' No nothing."

"Maybe her health plan changed and she's too embarrassed to tell you."

"Maybe," Tucker said. "Or maybe I didn't return a phone call fast enough, or maybe I wasn't as sensitive as I should have been. Or maybe a friend told her about this wonderful new doctor. Who the hell knows." He sighed. "All I know is that I've invested a lot of emotional energy in this patient, and it hurts."

Ellen shifted a bit in her seat.

"To some people," Tucker went on, "a doctor is nothing more than a commodity."

Ellen said nothing.

"Well," Tucker said, "this is a good way to start. Sorry. I get this way sometimes. Coffee?"

"Yes please."

Tucker began pouring some thick black liquid into a large mug encumbered with an oversized blue and yellow logo: "Cleveland Park: Planning for the 21st century."

After a moment, he stopped, scratched his head, then dumped the liquid into the sink. "Dirty mug," he explained, then began looking in a nearby cabinet for a clean cup.

"Why'd you choose an oncology rotation?" he asked, as he tried again with a new mug.

Ellen shrugged. "I thought it might be interesting. And…" she paused, reaching over to take the coffee, "…everyone said you're a very good teacher."

Tucker nodded. "Thanks. That helps." He took a sip of his coffee. "You're my only student this time. The other one backed out a few days ago, so you'll get to see more cases."

He reached under a large stack of charts and pulled out a folder with Ellen's name on it. "Here's the plan: I'd like you to join me in hospital rounds in the morning, then see my office patients with me in the afternoon. I'll also ask you to see all the consults and present them to me."

Ellen shook her head up and down.

"You'll be very busy," Tucker said, "but with some luck you might even learn something."

He sipped his coffee and made a face. "Cold," he said. Then, "Aha! Look at this!"

Ellen took the proffered slip of paper, a lab slip filled with numbers.

"The white count has come up at last," Tucker said, his voice sounding excited. "At last."

"He's not married," Jill said a little while later on the phone.

"Hmmph. Is that all you can think of?" Ellen said.

"Apparently."

How'd she know he's not married, Ellen wondered later, walking down the hall to see her first two consults. He was wearing a wedding band.

"I'm Ellen White, the medical student," she said to the first patient, sitting in bed, surrounded by flowers everywhere – on the nightstand, the floor, the window ledge. Sunlight streamed in, bouncing off floral reds and greens and yellows. "I'm going to see you first, then Dr. Tucker will come in later."

The patient raised her hands. "I'm so delighted to see you," she said. "I do so enjoy the medical students. It's very important to help teach the doctors of tomorrow." If Ellen saw the woman in the next bed make a face, she didn't let on.

Almost knocking over a vase of flowers, Ellen drew the curtain closed, physically separating the patient from the woman in the adjacent bed. Speaking in a very loud voice, however, there was no illusion of privacy.

"I've been Dr. Tucker's patient for almost ten years," she started. "You know, when I first was diagnosed with cancer, I could hardly believe it. I said to my Jim – that's my husband - one morning, why do I have this jaw pain, and he said I should see the dentist. So I called the dentist's office and the secretary was on vacation, so I spoke to somebody I'd never heard of, and she told me the dentist was very busy. Did I have an abscessed tooth? she asked. Well, I told her, how would I know? Really," she looked at Ellen, "how would I know that? Anyway, I told her I needed to be seen right away, even if it wasn't an abscessed tooth, and she said...." The patient continued with her history, in every detail, reviewing the story not only of her jaw tumor, but also being sure to give a comprehensive overview of her health practically from the moment she was born. At first Ellen wrote notes carefully, but after a while leaned back and listened. The patient went on and on.

And on and on.

At last, during a brief break-in-the-action, Ellen beat a hasty retreat. "I'll be back later," she said.

"Oh please do come back." There was so much more to tell. "I can't remember. Did I tell you about my hepatitis from the blood transfusion?"

"See you later," Ellen said as she hurried out the door.

She wrote a consult note, but deferred on any conclusions, partly because she had no idea what to recommend. Dr. Tucker would see the patient later.

Ellen started the second consult. Already the day was beginning to wear late, and she was planning on rounds with Tucker at 5:00 p.m.

"I'm Ellen White," she greeted the next patient. "I'm a medical student working with Dr. Tucker."

The old man in the bed lifted his head, the listless eyes sunk deeply in their sockets, lips drawn tightly over an edentulous mouth. On the nightstand a solitary decayed bouquet of flowers rested in rust colored water.

"I don't want to see any medical student," he rasped. "I'm not here for experimentation. I'm not a guinea pig." He turned on his side and shut his eyes.

"I'm not here for that," Ellen said. "I just want to talk to you and then tell Dr. Tucker the details. He makes all the decisions."

The old man lay on his side, not moving.

"Dr. Tucker will see you later," Ellen said quietly as she walked out. She'd review the chart carefully and tell the oncologist as much as she could.

"Don't take it personally," Tucker said when they arrived at the old man's room. "It has nothing to do with you."

Tucker looked through the chart. The old man talked briefly to Tucker but had very little to say to him either. He was dying of metastatic cancer.

"What would you do?" Tucker asked Ellen after they'd finished seeing the patient.

"Maybe some chemotherapy might help shrink the tumor?"

"Maybe." Tucker leafed through the chart. "But look at him. He's old and tired. He's given up. With so much disease everywhere, our job is to make him comfortable."

The oncologist's note was short and direct. There were some suggestions about pain control. Tucker would be available anytime, night or day, for problems that came up.

The garrulous woman was next. Ellen tried to present her history but without giving every detail.

Tucker walked in and, moving a few vases of flowers aside, spoke with the patient who kept smiling and winking at Ellen. Tucker examined her, then shook her hand and left.

"How'd you do that?" Ellen asked.

"Do what?"

"Get out of there in fifteen minutes. I couldn't escape."

Tucker laughed. "Experience," he said. His note in the chart was brief and to the point.

"So how'd you like your first day as a cancer doctor?"

Ellen thought of the taciturn old man and the loquacious lady. "Challenging," she said.

Rounds finished, Ellen watched the oncologist walk down the hall, one shoulder lower than the other, a slightly shuffling gait. She guessed he must be in his late forties – her contemporary. As he turned the corner, he stopped, scratched his head, then looked back at Ellen and caught her eye for a moment. Then he continued on.

Hard to believe anybody would fire him, she thought.

CHAPTER 17

Brink walked up the final step and closed the basement door behind him. It had been more effort to go downstairs than he'd expected, and coming back up even more difficult. But lymphoma or no, he had no plans to give in; the cancer might have a physical presence but no tumor would dare temper or dominate his spirit. If Roland Brink wanted to go down- and upstairs, he would do it. Simple as that.

But it had been an unwelcome surprise to find his stamina moderated, lessened. Ever since the kidney stone two days earlier, Brink hadn't been able to throw off the feeling of being....dulled. The narcotics were long since gone, so the lassitude must have been either from the tumor or the chemotherapy. Certainly not from fear and uncertainty.

Brink looked at The Washington Post. The stories all seemed too familiar. Some of the players were different, but they were all following the standard scripts. It was hard to get interested. He set the paper down.

Brink loathed television, but maybe there'd be something worth seeing just this once. He went through the stations: the evening news, the weather, cartoons, Sesame Street. He turned it off.

Only a brief look at the chessboard. No new moves. Maybe tomorrow. Maybe.

Slowly, holding lightly onto the stair railing, Brink went up to his bedroom. He picked up a surgical journal and started to read, but couldn't find the energy to focus on it. A slight chill caused a brief shudder. He set the journal down.

The phone caught his attention. Except for a call earlier in the day from Tucker and a couple from Marcy, it sat silent.

Going into the adjacent bedroom he used as a home office, he picked up the bills from today's mail. The electric and water bills demanded his attention. He wrote those checks and set them in a small stack next to the telephone, which sat as quietly as the phone in the bedroom.

Another chill, mild, annoying, not serious.

It was only 7:00 p.m., much too early to go to sleep. There were still plenty of things to do. Plenty of things.

He tried a different journal, a symposium on some newer surgical techniques. Brink was *the* master technician. This was something he'd really enjoy. He pulled the covers down, climbed into bed, turned the bedside lamp to the brightest setting, and began reading.

After a few minutes, he rested the journal on his chest. It just wasn't going in. Tomorrow would be better; he'd see to that. A good night's sleep.

The telephone rang.

At last. The outside world touching bases with Roland Brink. Somebody needed the surgeon. Roland Brink, the master surgeon.

Brink watched the for two rings. Important not to seem in too much of a hurry. He reached over and answered.

"Is Roland Brink there?"

"Speaking."

"Mr. Brink, how are you tonight? I'm calling from B & J Rug Cleaning Service and we're having a one week special on..."

Brink hung up.

* * *

Somehow Roland Brink managed to stagger out of bed and reach the closet across the bedroom. The thick white pile of the carpet had always felt soft and caressing before, but now even the touch of his feet caused a burning. Shivering, trembling, he reached up to the top of the closet. It took three tries to get the two blankets down. They fell in an amorphous heap in front of him; he stared down through his shaking, and slowly bent over to pick them up.

He didn't have a thermometer at home, but Brink knew he had a high fever as shudders passed through his frame, consuming him, teeth chattering, every muscle vibrating, the aching threatening to overwhelm him.

The extra blankets didn't help. Brink lay beneath them, staring at the cream colored walls, unable to focus on the formless art work. Slowly – he did everything slowly this night – he looked at the clock. Eleven p.m. He tried to pull up the blankets further, even as great muscular quakes wracked his frame.

Eleven fifteen.

The bed shook, even as he tried to roll the blankets around him.

Eleven thirty.

Brink knew he couldn't hold out until morning.

Summoning his remaining strength, he fumbled over to the night table and removed his address book. The trembles made it almost impossible to turn the pages without ripping them. He found George Tucker's phone number.

"Hello?" Tucker's voice was foggy, thick.

"George, this is Roland." It was an effort to speak. "I've got… terrible shivers and muscle pains. I must have a fever."

A pause. "Can you get to the hospital?"

"No," Brink croaked. "I can barely move." An ambulance wouldn't do; it would take Brink to the closest hospital.

"I'll be there in thirty minutes. Can you open the front door for me?"

A pause. "I'll try."

Brink crawled to the closet and pulled down his bathrobe. Hunched over, half-crawling, half-walking to the stairs, he descended backwards on hands and knees, one step at a time. Unlatching the front door, he crawled into the living room, lying in the darkness, unwilling to reach up to get the light.

Tucker arrived with a neighbor. The pair helped the surgeon into the car, gently placing him in the back seat and covering him with heavy blankets. Tucker's car sped off in the darkness, only missing two turnoffs to get to Key Bridge.

"105.4°," the Emergency Room nurse announced after they finally arrived.

"Let's give him some IV Demerol to see if we can bring down the shivering. That may help his temperature."

Brink's arm shook as the nurses placed the IV line. He curled onto his side, grasping at the blankets, pulling them over.

"You hear that moaning?" one nurse asked another. "Human after all."

Within a few minutes of receiving 100 mg. IV Demerol, Brink seemed quieter, swallowing some Tylenol. The IVs ran in cool saline.

Even as the blood was being drawn, Tucker examined his patient, now lying quietly on the bed. His neck wasn't stiff. The lungs were clear. Incredibly, the lymph glands in the arms were much softer than they'd been only two weeks before, when he'd first received the chemotherapy. The spleen also seemed significantly smaller. He took note of the small skull and crossbones on the upper arm.

Blood counts, blood cultures, chest X-ray. A urinary catheter. And antibiotics – Rochephin and Amikacin – to start. They'd wait to see what the final cultures showed, but this was good broad spectrum coverage to start.

Another 50 mg. IV Demerol. Brink's temperature was down to 102°.

Tucker walked to the back of the ER and poured some coffee. It was bitter, but with some effort the oncologist got a few swallows down. Sitting quietly, his chin supported by his open palm, he watched the wall clock tick off the seconds.

After a few sips, unable to get tolerate the coffee any longer, he turned his attention to a small drama being played out in a nearby cubicle. An elderly drunk man was being abusive, a nurse was trying to calm him down, a concerned wife was wringing her hands. On the other side of the ER, a baby was screaming as an intern tried to look in its ear. A group of ambulance drivers was talking to a nurse.

"Here's the CBC," a nurse said. Tucker jumped, surprised.

The white count was normal: 4100. There was a decrease in the infection fighting cells – the neutrophils – but not enough to be associated with a blood stream infection.

The Infectious Disease consultant arrived and after talking to Tucker, examined the patient. The two physicians went to the vending machines to buy palatable coffee.

"I don't think he's infected," Tucker said at last, putting fifty cents into the machine and watching the coffee pour into a paper cup behind the plastic barrier. "I think it's all massive tumor necrosis."

Tumor necrosis: so much of the tumor had been killed by the chemotherapy that the body was unable to handle the massive quantity of dead tissue released into the circulation. Tucker and the I.D. consultant agreed to continue to cover him with antibiotics, at least to start, but wouldn't be surprised if all the cultures were negative for infection.

Tucker and the I.D. consultant sat down on plastic chairs. The oncologist blew on the coffee. Although the rest of the vending machine room was empty, a cleaning man wielding a large waxing machine looking and acting something like an untamed bronco, came towards the pair and asked them to move. They stood up and the cleaning man moved the chairs and buffed the floor.

Tucker thanked the consultant for coming in so late, then headed back to the ER. Brink had taken prednisone – a cortisone derivative – the first five days of the chemotherapy, but that bolus had long-since disappeared, so Tucker decided to administer another cortisone derivative by the IV route to attempt suppression of the inflammation from the tumor cell death. The nurse ran in 200 mg. methylprednisolone.

With the surgeon more relaxed now, not shivering, the abdominal muscles softer, Tucker reexamined him. No question about it – the spleen was much smaller, in fact hardly palpable.

The surgeon dozed, occasionally opening his eyes for a moment.

Tucker said something to Brink, but the surgeon heard none of it, his eyes closed, sleeping.

"I don't like this," Tucker said to himself after leaving the room. "The chemo has worked too well." After a few phone calls, it was decided that Brink would be moved to the Medical Intensive Care Unit, where he'd be watched for the next few days until there were more answers.

For now, at least, he seemed stable.

Brink was transferred to a gurney for transport upstairs. Tucker thanked the ER staff for their help, and took a quick look around. The drunk and his wife were gone, the screaming baby was gone, the ambulance crew was gone. They'd been replaced by a new group.

Unblinking, Tucker stared at the clock on the wall, watching the second hand for nearly a minute. It was 3:00 a.m. Tucker would feel like hell in the morning, and he had a full day scheduled.

The oncologist accompanied the stretcher to the ICU where a fresh bed was just being readied. Monitor leads were placed immediately, oxygen prongs pushed into Brink's nostrils, and the side rails put up. A nurse brought in a single flower from another room and set it in a makeshift vase.

"I'll be back in a few hours, Roland," Tucker said to Brink, who appeared to be sleeping as he walked out.

The oncologist thought he heard a noise from the bed, so he stepped back in.

"Thanks George," the surgeon whispered.

CHAPTER 18

By the time Ellen showed up at Tucker's office at 8:00, the oncologist had already made his hospital rounds and checked on Roland Brink. The surgeon's temperature was down to 101.2°.

"You look tired," Ellen said when she said Tucker. He looked up, his eyelids dragging behind.

"I had a helluva night," he said. "I'm not as young as I used to be. Coffee?"

The office was so swamped with charts, folders, Xrays, and odds-and-ends that even the oncologist seemed overwhelmed, so he invited Ellen to the exam room.

"This is Theresa's domain," he said, waving his hand around the exam room, then pulling out a seat for Ellen, and sitting on the edge of the exam table. He took a sip of the coffee. "Theresa's the ideal nurse. She disapproves of my office, but never says a word. But in here she rules with an iron hand." He looked in the mirror and adjusted his tie, pushing the back piece between the shirt buttons.

It was a wonder, Ellen told herself a few minutes later as she waited to see the day's first patient, that a man who was so physically disorderly – not only was his office a shambles, but his tie didn't match his shirt and his shoes looked like they'd never seen polish – yet this man seemed so exact and orderly in his care of the patients, knowing the precise dose of every medication, when and how to give it. Perhaps he was careful only in those things that mattered to him.

Ellen had a busy morning with the patients, feeling a bit more confident. It wasn't that she knew any more oncology, but she had a better feel for *how* to approach each person. It was her first real opportunity to see people in an out-patient setting and she was impressed by the difference from hospitalized medical care. Less dramatic. More personal and low key.

Theresa would speak to Ellen briefly before she saw each patient, giving a brief summary. The nurse knew their stories from memory. She'd introduce Ellen, who would take a history, examine the patient, then review the laboratory data . When that was all done, she'd present the patients to Tucker. He seemed to know each one well.

"You getting ready for fly fishing?" he asked one man.

"You don't happen to have any pictures of your granddaughter's wedding?" he asked another.

"That Indian restaurant you recommended was superb," he told a third.

"How do you know so much about every patient?" Ellen asked him later.

Tucker smiled as he tried to adjust his tie again. "Many people want to talk to their doctor, take him or her in as a confidant. You only have to listen and you'll hear."

"I know this surgeon who could take a few lessons from you," she said beneath her breath. Hmmph.

Morning rounds over, George called Ellen into his office, clearing a space away on one of the chairs. "Let's go over the hospital list," he said. "I admitted one man in the middle of the night, and I've gotten two consult requests this morning. All the others, you already know."

Ellen looked at the two consults: one was a fairly young man with a history of a melanoma, almost certainly cured; he'd been hospitalized for something unrelated and probably only wanted reassurance. The other patient was a woman with lung cancer.

"The patient I admitted last night," Tucker said, "is a fifty year old man with a particularly aggressive lymphoma. I'd like you to take a look at him."

Ellen nodded.

"It's possible you actually know him," George continued. "He's a surgeon in town named Roland Brink."

No actress could have adequately portrayed the surprise on Ellen's face.

"Brink?" she said, her voice croaking. "Brink," she said louder, more clearly. "Roland Brink? That miserable woman hating SOB?"

"Oh," said Tucker, smiling slightly. "I see you already know him."

"Know him? He's the most unpleasant arrogant person I've ever met. I just spent a few weeks with him on the surgery rotation and he turned me off to surgeons forever."

Tucker said nothing.

Ellen shook her head slowly from side to side, then abruptly hissed. "I refuse to see him," she said. "He has been unfailingly rude to me..." She looked at Tucker. "Unbelievably rude!" she said, voice rising. "More than once..." She sputtered. "...Any number of times he went out of his way to publicly humiliate me."

Tucker looked at the medical student across the desk, but still kept his silence.

Ellen shook her head rapidly from side to side.

"He's very sick," the oncologist said slowly, "quite possibly dying."

"No," Ellen said face reddening, jaw clenched. "No!"

The room was quiet except for the ticking of the quartz clock on the wall and the sound of a leaky faucet in the next room.

"You don't have to like him, Ellen," Tucker said, a seriousness in his voice and expression that Ellen hadn't seen before. No fly fishing or pictures of grandchildren here.

"He's a human being," Tucker said.

Ellen started to speak, then felt quiet. Her face, lined, was red, her eyes almost slits.

"Whatever you think of him," Tucker said after a silence, "he's a human being." He rearranged a few papers on the desk. The telephone rang and he spoke for a minute or two, then hung up and looked back at his student.

"He's better than many people, Ellen. Cold, seemingly indifferent, yes, but each of us approaches life in our own way. That's his way. It doesn't make him less of a person, just different. Over the years, he's saved many lives."

"So you think we owe it to him because of that?"

"No. We owe it to him because he's a human being. He's one of us."

Ellen shook her head again "I don't know if…" She stopped.

"You don't have to see him if you don't want to," George said after a moment. "And I promise you I won't think less of you for it. But, I believe you'll think less of yourself."

"I can't believe…" Another unfinished sentence.

"Medicine mostly isn't like E.R. on television, you know. It's much less exciting, less dramatic. But in the end it's vastly more satisfying. A chance to be a physician."

"But… of all people." A pause. "Of all people, *he's* the antithesis of everything medicine stands for."

"No, just the antithesis of what you stand for. Brink is a fairly unique surgeon; he's a kind of weapon to be aimed at a target. Which is all he wants to do. But I think you are cut out to be, if you'll excuse the corniness, a healer."

Raising both hands simultaneously, then shaking both fists in front of her, she puffed out her cheeks, then slowly let the air out.

"Okay, okay," she said. "I'll do it. I'll see him. I'll be the 'compleat healer.'" She shook her head again. "I can't believe you've talked me into this. Tell me, how'd you do it?"

Tucker winked. "Experience."

They spoke a few minutes longer, then Ellen left the office. She had a number of routine errands to run, including a trip to the dry cleaner.

"You don't seem very cheerful today," the woman behind the counter said as she handed over the blouses and other assorted clothes.

"I just got some bad news," was all she'd say.

There was nobody to growl at when she filled the tank up a few minutes later, but she managed to splash her foot and spray her skirt with gas while putting the nozzle back.

Damn! Was all she could think to say. Damn!

She found a worn pair of sneakers in the trunk. Wiggling her toes she could just see the little one sticking out the side. She wiggled them again. At last something to smile about.

It was only about five minutes to the hospital. She went to the Dean's office to make a scheduling change, then decided on lunch before starting the consults.

In the cafeteria Ellen eyed the various entrees, bought the daily special, and chose a seat in the corner. After looking at the dried fish, she tried a bite, then pushed it around on the plate. It had looked a lot better on the steam tables.

She could feel a sense of nausea growing.

Brink! How on earth did she have to end up with that SOB? She was finished with him, or so she'd thought. Visions of the surgeon mocking her, belittling her, trivializing her... all suddenly very real again.

Another attempt at lunch, but the smell of gasoline on her skirt overwhelmed the poor fish.

Brink! Served him right to get sick.

No, she couldn't think like that. Tucker was right. There'd been worse people.

Still, if anyone ever deserved the wrath of the gods...

Ellen put her tray on the conveyer belt and watched the uneaten fish disappear behind black plastic danglies.

Time to start the consults. She saw the melanoma first, a simple case, an easy problem. Any third year student could've handled that one.

Then the lady with the lung cancer – but she was down in radiology getting a CT scan. A few phone calls, then Ellen looked into the patient's room again. Still empty.

No new consults had come in, so the next stop would be Brink. Ellen felt a thumping in her chest, her mouth dry, her nervous system on "Code Red," high alert. She could delay the inevitable no longer. It was time.

Maybe Brink had died before she'd get there. Maybe... no! Tucker was right. She was a physician, couldn't think like that.

Still...

The walk to the ICU was a long one, heart pounding. She passed a couple of medical students she knew. After an apology for smelling like a filling station, they talked for a couple of minutes. It was the briefest of respites.

But before long she was on her way.

The ICU was in a distant corner of the old gray granite building. When Cleveland Park Hospital had been built, there was no such thing as an Intensive Care Unit, so the hospital created one out of other spaces in the early 1970s. Once inside the Unit, all vestiges of the old structure were gone, replaced by a dozen patient rooms that fanned, pear-shaped, off a short corridor. The nursing station with all the monitoring equipment, medical supplies and other accoutrements was at the top of the pear.

Ellen walked to the chart rack at the nursing station. There it was, BRINK, written in large red letters on a piece of tape across the spine of the chart. Still alive.

The third year medical student who'd written the initial history and physical was a friend of hers. She read his careful, lengthy note; although he was her exact scholastic contemporary, she was now the consultant.

The intern had written a note, followed by a brief "see and agree" note from the senior medical resident. The med student's musings were long with much detail and a lengthy discussion; the senior resident's was very short. Brevity equated with experience.

There were two notes from George Tucker. It required some effort to decipher the handwriting. "An extremely aggressive lymphoma," he had written in his first note.

Massive quantities of tumor had died after controlled doses of deadly poisons had been given to the patient. He'd gotten sick, had a fever, became dehydrated, had a lot of pain.

An ordinary man after all.

"Hello, Dr. Brink," she said very quietly as she walked into the darkened room. The EKG monitor was beeping away. IVs poured in fluids, a catheter came out of the bladder, oxygen prongs were jammed up the nose.

An ordinary man after all.

The surgeon was lying quietly on his side. He opened one eye, then the other.

"Dr. White," he said, his usual strong voice dulled. He didn't turn his head to look at her.

A silence.

Call me Ellen, she thought, but said nothing.

Although the lights were turned low, Ellen had no trouble making out the limp body of the surgeon on his side, a heavy white blanket covering all of him save the head. A solitary flower in a makeshift vase rested precariously on the windowsill edge. A yellow vinyl chair sat unused in the corner. IV fluids hung from the metal pole. The EKG monitor ticked away. A blood pressure cuff was suspended on the wall. Otherwise the room was empty, barren.

"I'm taking an oncology rotation with Dr. Tucker," she said. "I'd like to talk to you."

"Talk away," he said, still looking into the distance.

"No, I mean I want to get a history and examine you."

The surgeon sighed, the white blanket lifting slightly, turning his head to look at Ellen for the first time. "I've got lymphoma, about a 30-35% chance I'll survive. The details are in the chart. What else could *you* possibly need to know?"

You won't treat me like this, Ellen thought. "Dr. Brink, you once…" *Once what? Embarrassed me? Humiliated me?…* "You once admonished me to always take a history. That's what I'm doing."

"Practice on somebody else," he said, not raising his head.

"No!" Ellen said, her voice sharp. "You won't humiliate me once more. You may throw me out of here if you wish, but I won't be demeaned by you again, no matter how sick you are."

Ellen heard a noise and looked over her shoulder to where George Tucker was standing in the doorway, his body a dark shadow against the bright light of the ICU.

"You two are going to have to reach some kind of rapprochement," he said.

"I already…" Ellen started.

"Well?" the oncologist said, sniffing the air.

"Well what?"

Nobody said anything for a moment. The EKG monitor beeped along.

"George," the surgeon said, turning his head slowly and deliberately, looking at the oncologist. "Dr. White has already told me I'm an insensitive doctor, a woman hater. Do you now expect me to talk to her?"

Ellen began to speak, but Tucker held up his hand again, then pushed errant hair off his forehead.

"Every day," he said, shaking his head, "something new and different. I've never been an arbitrator before." He sniffed again. "Smells like gas in here," he said.

Tucker walked towards the surgeon.

"Truce?" he said, casting his glance back and forth between the two antagonists.

No response.

"C'mon dammit. A truce."

Brink slowly nodded his head. Ellen followed, even more slowly.

A few minutes later, Tucker left. Ellen moved next to the surgeon's bed and questioned him, never sitting down, hands held stiffly in front of her. Brink lay on his side, giving monosyllabic answers to the wall. When it came time to examine him, he turned without word onto his back. Ellen pulled the white blanket down.

Good God, she thought, *he looks thin, even a little wasted.*

"Are you eating enough?" she asked gently. Brink must have noted the sudden change in tone, because he turned to look at her in full, picking his head up slightly.

He shook his head. "George is making me drink nutritional supplements if I'm not hungry," he said.

Ellen examined the surgeon, making him sit up, breathe in and out. Brink's hands stayed quietly at his sides; even when she leaned over him to palpate his belly, Ellen made certain not to graze against him. She listened to his heart, poked his abdomen, checked his reflexes, saw the small skull and crossbones tattoo on his arm.

"Thank you," she said at last, turning to walk out.

"Could you get me some water?" He paused. "Please."

Ellen filled a cup, and held it for Brink, who sipped through a straw. "Thank you," he said.

Ellen sat down at the nursing station desk rubbing her eyes, then began to carefully write her note in the chart.

"Tell me about his social situation," Tucker asked when he came later to hear the details.

"He's not married," Ellen said.

"And?"

She shrugged her shoulders. "And?"

"He lives alone," Tucker said. "There's a brother who apparently lives someplace in New York, and a mother in New Jersey. He never speaks to them. Should we call them?"

The oncologist looked at his student. "He's all alone in the world, Ellen," he said slowly. "Dying, and all alone."

CHAPTER 19

"Dying?" Jill asked.

"That's what he said," Ellen answered across the kitchen table. "He said this is a particularly aggressive lymphoma and he's not very sanguine about Brink's chances for recovery." She brought a forkful of salad to her mouth.

"Tucker wants you to talk to him about his personal life?"

"I'm not sure." Ellen shook her head from side to side. "It'd be like trying to sell Girl Scout cookies to Mephistopheles. It just doesn't compute."

Ellen sighed.

"You're really upset about having to see Brink, aren't you?" Jill asked

Ellen bit her lower lip. "There's something else too."

Jill said nothing.

Ellen sighed again. "I heard from Dave today. He's in California now, but is heading – would you believe? – to Asia for at least the next few weeks, maybe longer. He said it was completely unexpected. Big case."

Jill still said nothing but came over and gave Ellen a hug.

"I'm just not very lucky," Ellen said. "Dave seemed to be the first ray of sunshine in a very long time, and now it's clear that I..." She stopped.

Jill went into the kitchen for a moment, and Ellen sat quietly, humming to herself.

"Chopin," she said when Jill returned. "The first Ballade. Deb hasn't said a word to me, but I've heard her playing several times. Mostly scales and exercises, but also a few short pieces."

"So there *is* something positive in the life of Ellen White, standard bearer of tribulations."

Ellen smiled. "Am I *that* bad?"

Jill responded with a smile.

"You know, Deb was really quite a talented pianist," Ellen said. "I was sorry when she quit." Ellen looked around. "She said if she couldn't be perfect, she wouldn't even try any longer."

"Her mother's daughter," Jill said.

Ellen took a sip of the soup. It was cold. She looked at her watch.

"I've gotta go back to the hospital. I told George, that is, Dr. Tucker, that I'd see one of his patients tonight. And he wants me to check in on the star patient."

"So it's 'George', is it?"

"It was his idea, not mine."

Jill looked at her friend. "Look," she said, trying to suppress a smile, "forget Dave. Maybe George is available."

Ellen smiled. "Hmmph. You're incorrigible," she said.

It had started to rain when Ellen left a few minutes later. A week before, the cold rain had still been in the thrall of a northern master, stinging the skin; now it was carried on a warm southern wind. It might be mid-March, still winter by the calendar, but this rain was soaking the earth with the scent of spring. Even in the darkness, Ellen could see reddish flowers atop the red maples against the street lamp.

She pulled into the hospital parking lot and walked in the side entrance, feeling the brooding in the unsmiling gray granite. No smell of the spring here; Ellen could almost sense the presence of sickness as she passed down the dimly lit corridor. Each stone in this land without seasons seemed to add its weight to her shoulders. For a moment, Ellen felt like turning and fleeing outside to the rain.

But she took the elevator to the fourth floor to see a new patient who'd just been admitted to George's service.

The elderly man lay in his bed on the oncology ward. Ellen looked through his chart; he had chronic myelogenous leukemia. He'd tried all the new drugs, the new immunotherapies, and now there wasn't much left to offer him. His white count was increasing. Sunken cheeks echoed the flaccid flesh outlining his bones. The dull eyes hoarded whatever light reached them, reflecting nothing.

"Hi Mr. Rigby," Ellen said, trying to sound cheerful. She'd met him several days earlier in Tucker's office.

Mr. Rigby turned his head, then extended his thin hand. "Please," he said, "sit down."

"Is that your family?" Ellen asked pointing to a picture of three smiling children.

"My grandchildren," Rigby said. "They live in California. I haven't seen them in half a year."

"Do you have any family around here?"

"My daughter lives in Frederick."

Ellen looked over to a few cans of unopened nutritional supplements. "Why aren't you drinking those?" she asked.

"What for?" he asked. "So I can live two weeks longer?"

Ellen reached over to hold the old man's hand. For a few moments they spoke quietly, Mr. Rigby's voice as weak as his muscles. It was an effort but Mr. Rigby wanted to talk about his family, his business, his life.

"I would always hit the ground running," he said. "Nothing could keep me down." Up and down went his head slowly. "I used to be a man. Now," he said, his voice trailing off, "I'm a nothing."

"That's not true," Ellen said.

"Of course it's true," Mr. Rigby said, his voice now so feeble he could barely whisper. "I'm so weak...." He began to cry softly, a thick strange muffled sound coming from the back of his throat.

Ellen squeezed his hand harder.

"I'm so weak...." he started again, "...that I can't even put up a fight anymore. A hell of a finish."

Ellen looked away, out the darkened window, into the rainy night. She could feel the sting in her eyes.

Mr. Rigby closed his eyes, drifting off to sleep. His chest moved slowly up and down.

For a minute, Ellen sat quietly, then withdrew her hand, wanting to say something, anything. At last she got up and left.

"God bless you, Mr. Rigby," she said and walked into the hall.

She wiped her eyes. Why did I ever take this elective? she asked herself. Why did I even go into medicine?

There's still time to change. I could get a very respectable job in some high powered firm. I could spend more time with Brett. I could....

The Chopin 'Revolutionary Etude' suddenly teemed out of the car radio....It had been this piece that had defeated Deb. She'd quit the piano, unwilling to continue the struggle for mastery. Too hard, she'd said. Too much effort. And now the Chickering sat in the living room, more occupied with the gathering dust than with Chopin.

Well, I won't gather dust. Ellen chased the few tears from her eyes, stood up straighter, and checked her patient list.

And anyway, Deb's started to play again.

* * *

After looking in on a few other patients, Ellen crossed over to Roland Brink's ward. The chart said nothing new: blood counts stable, temperature coming down, IV fluids in, urine out.

She stopped in front of the surgeon's room, staring at the closed door.

Ellen was coming to see Brink, but couldn't get the image of Mr. Rigby out of her mind. Would Brink follow in the same footsteps? Would he give up a fight if it were time?

'You can't just quit!'

A few knocks and she entered.

"Hello," she said softly. "It's Ellen."

For a few moments, silence, then the surgeon turned his head.

"Dr. White. It's rather late for you, isn't it?"

"Please call me Ellen, and no, it's not too late. Dr. Tucker asked me to see his patients."

"Even the contentious and difficult surgeon? The misogynist?"

"Look, let's stop all that."

Brink nodded, but said nothing.

"What are you going to do when you leave the hospital?" Ellen said, pulling up a chair.

Brink smiled. "I can almost hear George's voice behind that question," he said. "Well, I'm going to go home."

"Do you have any family?"

The surgeon squinted at his interlocutor. "Why?"

"Who's going to look after you?"

"No one."

"Don't you have some friends or family to check on you?"

Even in the dim light, Ellen could see the red rising in his cheeks.

"I can manage on my own," Brink said.

"Don't you ever get lonely?"

"Playing the psychiatrist, Dr. White? You…"

"Ellen," she interrupted.

"You already know what I think about psychiatrists. I would prefer not to talk, thank you."

Ellen got up, pushing the chair back.

"Okay," she said, "I'll leave you in peace." She began to head out.

"Wait…" Brink said.

Ellen turned around.

"You can stay to talk about medical things," he said. "It's just that I'd rather not talk about personal things."

For a moment she looked at the surgeon, then pulled the chair back and sat down.

CHAPTER 20

One week after leaving the hospital, Brink was beginning to feel better. The fevers had resolved, the muscle aches were gone. Only the weakness remained, a pervasive debility, hobbling vigor, sucking energy.

"I'm not going to let this thing beat me," he told Tucker, force feeding himself and taking long walks to improve endurance and stamina. He called Marcy to have her schedule a few patients. Further, with his strength marginally improved, Brink decided to try his hand at some elective outpatient surgery. But first, he had to go in to the office and get things cleaned up.

The desk was buried under charts, papers, letters, journals. Everything was neatly stacked, but it was still an unaccustomed and unwelcome intrusion into the usual precision in his life.

It took him most of the morning to go through everything. Several times he had to stop, lean back, close his eyes, and rest for a short while before resuming the straightening up chores.

"An orderly desk helps an orderly mind," he explained to Marcy and, indeed, by the end of the day, the office was immaculate once again. Everything was in its proper place; precision was a defense against sloppiness and disorder. After the last paper had been cleared, he carefully positioned the carved green Duesenberg Model A Phaeton where it belonged.

"How many patients have I got for tomorrow?" he asked Marcy.

"Two," she answered. "Mrs. Flaherty and Mr. Gaines."

Two long-term patients he'd been following for years.

"Nobody else?"

"I've been sending your patients to see other surgeons," Marcy said. "There's nobody out there waiting."

"What about those hernias? I had a couple of elective cases that could be scheduled."

Marcy coughed. "I couldn't reach those patients."

"What? What do you mean?"

"Nobody seemed available."

Brink's eyes narrowed. "What is it you're trying to say?"

"Nothing."

The surgeon's face reddened, his breathing becoming more rapid and shallow.

"I'm as good as I ever was," he said, measuring each word.

"Yes sir."

"Yes sir?"

"Dr. Brink," Marcy said, her cadence matching his, "since you got sick, nobody's been sending you patients. Everybody knows you were in the hospital, so they sent their cases elsewhere."

Brink squeezed his fists together, then hit the desk with his right hand.

"I am fine," he said. "Fine! Get it?"

Marcy nodded.

"Good. Now get me that guy who needs the new mesh put in his abdominal hernia. You know the man I mean?"

Marcy nodded.

"Call the OR and tell them I'll start at 8:00 tomorrow, and arrange with the patient to be ready."

"Are you sure?"

"Dammit!," Brink spat out. "Of course I'm sure."

Marcy came to Brink's office ten minutes later.

"Well?"

"He can't be ready by tomorrow," she said softly.

"Then, get me that woman who wants a reduction mammoplasty."

Marcy returned a few minutes later. "She's already had it done elsewhere."

"I'll do a colonoscopy," Brink said. "A colonoscopy. Do you understand?"

Brink lifted his head up slightly, chin pointing upwards, lips slightly downturned. "I have a whole lot of patients who need that," he said. "You find me one for tomorrow. Understand?"

"Dr. Brink, I really don't think..."

"You are not paid to think," Brink exploded. "You are paid to be my secretary."

"I've been your secretary for twenty years," Marcy said very quietly. "I deserve more respect than that."

Brink pounded the desk. "Is this a conspiracy?" he asked. "No referrals, no patients. Now my secretary."

Marcy turned and walked out.

She returned fifteen minutes later. "Mr. Fliss is scheduled for his colonoscopy at 8:00 tomorrow," she said quietly.

Brink got up, walked out, slamming the door behind him. Moments later the Porsche squealed out of the garage and onto Massachusetts Avenue. Weaving in and out of the traffic, the surgeon sped down Wisconsin Avenue on his way to Key Bridge.

"I'm as good as I ever was," he snarled through clamped front teeth, the Porsche shrieking over the Potomac and into McLean. The tires screamed as he careered into the driveway. The Porsche rocked momentarily after the car door crashed closed. Brink pushed open the front door to the house, nearly tripping on the mail which had been pushed through the mail slot.

"As good as I ever was!" he shouted to the empty house. "Do you hear me? As good as ever!" The mail flew over the foyer from his vigorous kick.

The surgeon loosened his tie, walked to the bar and poured a large Johnny Walker, downing it in a few gulps.

He turned on the computer. The chess board came into view, matching the board on the table. Brink closed his eyes for a moment, then moved a pawn forward one space. He repeated the move on the computer, then pushed Enter.

He'd not even brought his hand back when the computer responded, swinging a bishop over three diagonals, directly jeopardizing a rook.

"Shit!" Brink muttered, repeating the computer's move on the cut glass chessboard, before flipping the computer switch off.

He started up the stairs, passing his reflection in the hall mirror.

"As good as I ever was!" he spat to the image.

Setting the alarm to sound early, he read a surgical journal for a few minutes, then turned off the lamp. A few minutes later, he adjusted the pillow to find a more comfortable position and turned on his left side. Then onto the right side, then the left side again.

Overhead, he heard the distant howl of a jet in the final descent into Dulles. He adjusted his pillow.

He turned on the lamp and picked up the surgical journal again, but after reading a few pages, he set it down. Roland Brink wasn't going to let *his* mind play tricks on him; Roland Brink controlled *his* emotions. If he needed to go to sleep, then he would go to sleep. As simple as that. He turned off the lamp.

The night passed slowly as Brink adjusted and readjusted his pillow in the dark room, hearing the occasional jet passing overhead, turning from one side to another until at last he fell asleep.

* * *

With the abruptness of the alarm, Brink got up, shaved, showered, dressed, had a quick breakfast, and headed to the hospital.

He arrived at Cleveland Park at 6:00 a.m., his usual hour, but had nobody to see. No consults had come in overnight. There were no patients on the wards, no patients in recovery.

Although he'd lost a taste for coffee since starting the chemotherapy, he decided to go to the cafeteria. He'd take a surgical journal with him and humor a decaf. If people saw him, looking his usual self, they'd know that Roland Brink was back in business.

A nurse he knew looked slightly surprised seeing him, then smiled. The cashier in the cafeteria, who'd worked there forever and was reputedly older than God, appeared a bit startled when she made his change.

It didn't take Brink long to realize they were looking at his scalp. He'd combed his hair carefully this morning, but gaps from the chemo were still evident, where clumps had fallen out. No matter how straight he stood, no matter how firm his jaw line, no matter how well pressed the slacks or well knotted the pure silk tie, he looked different. He'd think about a hairpiece. Or would he? Wasn't that giving in to the disease?

The cafeteria still empty at that hour, nobody spoke to him, so he decided at 6:45 to go to the OR lounge. He had more than an hour to kill, a new and unwelcome experience for the perpetually busy Dr. Brink. The surgeon walked briskly, with purpose, down the long corridor leading from the cafeteria. He could feel the heart beating; he became slightly short of breath. Still he kept walking without changing his stride.

A distant figure with the shape of a youngish middle aged woman, slowly resolved itself into clear focus. The woman was walking towards him.

"Good morning, Dr. White," he said as he neared her, slowing down.

"Hello, Dr. Brink." She stopped for a moment.

For a moment, neither said anything. Brink's chest was heaving; he struggled to control it.

"How are you feeling?" Ellen asked.

"Very well, thank you. Actually, I'm on my way to the OR now. Busy day." He looked at his watch. "In fact, I'm a bit behind. Gotta go."

They nodded at each other.

"Good luck," Ellen said.

"Thank you," and immediately he regretted having answered. Nobody ever needed to wish Brink 'good *luck*' – Brink didn't believe in *luck*. He was

Roland Brink, and it was his skill that made him the surgeon he was.

For the next hour, he sat in the OR lounge, reading, speaking concisely with the other surgeons and anesthesiologists who were now beginning to arrive. Each was briefly solicitous.

"You're looking well, Roland."

Of course I am; why shouldn't I look well?

"Back to full speed?"

Certainly. Would you expect otherwise?

At 8:00, he was ready, clothed in his OR green, mask over his face. He went to the colonoscopy suite, spoke briefly to Mr. Fliss, then administered the anesthetic. The patient, although arousable, slept soundly. Brink inserted the colonoscope, watching the television screen as the device advanced.

It felt good to be in the OR again, even if was only a colonoscopy.

Brink negotiated the first and then the second turn in the large intestine, pushing and retracting slowly, pumping in air and suctioning, all the while watching the monitor. A large polyp, quite possibly an early malignancy, came into view. He took out the biopsy forceps and began to advance the colonoscope, at the same time steadying it with his left hand. Peering intently at the television screen, Brink felt sweat begin to prickle beneath the mask.

His right hand began to shake, to tremble. Renewing his effort to concentrate, the shaking began to envelop his whole right arm. The sweating increased, a profound weakness swept over him. He advanced the biopsy forceps further, the instrument now shaking so much that the television image was blurry. Brink applied the wire loop around the base of the polyp, at the same moment that his right hand slipped and the colonoscope fell towards the floor. He arrested its movement with his leg. The polyp was now out of sight; a blur of red appeared on the monitor. He'd have to advance the scope at least another foot. His heart pounding, he heard his own heavy breathing, felt the sweat in rivulets. And he could hear the rustles of uncertainty made by the two assisting nurses.

Brink took a deep breath, then advanced the scope again.

"Ow!"

He'd pushed the colonoscope so vigorously that he'd actually hurt the lightly anesthetized patient.

He pulled it back again, turned the scope around by 15°, then readvanced.

"Ouch!"

Brink couldn't locate the polyp again. Back and forth he moved the colonoscope, but only a red blur filled the monitor screen. No polyp. The scope was rotated another 30°, but still no polyp. His arm was shaking wildly. Sweat poured off his face. His head ached. He stopped, closing his eyes, hunching forward, and slowly rocked back and forth a few times. He opened his eyes and saw the red blur on the screen.

Then, all at once, he pulled the colonoscope out, practically throwing it on the floor.

"Tell him I'll have to reschedule," Brink said and walked out.

Word of the surgeon's failure raced around the hospital. Within moments everyone at Cleveland Park, maybe Washington, perhaps the whole world, knew that Roland Brink hadn't been able to finish the procedure, that Roland Brink had failed. Certainly Ellen White, seeing outpatients in George Tucker's office, had heard early on, even as the surgeon walked into the oncologist's suite.

"Can we move up the next chemo?" she heard Brink ask through the closed door.

"No, not yet," was Tucker's answer. "I've decided to delay a week, to allow you time to recover. I think we'd better stick to the plan."

"I haven't got the patience to wait," she heard Brink respond. "Let's move it up."

"No," Tucker replied. "It's my call. This time, you're the patient."

She heard the door slam behind the surgeon as he walked out.

Ellen looked out the window to the parking lot where she'd seen Brink's Porsche earlier. Even from the distance, she could see the flat right front tire.

Serves him right, she wanted to tell herself. But no: she thought of the man so recently in the hospital bed, the man she'd seen in the hall this morning – thin, hair falling out, complexion sallowed - trying, not completely successfully, to appear normal.

She saw Brink come into view on the far end of the parking lot, still unaware of the flat tire, and she saw him periodically throw his shoulders back, straightening up, his gait variably strong, then slower. She saw him look away from someone approaching from the other direction. She saw him take leather gloves from his pocket and drop one in a small puddle of mud and she saw him slowly – very slowly – reach down to pick it up. And she saw him stop in front of his right front tire.

"I'll be back in a few minutes," she told Theresa without explanation, reaching for her overcoat.

The man in the parking lot was leaning on the door of his Porsche, and didn't see the medical student approaching. The arms were folded on his chest, eyes staring off vaguely into the distance. Ellen broke into a trot, coat still open, hair flying behind her in the late March wind.

As Brink grew larger in her horizon, she could begin to make out his features more closely, even as she ran through the parking lot. The surgeon turned his head towards the sound of her footsteps. He watched her draw closer, showing no surprise, saying nothing.

Breathless, she came within a few feet, then stopped.

"You looked like you needed some help," she said, panting, pushing the loose hair off her face.

Brink looked at her with his unyielding blue eyes.

For a moment, the two stood five feet apart, the cold March wind sweeping down, brittling their cheeks.

"It was nice of you to come.... Ellen," the surgeon said slowly, "but I can manage for myself, thanks."

Ellen!

"Can I help you with the tire?"

"I was going to call a local garage."

"I'm good at changing tires," Ellen said.

"But, you're a...." he stopped.

The two briefly stared at each other, then Brink went over and opened the trunk.

"I'm feeling a little weak," he confided, "but can still manage. But I could use some help." He reached into the trunk. "I suppose."

CHAPTER 21

Warner Millstone put his hands on Brent's abdomen and pushed gently. "How long have you had this?" he asked.

"I'm not sure," Brent answered. "How long do you think?" he said, looking over at his mother.

"I'm not the patient," Ellen said. "Why don't you tell Dr. Millstone yourself."

Brent blinked a few times. "Maybe I've had this pain for a couple of weeks," he said. "Sometimes it's worse than other times."

"Where is it the worst?" Millstone asked.

Brent swept his hand over the entire abdomen. "Everywhere," he said, "but when it hurts a lot, it's worst here," pointing to the right lower quadrant.

Millstone pushed, poked, prodded once again. "Pretty soft," he said, looking at Ellen. "How have you been feeling otherwise?" turning his attention back to Brent.

The teenager shrugged. "Tired I guess, and a little bit achy."

Millstone nodded. "Let's get some blood work and see what that shows."

"I think it's stress," Millstone told Ellen while Brent was getting dressed.

Ellen shook her head. "Maybe...." she said slowly, "but you've been his pediatrician for a long time, and you've never seen him like this before."

Millstone shrugged. "I don't pretend to understand why things like this happen, but maybe his GI tract is his 'weak spot.'"

The pediatrician reached into a drawer and took out a business card. It had a psychiatrist's name and phone number.

"Give Brent some Metamucil for the next few days," Millstone said, "but if things don't get better, then," tapping the business card, "give him a call. He's helped a number of kids I know who've had divorced parents."

An hour later, after dropping Brent off at school, Ellen headed to George Tucker's. At a traffic light, she watched an unscheduled performance. A woman was gesturing furiously at the crunched back of her car, and a man from the ramming vehicle was approaching slowly. Within a moment, they were yelling at each other. Traffic was blocked in Ellen's direction. Soon a police car flashed in. The woman and man were both pointing wildly and yelling at the policeman, who walked away and began to direct traffic around the accident. The woman and the man continued their pointing and yelling.

Hmmph. Everybody's got their problems, Ellen thought. Now Brent had his as well. It didn't seem quite right, but Millstone was probably correct. It had been very difficult for Brent. Schoolwork was tough; the tutor had been able to help with that, but she knew that Brent felt the loss of close contact with his father acutely. Jeff had become a 'virtual' father, only spending every other weekend with his son.

A boy needs time with his father, she reminded herself, nodding her head up and down.

But maybe she was neglecting him too. Although Ellen set aside extra time for her son, sometimes she was just too overwhelmed with medical school work. At least the oncology elective wasn't nearly as demanding as the surgery rotation had been in terms of time, but the strain of seeing so many terminally ill patients – *so many terminally ill patients!* - was very emotionally exhausting. Some of that must have rubbed off on Brent.

Ellen walked into Tucker's office.

"A pretty busy morning," the secretary said. "Dr. Tucker got lost on his way here this morning and..."

"Got lost?" Ellen said. "How could he get lost?"

"He's done it before," Theresa explained. "Maybe he made a house call or stopped at Starbucks for a cafe latté. Anyway, he'll be a little late, so he wants you to see a couple of patients for him before he arrives."

"Don't look so doubtful," the secretary said. "Dr. Tucker thinks you're really doing a good job. He never let the last two students see patients for him."

"But I have such limited experience," Ellen said back, "and some of these people are so sick." She stared at a vase filled with daffodils. Each flower seemed to catch the sunlight as if the sun had been especially created for just it. For a moment, the radiance of each daffodil dulled everything else in the room.

"I hardly know what to ask these patients," Ellen said, looking back at the secretary, "let alone telling them what to do."

"That doesn't matter," said George Tucker's voice behind her. Ellen jumped, then turned around. "The mere fact that you're interested is enough for many of these patients. Just be yourself."

So Ellen went off to see patients while the oncologist returned some phone calls.

Just being myself, she thought. Sometimes there were pauses, but it almost seemed that the patients knew what to say in each hiatus, sometimes asking about Ellen's family or her medical school career.

Tucker joined Ellen and saw the patients with her. Today was a better day; everyone seemed to be doing well. A couple of cancer cures, a few prolonged remissions.

"Some days it all seems worthwhile," Tucker said, "at least for a while."

Tucker wove in and out of the various rooms, never appearing hurried, somehow always having plenty of time to spend with each patient. Ellen tried to hide in the shadows, but the oncologist actively brought her into his discussions.

Watching Tucker work, Ellen discovered that he never made an important point when standing. He'd always look for a chair or bench or even the corner of an examining table before speaking. After sitting, he'd rub his chin a couple of times and run his hand through his thinning hair; he always gestured with his right hand when he spoke, using his index finger for emphasis.

The morning drew to a close. "Lunch?" he asked Ellen.

She pointed to a brown paper bag she'd brought. A turkey sandwich and an apple.

"I think you can do better than that," Tucker said, inviting Ellen to a nearby restaurant.

"When the afternoon patient comes in, tell him we'll be back around 2," the oncologist said to his secretary.

"I thought you didn't have any office patients this afternoon," Ellen said, walking through the door Tucker was holding open. Tucker shrugged.

"Just one," he answered.

The restaurant on Wisconsin Avenue was noisy and looked like it always ran at a frenetic place. Waiters and waitresses called across the small room filled with Swedish Modern tables and Georg Jensen tableware. Black and white pictures of Georgetown from the 1920s lined the walls. Daily specials were written on a blackboard. The waiter introduced himself ("I'm Robert, your server") and handed them menus.

Tucker's beeper sounded. Reading the message, he answered on the cellular phone. Ellen looked intently at the menu.

The waiter stopped over, but Tucker was still on the phone. He talked and wrote notes on a scrap of paper, then pushed it into his wallet.

The beeper sounded again. Tucker made a face. Another phone call. He gestured to no one as he spoke on the phone, sometimes shaking his head no, othertimes yes.

Another visit from the waiter. Ellen continued peering intently at the menu, avoiding the waiter's stare. A line was forming outside the restaurant. Inside, the pace continued as before, waiters and waitresses running and calling out, dishes and glassware clanking.

Tucker was busy speaking quietly, writing down notes. He disconnected from one call, and dialed another. More conversation.

The waiter stood directly in front of Tucker and smiled, a saccharine smile.

"Sir," the waiter said. "Excuse me, sir."

Tucker continued talking intently into the mouthpiece. The line outside the restaurant was slightly longer.

"Oh sir," the waiter said, and at last Tucker looked up at the supercilious smile. "Sir. Now that I have your attention. Were you planning on ordering something?" Tucker looked slightly perplexed. Ellen tried to look away. "Sir," the waiter came back, "this is a restaurant and it's lunch." He raised his eyebrows. "There are people waiting," he continued, sweeping his arm towards the line. "Perhaps you'd like to order."

"Sorry," Tucker said, "I haven't looked at the menu yet. Just give me a minute."

"Of course, sir," the waiter said. "I'll be back soon – *very* soon sir – to take your lunch order."

Tucker glanced at the menu, then made a quick phone call.

"How can you do it?" Ellen asked a few minutes later after they were served by the suddenly speedy waiter, as she pushed the salad onto her fork. "Day after day, you see these sick people. Me? I know that in a few weeks my rotation will be done; I move on to something else. But these people you look after – you never 'rotate off service.' They're always there."

Tucker took a sip of his ice water.

"I hadn't planned on going into oncology," he said. "It happened by accident. The details aren't important." He took a bite of his sandwich; some mustard squirted out the side and caught his suit coat. "Damn!" he said quietly, dipping his napkin in the water glass and rubbing it on his jacket.

"Where were we?" he said a minute later.

"How you can be an oncologist and stay sane."

Tucker nodded and rubbed his chin a couple of times, then ran his hand through his hair. "It would be easy to become a philosopher in this business," he said, wiping off his jacket again. "I know this cancer doctor who used to read Sartre and Camus to try and understand."

"Any success?"

A short laugh. "Of course not. After a while, he gave up and went back to reading best sellers. Pretend worlds are sometimes a lot easier than the real ones."

Ellen pushed more salad onto her fork.

"Is everything alright?" the waiter asked. They both nodded yes.

"But how about you?" Tucker asked. "Is it any easier for you? You've had your share of problems."

Ellen opened her mouth for a moment, then shut it, and returned to chewing her salad.

"Today," she said, after a few more mouthfuls, "I learned that my son is somatisizing symptoms. His appetite is down; he's got a stomachache. That makes me feel pretty badly."

"Because you feel responsible?"

"Yes."

Tucker shook his head slowly. "But," he said, rubbing his chin, "you've already told me how much time you try to spend with your son." He took a bite of his sandwich. "The problem with you," he said, speaking with his mouth full, "is you're too much of a pessimist. The world can't manage its problems alone, so you try to appropriate some of them for yourself."

Tucker called for the check. "Speaking of which, we've got to get back to the office to see my afternoon patient."

In the short ride back to Tucker's office, Ellen said nothing, looking at jonquils and daffodils celebrating spring on sunny patches of land; the shadowy corners still hadn't heard about the new season. Japanese cherries and magnolias were almost ready to flower, but though a mild late March day, the imprint of winter was still all around, even to the overcoats and the closed car windows. Tucker pulled into the parking lot, tarred with white lines, a world that seemed oblivious to the seasons.

Ellen was not surprised to see Roland Brink in the chemotherapy chair, sleeve rolled up. The nurse was just putting on the tourniquet, getting ready to start the IV.

Brink looked so much older. Ellen remembered a man of physical vigor and strength only a few months before, but now saw the physical robustness gone, thinner, pasty yellow skin with flesh hanging from the frame like a vine dangling from a tree; much of his full head of black hair was gone, and what remained was an abrupt and unexpected gray.

But the eyes revealed none of that, blazing from sunken sockets, fiery, defiant.

"Hello Dr. White," the surgeon said, the voice less resonant but betraying no weakness.

"I'll be back in a few minutes," Tucker said, walking out.

"How are you?" Ellen asked, taking the stethoscope out of her pocket, putting it around her neck.

"Fine, thank you."

"Isn't this is your second chemotherapy?"

"Yes."

"Any fevers?"

The surgeon's eyes narrowed a bit as a thin bitter smile crossed his lips.

"You'd better examine me, Dr. White, so you can get a good grade from Dr. Tucker." Ellen walked over towards Brink, then abruptly, face reddening, hit her fist onto the side of the reclining couch.

"Look at me!" she commanded.

Brink's head turned.

"I've had enough of this bullshit!" she said. "From now on, Roland Brink, no more role playing or games. You betrayed some civility in the parking lot the other day, and from now on, I expect nothing less. Do you get it?"

Brink stared at his Torquemada.

"Do you get it?" she repeated.

Slowly the surgeon's head nodded up and down.

"Better," Ellen said in a low voice, trying to moderate her tone. "Now, Dr. Brink, sit up so I can listen to your lungs."

He sat up.

"Good," she said, putting the stethoscope in her ears, "now, take a few deep breaths through your mouth."

In and out. In and out.

Through the earpiece Ellen heard a muffled noise; she took the stethoscope out of her ears.

"What did you say?" she asked.

"I said 'Call me Roland'," the surgeon repeated softly.

The nurse came in and hung up the IV bag with the medications. Tucker walked in a moment later.

"Roland," he said, sitting on the edge of the window sill, then rubbing his chin and smoothing out his hair, "I've decided to risk giving you another full dose. My best guess is that your tumor burden is dramatically down so I'm not expecting you to have another episode like before. Of course," he said, voice trailing off slightly, "I wasn't expecting anything funny the last time either."

The IV chemotherapy began to run in, the nurse checking each line and syringe with great care. She left, followed by Tucker. Only the medical student and the surgeon remained.

Ellen watched the red doxorubricin drip in. Once inside the bloodstream it would travel to God-only-knew where, doing God-only-knew what. Controlled poisoning. Kill the bad cells without killing the patient.

Ellen watched the red liquid, one drop after another, disappearing through the IV tubing into the surgeon's bloodstream. Each drop had its assignment, to kill tumor; would they complete their task?

She turned and looked at the surgeon, who'd been watching her. For a moment, a brief moment only, she saw it, an uncertainty in Brink's face.

"Good luck....Roland," she said, getting up and walking out, closing the door behind her. Brink lay quietly in the chemotherapy chair.

"Thank you....Ellen," he said to the blank face of the door.

CHAPTER 22

Ellen pushed the fish around on her plate.

"You alright?" Jill asked.

Ellen nodded yes, taking a small bite of the halibut.

For a few seconds, Jill watched her friend closely.

"Do you want to tell me about it?"

"Nothing to tell," Ellen answered.

Jill got up and turned the CD player down, then, as an afterthought, changed the selection entirely. Bass notes replaced the violin.

"Mingus," Jill said. "Old recording from the early seventies."

Ellen tapped her fingers on the edge of the table, the rhythm not coordinated with the music.

"You like Mingus?" Jill asked.

"Never thought about it."

"I heard him once, up at a small club in Boston. Long time ago. Big man, quiet." Jill paused. "But electrifying."

Ellen opened her mouth for a moment as if to speak, then shut it.

Jill went to the bar and came up with a bottle of scotch.

"On the rocks or with soda?" she asked.

"Me? I don't drink scotch. Can't stand it."

"I'm going to force you to drink it until your resistance is down, unless you tell me."

"Tell you what?"

"You tell me."

Ellen pushed her plate away.

"I could swear I saw tears in his eyes, Jill. Just a little wet, but still a sign that he's a real human. Like Tucker said."

"That surgeon again?"

An up and down head nod. Mingus's bass plucked away in the background.

"Did I miss something?" Jill said. "I thought you didn't like him."

"I...." She looked at Jill, leaning forward on her elbows. "Dammit Jill! Will you stop nosing around so much in my life. It seems you have nothing better to do than put your two cents in every time I try to do anything." She pushed the chair back abruptly, the feet stuttering against the wooden floor.

"And I don't give a damn about Mingus either," she said, voice rising.

"I'm sorry. I really didn't mean..."

Ellen took a deep breath, then walked over to the window. She pulled the curtain back and stared outside for a few seconds, then sat down on the sofa, rubbing her hands over her eyes.

"I'm sorry," she said, putting her arms around Jill. "You know I didn't mean it." She laughed quietly. "Maybe you were right. I should've had that scotch."

Now it was Jill's turn to say nothing.

"So much going on," Ellen said." It sounds like a broken record, doesn't it? But there's something different and I don't know what it is." She let go of her friend and settled back on the couch. "Here's this guy I swore I'd detest forever. And now...." She stopped. "And now..." She closed her eyes and took a deep breath. "And now, there's something about this man that makes me interested in...well, in his case. Suddenly I see him struggling in this new role of dependency, trying to understand something he may be constitutionally incapable of understanding. And I wonder, do I have a responsibility to help him? I'm sure George Tucker thinks *he* does and since I'm his surrogate, I do too." She stopped. "A least I think that's why I feel this way." Ellen frowned. "I think?"

Jill got up and turned off the CD. Ellen didn't seem to notice.

"And I'm worried about Brent," Ellen went on. "He's just not his usual self, dragging around so much. He's lost some weight and doesn't feel like eating."

"That doesn't sound like him."

"His doctor thinks he's depressed."

"And you?"

"Not sure."

Ellen walked over to the CD player. "How do you turn this thing on?" she asked. "I really would like to listen to Mingus." She pushed a few buttons randomly. Nothing happened.

"And I gotta tell you, Jill, the oncology rotation is *so* depressing at times. Tucker says it's not usually so bad, but we've had a run of really sick people."

"For what it's worth, *I* think you're lucky," Jill volunteered. "You get a chance to do something noble, actually making a difference in some people's lives."

"Tucker says we're just ordinary people in extra-ordinary places."

"Tea?"

Ellen shook her head no.

"You know what really bothers me about Brink?" she said. "I can't tell if he even really understands what's on the line. Where is the pathos, the humanity? Sometimes I think his seeming indifference is even sadder than the people who are so scared."

"Sadder to you, maybe. But to him?"

"You're probably right. I shouldn't judge him by my values. Still...."

Ellen drove home a few minutes later, listening to an 'all news' station, trying to distract herself. Jill was right. She shouldn't use her values to assess Brink.

She headed down Canal Road. The news station was too distracting, so she changed to find some music.

She found a station playing Oldies from the sixties.

I can still be humane and compassionate. I'll just have to distance myself emotionally.

"She loves you," the Beatles were singing. Ellen began humming along.

Resolved. No more appropriating other people's problems. No more being distracted. Done. Finished.

"She loves you."

Well, I certainly don't love him. I....damn!

The car sped past the turnoff she usually took to get to River Road. Ellen looked for an exit to get off. She hardly ever came out this far.

"I only want to be with you," Dusty Springfield began.

What the hell is this? A conspiracy? I sure don't want to only be with him!

She turned off the radio.

Ellen found an exit at Carderock Springs and followed it around until she found herself on River Road. She was home a few minutes later.

Brent intercepted Ellen at the door.

"How are you?" she asked, kissing him on the head.

"A little better," he said. "Dr. Tucker's called a whole bunch of times. He wants you to call him right away. One of your patients, some surgeon, has been admitted to the hospital. Dr. Tucker says he's real sick."

"What else did Dr. Tucker say?"

"That this surgeon guy wants *you* to come to the hospital and help take care of him."

CHAPTER 23

The hospital of the night is very different from the hospital of the day.

During the day, the organism pulses with a diffuse energy. Everywhere someone is doing something, each in his or her own way contributing to the intensity and vigor of the institution. Patients fill the corridors, from the gift shops to the wards themselves; some walk vigorously, others only move slowly, grabbing onto walkers or other people, still others sit reclining in large chairs in the halls; some are watched over by their families, alternately joyful at a good prospect or numbed by a sad outcome. Physical therapists abound on the wards, cajoling the infirm and the injured to exercise, to walk; dieticians exhort patients to eat, planning menus or doing calorie counts; clergy request divine beneficence for the infirm. Doctors, singly and in groups, roam the halls and conference rooms and patient bedsides, talking and examining, writing in charts, reviewing X-rays. The Operating Rooms are filled with anesthesiologists, surgeons, nurses, and patients, abetted by the whir of sophisticated machines. The accounting office rumbles with life; medical records staff move charts from one place to another. And the nurses are ubiquitous, checking vital signs, dispensing medicines, talking to patients and comforting them, taking calls from family members, cleaning urine from soggy bedsheets, encouraging patients to eat their lunch. Maintenance men repair faulty wiring and plumbing; housekeeping sweeps and mops the vast corridors; delivery trucks pull in and out of loading docks. Everywhere kinetic energy abounds, in every hallway, behind every door.

At night, the great institution becomes a study in potential energy. The dynamism is condensed, confined to a few areas. There is still a daytime energy in the emergency room and sometimes an intensive care unit; perhaps in one or two operating rooms. But elsewhere it is darkened and quiet. Patients rest in their rooms, their families home in their own beds. Nurses quietly trod the hallways, taking vital signs, administering medicines. A sleepy guard watches television monitors; a nighttime supervisor opens medical records to get a needed chart; an X-ray technician reluctantly comes in to perform an emergency study. The cafeteria is darkened, the conference rooms and the slide projectors are quiet.

It was almost midnight when Ellen White walked down the main hall of Cleveland Park Hospital. Many of the lights had been turned off; those that remained on gave dark shadows – pent up and hidden all day – the chance to spring out and caress the walls. At the elevators, Ellen pushed the button and waited. Pictures of some of the hospital's most notable physicians watched her impassively in the half-light. She squinted to see their faces, but they didn't return the squints through the darkness.

She got off at the sixth floor. The small foyer in front of the elevators was dark. Ellen turned to the right, passing patient rooms, their doors closed. It was quiet, save for a low moaning sound behind one of the doors. Ellen went to the nursing station, where a couple of nurses were speaking softly; a secretary was typing something onto a computer screen.

"Where is Dr. Brink?" she asked.

The secretary rummaged around on the counter and produced some sheets from the chart that hadn't yet been assembled, then pointed down the hall.

Ellen read through the papers. There were some brief notes by a nurse and a medical student, and a longer note by the ER physician. "Elderly male physician ..." the note began. Closing her eyes, Ellen searched for an image of the fifty year old man she'd first met only a few months before, the man who had aged – what was it? -maybe twenty years in the past month since becoming so violently ill and taking such powerful medicines. She opened her eyes and continued reading.

"Elderly male physician admitted with fever and nonproductive cough. Known history of lymphoma...."

Ellen walked briskly down the darkened hall to Brink's room. The clatter of her shoes against the tiles, bouncing the sound off the walls and returning it louder, coming from everywhere, forced her to slow her stride slightly as she passed by the closed doors of the other patients.

George Tucker was sitting on the side of the patient's bed, speaking quietly. Someone she didn't know was sitting on a chair on the opposite side of the room, writing something in the darkened room. Tucker nodded at Ellen.

Brink lay in bed, sheets and blankets pulled up over his shoulders. It had only been two days since she'd seen the surgeon, but he'd aged yet another twenty years, the cheeks hollowed, fragile skin barely embracing the facial bones, complexion yellowed.

But the eyes burned.

'*Elderly male physician.*'

"Hello Ellen," he said, his weak voice trying to project strength as it escaped from the dried mouth, the crusted lips.

"Hello Roland," she said, "how are you?" and she felt stupid as soon as she asked.

"Fine," he said, abruptly shaking beneath the blankets as a chill enveloped him.

"Ellen," Tucker said, "this is Dr. Raymond Elgin," pointing to the man on the other side of the room, who was still writing. Elgin looked up and nodded.

"He's with the I.D. folks," Tucker said. Infectious Diseases. He looked so young, Ellen decided, that he must be a trainee. Of course, a lot of them looked young these days.

"Roland's had a fever for about twelve hours," Tucker said, "probably maxing out at about 102°."

Ellen stood without moving. A small light over the head of the bed was trying to fill out the corners of the room but only managed to produce shadows that accentuated the night.

"After a few hours, he called me," the oncologist continued. "By the time he got to the ER, he was already complaining of some shortness of breath."

Ellen looked at the small prongs hooked into his nose, a tube leading from an oxygen spigot on the wall.

"The chest film shows a pneumonia," Tucker said.

"Er, I'll, um, write a note in the chart, George," Elgin said, looking at the floor, away from the oncologist, "and we'll, um, get him started on some antibiotics." Elgin's swallowed words almost seemed to seek out unlit corners of the room.

George. First name basis. So this guy probably wasn't a fellow, but a more senior physician.

Elgin looked at Tucker, then stood up. With staccato movements he took two steps to the surgeon's bed.

"Um, Roland," he said, the words muffled, "I'll, uh, see you in the morning. I hope you, um, feel better."

For a moment, the I.D. doctor stood motionless. Brink nodded, and then Elgin turned, took a few hesitating steps, and was gone.

"Doesn't inspire much confidence," Ellen mumbled to no one.

Tucker's beeper sounded. The oncologist fumbled a bit but finally found the button to stop it. He looked at the message.

"I'll be back as soon as I answer this page," Tucker said. "Ellen, why don't you stay here, take a history and examine your patient."

Ellen looked at the corner of the bed, but then her eyes settled on the chair, and she pulled it over.

"You've been sick for about twelve hours?" she asked.

Brink nodded.

"Do you have a cough?"

"A little."

"Is it productive?"

For a moment, Brink closed his eyes, almost shaking his head from side to side. But after a few seconds, he spoke. "No," he said, looking directly at Ellen. "It's dry."

A huge chill enveloped him at that moment and, as he shook on his own personal Richter scale, he bent his knees up, tugging at the covers. Ellen stood up and pulled another blanket over him.

When the violence had subsided, the surgeon looked still more pallid than before.

"Are you having trouble breathing?" Ellen asked.

Brink looked up at the medical student.

"Ellen," he said, his voice weak, "I know what you think... about my attitude towards you." He stopped, breathing shallowly. "But I don't have the.... energy to speak. Please..." he stopped. "Please talk to George."

Deb had banged her fists on the keyboard. "Chopin wins! Chickering wins! I quit!"

'You can't just quit!' Ellen had said.

"No? Watch me then," Deb had said, storming out.

For a moment, Ellen looked uncertain... but only for a moment. "I'll examine you," she said.

"Must you?" Brink asked. Did the light in the surgeon's eyes seem dulled for a moment? Ellen looked again; no, they burned with all their usual ferocity even in the dim light.

"Yes," Ellen said, surprised by the firmness in her voice. "It's part of being a doctor."

Brink felt very warm. The throat and tongue were parched but otherwise clear. The neck was supple. The lymph nodes in the axilla seemed firmer and larger than when she'd last checked him only several days earlier. The spleen tip was palpable. He was breathing quickly, nostrils flaring with each inhalation, but the lungs sounded clear; no moist or gurgling sounds.

"I'm going to look at the X-rays," Ellen announced in the newfound firm voice.

She went to radiology to locate the films. The receptionist, apparently talking to her boyfriend, looked up briefly when Ellen arrived. Loud music from a radio on the end of the desk competed for air supremacy.

"X-rays are in the reading room," the receptionist said, vaguely pointing to the left.

Ellen found the reading room, and went through the X-ray jackets. Smithson, Scarpetta, Nussbaum, Hillmead, Gomez. One after another. But no Brink.

"I can't find them," she said on her return to the receptionist.

The receptionist said something into the phone, then looked up. "Must be in the ER then," she said, returning to the telephone.

"Are you sure? It's really very important. This man's very sick."

The receptionist shook her head. "The ER," she said again.

"Don't ever say that to me again," Ellen heard the receptionist say into the phone as she headed to the Emergency Room.

"They're not here," the nurse said after looking for five minutes with Ellen. "Let me go to X-ray with you."

The receptionist looked up. What is it now, her look demanded.

"It's very important," Ellen started. "I really have to...."

The nurse looked at the receptionist in the flickering fluorescent light. "Please put the phone down," she said, "and help us find these films."

"What?"

The nurse took two steps and turned the radio down, then repeated her demand.

"Call you later," the receptionist said into the receiver, and got up slowly, accompanying the two women to the file room.

"Been checked out," she said after looking at the log. "To Dr. Tucker."

"Thank you," Ellen said, and then felt stupid for saying it. Thanks for what?

She arrived at the sixth floor. Tucker was standing, still on the phone, his back towards Ellen. She could see his reflection in a paper towel dispenser. His eyes were half-closed, cheeks sagging, somehow echoing his sagging middle, the posture of someone old beyond his years. Tucker nodded from time to time, sometimes speaking into the phone. Was he bored or just tired? Or was it something more? Not sensing Ellen's presence, Tucker seemed drawn inward, exuding a weariness, both physical and mental, that she'd never noticed in the few weeks since they'd met. The resilient oncologist, the sometimes messenger of the angel of death, suddenly stood in front of her, revealed as ... what was it?... the man of infinite patience? The man of infinite compassion?

The man of infinite weariness?

She thought about the thick glasses, the messy office, the chronically ill-fitting suits with ties that never quite matched. No, this was very much a real human being, even though the warts sometimes didn't seem to matter quite so much.

Ellen stood quietly for a few seconds more, then saw Tucker's posture stiffen slightly, stomach pulled in, as he caught her reflection in the towel dispenser. The phone conversation ended in a moment; he turned around towards Ellen. It was the compassionate healer once again who faced her.

But Ellen had seen him. She knew.

"X-rays?" she said.

He scratched his head, then reached over behind a chair and produced the folder.

Ellen brought them to the ancient yellowed view box, a renegade from a former era, hanging next to a cabinet. She hunted around until she found the electric switch. The fluorescent light considered it for a moment, then grudgingly sputtered on.

The right lung seemed normal enough, but the left showed a fuzziness, a "ground glass" consistency, especially on the inside, or medial, part of the lung. She looked around to see what Tucker thought of the x-ray, but the oncologist was nowhere evident.

Ellen reviewed the chart again. Brink's white count was nearly normal, although he was fairly anemic. The kidney and liver functions were acceptable.

She returned to Brink's room, walking in quietly. She needn't have taken the precaution. The surgeon was alert, his deep black eyes following her.

"What ... did you... think of the X-rays?" he asked, the voice somehow less strong than usual. Ellen's surprise at his tone must have been noted, because he repeated the question, this time with more effort, but also greater force.

"I'm not very good at reading X-rays," she said, "but there seems to be a haziness in the left lung." She paused. "The ER doctor's note said it's in the lingula."

"Don't always depend on others," Brink said. "You must... trust your own judgment."

"I'm only a medical student," Ellen said. "I don't know how..."

Brink raised his hand from under the sheet.

"Others may try to... sound learned and smart," he said, "but...Ellen...you have to believe in yourself." He slipped down almost imperceptibly under the covers and closed his eyes. "And your patients... must believe in you."

She thought of Elgin, the infectious disease man.

Ellen sat down in the half-darkened room, trying to recall the X-ray, trying to think harder about Brink's problem, trying to believe in herself. She watched her patient breathe. He didn't seem *too* short of breath, did he? Believe in yourself, she reminded herself. From time to time, a brief chill would shake beneath the covers.

Still no George Tucker.

Ellen's attention wandered a moment and abruptly she could sense Brink's gaze. She turned to see his eyes open, fixed on her.

"Do you have ... children?" he asked.

Ellen's surprise at the question must have been evident, because a faint smile managed to appear on Brink's thin cracked lips.

"Well?" he said.

"Two," she answered.

"Is it hard," he asked, his breathing suddenly becoming more labored as he spoke, "to be a student and... not be with your children?"

"Sometimes, yes," she said almost too quickly, eyes narrowing.

Brink nodded. "Don't be so defensive," he said. "It's..." he stopped to take a few shallow breaths. "It's a reasonable question. Don't always sit..." another few breaths "...in such harsh judgment of me." He closed his eyes for a moment, the breathing rapid and shallow, coughing intermittently. "I'm sorry I never had children...." he said "...but maybe it's... just as well."

George Tucker returned.

"Roland," he said, "we're going to start you on triple therapy. Amikacin, Rocephin, and IV Erythromycin. If you're not starting to get better in twelve hours, I think we'll bronchoscope you."

Brink's eyes were closed now as he nodded.

"See you in a few hours," Tucker said. Down the dark hall some type of electronic instrument was beeping softly. In the next room, the sounds of a television were just audible.

Brink opened his eyes. "Thanks for your help George," he said. His gaze shifted to the medical student. "And thank you ... .for coming in, Ellen."

Ellen nodded and turned. When she reached the door, she felt herself being held hostage, turned around by an unrecognized force. The surgeon was watching her. A brief smile –almost finished before it was given - and she walked out.

Tucker and Ellen walked down the hall, saying nothing.

137

"Coffee?" Tucker asked when they got to the nursing station. "They've got a pot of decaf."

Ellen shook her head up and down, a chill enveloping her, numbing even as she shivered. There was an internal void, her skin quivering gelatin.

Tucker poured the hot coffee. Ellen held the cup between her hands, fighting for its warmth.

"I used to smoke," she said, taking a small sip. "I could really use a cigarette now."

CHAPTER 24

Ellen walked up the stairs quietly and went into Brent's room where the teenager was sleeping. She kissed him on the top of his head; he didn't even stir.

She'd thought about staying at the hospital to look after Brink, but quickly decided in favor of her son. Looking down at the sleeping boy, posters of his favorite Washington Redskins players on the walls, she felt a terrible loss. Of course she'd planned on staying home that night, but Brink's sudden admission quashed that.

A fifteen year old shouldn't have to sleep at home alone.

She sat down on the bed next to Brent, and gently stroked his head. The boy barely moved. At first she felt only the sting in her eyes, followed by the blurriness, even here in the partly darkened room, then finally the droplets rolling down, spilling over her cheeks and onto her lap.

It was 4 a.m. In two hours, she'd get up and ready herself to go to Tucker's office; it'd hardly be worth the effort to sleep, or at least to make the attempt, but she wanted to shower and just stretch out a bit. And, at least she'd have a chance to spend a few minutes – a few minutes, that was all – with Brent, before he left for school. Not even enough time to ask him about his classes let alone make pancakes.

The bed felt soft and cool when she lay down after her shower, the smooth silk of the nightgown reassuring and comforting against her skin. She closed her eyes, waiting for the inevitable sleep.

But the goddess of sleep was nowhere near. Although too tired to think, images of the Chickering and Brent and Brink raced around her brain, mercilessly demanding her attention, brooking no distractions. No other visions need apply.

Brent and the Civil War paper; running off with his father on alternate Saturdays; sleeping home alone. Alone in his bed.

The surgeon's dry cough, the strong voice, the I.V., the chills and shaking from under the blanket, the weakened voice. The thin drawn face. And then: the proud arrogant surgeon of old, cold master of daily hospital rounds. Scrubbing pots and pans instead of scrubbing her hands for the Operating Room.

The dusty Chickering. The untouched scores – Bach's Well-Tempered

Clavier, Chopin's Preludes, Brahms' Intermezzi – atop the piano. The furtively played scales and hesitant stumbling of the reinvented pianist.

Brent in the next room. He'd been feeling a little better the past few days. Still not up to his usual athletics, but otherwise at least some improved. He'd stopped losing weight. The pediatrician seemed satisfied, although Brent's sedimentation rate, a measure of inflammation, was still somewhat elevated. Still, he seemed more like his old self. In fact, he hadn't complained about a stomachache for at least three or four days.

Brent. A good boy....too good for me, she thought. Supportive, understanding. She wanted to spend the coming evening with him tonight, but knew she'd be too wiped out. She'd spend the evening in bed.

Maybe she should be scrubbing pots and pans.

Deb banged her fists on the keyboard. "I quit!"

"You can't just quit!" Ellen said.

Brink's image intruding again. The surgeon who had asked her to come to see him.

The earliest morning gray began to outline the small cracks around the window shades. Songs of the chickadee and the titmouse sounded in a nearby tree. The sound of April raindrops started to...

The alarm began squawking. The raindrops and the birdsongs vanished. Ellen reached over to shut off the offending screech.

She dressed and shuffled downstairs to make Brent's lunch, then went back upstairs to awaken her son.

"That guy's weird," Brent announced when she kissed him.

"Who?"

"That surgeon. Didn't you tell me a few weeks ago that he hated you? Then he calls you when he's sick."

"I'm beginning to believe he's not quite as awful as I'd thought," Ellen said.

"Yeah? Well, he's weird if you ask me."

"Which I didn't. By the way, what time did you go to bed?"

A cough. "About ten." A sidelong glance, and Ellen knew he'd been watching TV long past his bedtime.

No matter how many cups of coffee it took, she'd stay awake for her son tonight.

* * *

Ellen arrived at the doctor's parking lot about 45 minutes later. Already crowded with cars, Ellen recognized Tucker's jalopy. Overhead, the overcast sky was answered by the hospital's thick gray granite blocks.

Brink's hospital room was filled. Tucker was speaking to someone at the end of the bed, while two doctors she didn't recognize huddled over the patient. The nasal prongs were gone; an oxygen mask now covered his face. A couple of nurses were fiddling around with the IV, and a burly man who looked like a football refugee, was cranking the bed down.

"We're moving him to the ICU," Tucker said, spying Ellen. "He's a lot more short of breath." The oncologist showed Ellen a paper with the data summary. Clearly Brink's oxygenation was becoming rapidly impaired.

"I hope we don't have to intubate him," Tucker said quietly to Ellen, "but he looks pretty sick."

The burly man left, returning in a minute with a stretcher. Brink lay under the covers, his chest heaving with each breath, nostrils flaring, ropy veins on his forehead suffused with blue.

Brink opened his eyes and immediately fixed on Ellen.

Was that a hint of a tenuous smile on those thin desiccated lips?

The burly man pushed the stretcher next to the bed. With the aid of two nurses, Brink was lifted up, sheet and all, from the bed to the stretcher. A portable oxygen tank was shoved onto the side of the stretcher. The IV was moved.

The burly man pushed the stretcher out of the room quickly. Brink's eyes were open, staring up at the ceiling. His chest heaved. He coughed, a dry cough, a hacking dry cough, sometimes in brief spasms. Tucker, the two unnamed doctors, and Ellen followed the stretcher down the hall.

The burly man pushed the elevator button. An interminable wait. Brink's chest heaved, interrupted by the dry coughing spasms. The burly man tapped his fingers on the side of the stretcher.

Waiting.

Another coughing fit.

At last the elevator arrived. A dolly with food got off, followed by two nurses, discussing their vacation schedules.

Brink's stretcher got on with two of the doctors and Ellen squeezed in. There was shaking from under the blanket, gasping from the mouth.

A team of nurses and orderlies were waiting for the patient in the ICU.

A fresh blood oxygen level was taken even as a radiology technician was shoving a hard X-ray plate under the surgeon's back. He shivered as the cold plate touched the skin.

"X-ray," the technician yelled and everybody cleared out. For a moment, Roland Brink was alone in the room.

Alone, Ellen thought. Like always.

The X-ray taken, the nurses reentered.

"I don't like this," Tucker said to Ellen outside the room. He introduced her to one of the doctors. Dr. Pamela Wilkinson, a lung specialist.

"I think he needs to be 'tubed," Wilkinson was saying, "if there's any worsening."

"It'd be easier to bronchoscope him then, wouldn't it?" Tucker asked, scratching his head.

Wilkinson nodded.

"Then," Tucker said, "I see no sense in waiting. Let's intubate him and then move ahead." He spoke clearly and to the point, his voice more resolute than Ellen had ever heard it. Was this the same man who got lost on his way to work?

Ellen thought about the man in the bed. He'd probably approve of Tucker's decisiveness.

"Roland," Tucker said, approaching the bed, "I want to intubate you. Pam Wilkinson and one of the anesthesiologists will help."

For a moment, Brink was fully alert, all his energy and attention suddenly concentrated on the oncologist.

"No," he said between labored breaths, "not yet."

Ellen stood at Tucker's side, bedraggled hair tumbling over her face, white coat hanging limply to the waist. Brink spied her, even as she was working to maintain a neutral, impassive face.

"Dr. White, " he said, and stopped. "Ellen," he said in an even quieter voice, "what ... do... you think?"

It would be so easy to equivocate, to say she's a student, that she doesn't have enough experience, to defer to the judgment of Drs. Tucker and Wilkinson, the oncologist and the pulmonologist. So easy to waive her decision.

So easy.

"I think," she said, straightening up, trying to muster up her firmest voice, "that you should be intubated."

Brink's eyes narrowed. Light from those dark eyes pierced the glasses still on his face, burning into the eyes of Ellen White, third year medical student.

"You've ... already learned a lot," Brink said gasping. "Okay," he said, turning to Tucker, "intubate me."

A nurse left, returning back a moment later pushing a small cart with the equipment. Some of the people who worked in the ICU came over to watch.

The anesthesiologist gave a small dose of I.V. Demerol and Versed, then pried open the surgeon's mouth. The tube slid in easily. The small balloon that would hold the endotreacheal tube in place was inflated, and Brink was hooked up to the respirator. Roland Brink, fifty years old, now completely dependent on others. His breathing had been taken away, was in the control of others. He had surrendered a primal function.

"I would always hit the ground running," Mr. Rigby said. "Nothing could keep me down." Up and down went his head slowly. "I used to be a man. Now," he said, his voice trailing off, "I'm a nothing."

"That's not true," Ellen said.

"Of course it's true," Mr. Rigby said, his voice now so feeble he could barely whisper. "I'm so weak..." He began to cry softly, a thick strange muffled sound coming from the back of his throat.

Ellen squeezed his hand harder.

"I'm so weak..." he started again, "...that I can't even put up a fight anymore."

Dazed from the medicines and perhaps the shock of the tube, Brink lay quietly. An occasional shiver came out from under the blanket. The monitor recorded every heart beat and every few moments, an automatic blood pressure cuff inflated.

The X-ray was on the view box behind the room.

"It looks a lot worse, even in the past few hours," Wilkinson was saying. "Look here," and she pointed to the right lung. So clear recently, now it too had a ground glass appearance.

"Get me the bronchoscopy tray," she barked out to the nurses.

Another injection of Demerol, and the surgeon now slept peacefully, unaware of the presence of the bronchoscope tube that was placed into his airways. The pulmonologist carefully suctioned out a small amount of fluid, then performed lavage, taking out quantities of bronchial cells in saline solution.

Brink rested quietly. The procedure done, the interested crowd dispersed, and the specimen was rushed to the pathology lab where, given the status of their important patient, the Chief of Pathology himself had mobilized a whole team to hustle things along.

"I have to go to the office," Tucker said to Ellen. "There are already plenty of patients there and they're probably all mad because I'm showing up late." He shrugged his shoulders. "Can't win in this business."

He reviewed the other patients he was following in the hospital.

"You check on them and call me if there are any problems," Tucker said, handing a list to Ellen at the same time he knocked the stethoscope out of his pocket. Bending over to pick it up, his glasses fell off. Ellen chuckled, quietly at first, then more until it was a full fledged laugh. It felt so good to laugh! Tucker seemed to pay it no attention.

It felt so good to laugh!

"Tell the patients I'll see them before I go home tonight," he said, adjusting his glasses.

It would be a long day for the oncologist. Ellen hoped she'd get out sooner. Maybe she could spend a little time with Brent.

She sat down for a cup of coffee, and all at once felt overwhelmingly tired, suddenly realizing she'd hadn't slept for well over one day.

Over the top of the central monitor bank, she could see the surgeon's room. A nurse was readjusting his I.V. and checking settings on the respirator. Except for an oval — the head – sticking out, there was no evidence that the bed actually contained a human. And that head had a large plastic tube running into it, connected to the respirator.

"C'mon Ellen," Wilkinson said. "Let's go down to pathology and see what they've found."

Ellen shook herself out of a trance, an exhausted torpor, and rose slowly, face droopy as worn drapes, posture sagging like an old stretched out dress. Left foot, right foot, she followed the pulmonologist's sprightly step, the bounce of someone who'd slept all night.

"Pneumocystis," the Chief of Pathology announced.

Wilkinson nodded.

"Pneumocystis?" Ellen gasped. "But he doesn't have AIDS. How..."

The pulmonologist raised her right hand. "There was pneumocystis before there was AIDS. This man's very immunosuppressed, and obviously the stage was right."

Ellen thought about the X-ray. No wonder he was so short of breath but had such clear sounding lungs. A typical pneumocystis story.

Within an hour, Brink, still asleep, still so dependent on the respirator, had received his first dose of I.V. Pentamidine.

"What are his chances?" Ellen asked Wilkinson. "I mean, he is going to be alright, isn't he?"

The lung doctor gave a total body shrug, forehead, chin, shoulders, arms, even torso all pointing up in a large question mark.

"Can't say. He might make it."

Ellen looked for a chair.

"Don't look so down," Wilkinson said "It's not your fault."

Ellen felt a terrible emptiness. Why? she asked herself. I hated the man. What do I
care?

Resolved. I'm simply not going to let the patients bother me so much. I'll erect some kind of barrier. Nothing unreasonable about that. Ellen White has her own life too.

After Wilkinson left, Ellen went to the cafeteria, bought a small pastry, and sat down. She stared at the pastry, took a few bites, then set it down.

Why? she asked herself again. I hated the man. What do I care?

She made her rounds, seeing all the other patients, and began feeling more energetic, the storm after the calm, as if activated by an outside energy source. Something seemed to be driving her as she moved quickly from one floor to the next. Tucker had a goodly census of hospitalized patients, keeping Ellen busy for a few hours, reviewing charts and X-rays, talking to and examining patients, moving from one floor to another.

Her other duties finished, she returned to Brink's room. He lay there, eyes still closed, chest moving up and down in concert with the bellows.

The room was busy even now. Nurses, lab personnel, respiratory technicians, doctors.

But no family. No next of kin. Nobody.

Chest moving up and down. The room so full of people, but the surgeon was alone. All alone.

CHAPTER 25

For a moment, Ellen continued to stare out the kitchen window, letting the doorbell ring. An unusually warm day for early spring, the southwest wind carried not only tropical air but a pervading buoyancy. Spirits were lighter, humor was higher. And if everything didn't seem quite right to Ellen, still it was hard to ignore at least a semblance of well-being. The yellows of the forsythia kept pace with the brilliance of the sun; the cherries were already beginning to bloom along the Tidal Basin.

Ellen had seen Brink in the morning, but had taken the Saturday afternoon off to do some shopping. Brent was with his father, Deb was off with friends. Ellen still had an hour until she'd head into Georgetown to have dinner with Jill.

Who could be ringing the doorbell?

A man she didn't recognize was standing at the front door with something – it almost looked like flowers – in his hands.

"Ellen White?" the man asked. "These are for you," handing over a dozen red longstem roses.

Who would send her roses? Her hands trembled as she took off the small envelope. For a second she closed her eyes, trying to imagine, then fumbled to open the card.

"I have to stay in Thailand longer than expected, but I look forward to returning to D.C. soon. Hope to see you then. Sincerely, Dave."

He'd disappeared so abruptly from her life. In a Peruvian restaurant one day, off in Thailand the next. She hadn't forgotten him, but he'd lost his relevance.

And then a dozen roses.

Her life had been so taken up with the oncology elective. And more recently with Brink. It was three days since he'd been intubated. Only three days?

And now a dozen unsolicited, unexpected, unimagined roses. Roses from the periphery of her life.

Ellen couldn't remember the last time anyone had sent her roses. She rummaged around in a big closet until she found the vase, terribly dusty. A little soapy water and it came to life.

She set the roses on the dining room table, but it seemed too dark. Looking around, she decided on the Chickering, which was in full sunlight. The roses sat there pulling in the rays of the late afternoon sun through gauzy curtains. The tired and worn living room lit up, became three dimensional in an instant.

A dozen unimagined roses.

* * *

"I knew you'd say that," Ellen said. "I almost didn't come over."

Jill laughed. "I'm glad that I'm so predictable."

Ellen shook her head. "The guy disappears to the other side of the planet, then sends me a dozen roses and I'm supposed to be excited, or to use your word, 'thrilled.'"

"He had no long term commitment to you," Jill said. "You'd had exactly two dates with him; I don't see why he had to report to you when he went off on business. I think it's pretty nifty that he's thinking of you at all, especially in Thailand." She sighed. "Rick hasn't sent me roses in years, and *he* has a commitment to me."

"I'll think about what you're saying, but right now my life is so filled up with other matters... ." Like Brink, still on the respirator in the ICU.

And like Brent.

Brent. It looked like the pediatrician was right.

Ellen shook her head. A fifteen year boy had no business getting depressed. She'd failed him as a mother.

Ellen looked across the table at Jill. Should she share this sadness with her friend? There really was nobody to talk to. Ellen White, the medical student who spent so much time listening to her patients, had no one she could talk to.

Should she share it with Jill?

Her closest friend, but sometimes Jill could be so flip, so judgmental. If she told Jill about how badly she felt about Brent, how she felt so responsible...

"You're crying?" Jill said softly.

Ellen nodded. "Just thinking about those roses."

The dinner was soon over and Ellen began the short trip to the hospital for her late evening rounds. At least it gave her something to do, some purpose.

The moon was just rising, trying to hide behind some tree branches covered with an early leafy fuzz. The unexpected daytime spring warmth was replaced with an evening chill.

Ellen pulled into the parking lot. The hospital seemed even darker than usual this evening. She watched a mother berate a youngster who was screaming in the long hall; a guard at the nearby door looked away uncomfortably, his attention suddenly arrested by a photo of the Washington Monument on a nearby wall. The woman at the gift shop was just closing the door when a man came up and asked her if it was too late to buy a paperback for his wife. "She's bored out of her mind," Ellen heard him say. The gift shop woman hesitated, then opened the door, almost furtively. "Shh," she warned as they went inside. The woman berating the child was gone, and the guard's interest in the Washington Monument waned.

Ellen's first stop was the gynecologic oncology floor; the woman there was dying and was terribly frightened. So terribly frightened. And Ellen found it uncomfortable to sit with the woman and her husband as they asked all kinds of questions she couldn't answer. Here was this woman dying and Ellen wanted to help, but all she could do was admit her ignorance.

What would George Tucker think of her?

Always saying "I don't know." What would Roland Brink think of her?

Ellen felt like getting up and kicking the door. She was a complete failure. When her time with them was finished, she hadn't told them anything, hadn't helped them a bit. Whatever on earth possessed her to want to be a doctor?

The world would probably be better off if she just plain quit.

The Chopin 'Revolutionary Etude' suddenly teemed out of the car radio, great scales heaving up and down....

It had been this piece that defeated Deb. She'd quit the piano, unwilling to continue the struggle for mastery. Too hard, she'd said. Too much effort.

And now the Chickering sat in the living room, more occupied with the gathering dust than with Chopin.

Too hard. Too much effort.

"Thanks so much for coming by," the husband said as Ellen left. "Your visits always mean so much to us."

She saw a few more patients, saving her sickest until last. Up the stairs to the Intensive Care Unit. Past the elevators, past the restrooms, past the nurses' lounge. Past the small ICU waiting room. She glanced in.

For a moment – just the briefest second – Ellen was startled. She thought she'd seen Roland's face, but there was only an elderly woman sitting in the waiting room corner. Ellen wasn't happy admitting it, but Jill was right. Roland Brink *was* having a profound effect on her. More and more, every time she saw a cancer patient she'd wonder not what Tucker would think of her, but what Brink would say. And now she was even seeing his face where it didn't belong, here in the waiting room.

The ICU was dressed in its usual quiet evening garb. Ellen looked at the flow sheet.

It was three days since Brink had been intubated. Although the pneumonia was beginning to clear up on the pentamidine therapy, it wasn't yielding without a good fight. The surgeon's white count remained profoundly depressed, but Tucker had said it should start to come up in a day or two. All kind of bone marrow stimulants were already being given.

The blood pressure remained stable. Urine output was adequate. Brink was becoming protein depleted; soon he'd be getting intravenous feedings.

Every manner of doctor wrote notes in the chart, each conveying the same sense of gloom. The prognosis was not good. And even if the surgeon survived this episode, what then? He still had the cancer to fight.

Except for interludes when sleeping, Brink was alert. The respirator tube made communication very difficult; he would nod yes and no to the questions of doctors, nurses, and others, but unlike many patients, the surgeon made no particular effort to write notes. But he watched everything, never releasing his gaze for even a moment.

It was past midnight. Ellen was tired – no, more than tired. Weary. She'd examine Brink quickly, then go home.

His eyes were open when Ellen came in. The monitor on the wall flashed the surgeon's vital signs continuously; the bellows of the respirator went up and down; urine filled the drainage bag hanging from the bedside.

Brink's eyes followed Ellen as she took in all the monitors.

"Are you feeling alright?"

He nodded yes.

"Any pain?"

No.

"Is there anything I can do to make you more comfortable?"

No.

She examined him, suddenly feeling the unexpected alertness return, her fatigue gone. He was somewhat wasted, his cheeks drawn in. The ribs were still more evident on his chest. Only the eyes were unchanged – brilliant, burning.

The lungs sounded clear. The heart tones were normal. The abdomen was soft. There was mild atrophy of the muscles of the arms and legs. Once again, Ellen noted the small skull and crossbones on the upper arm.

The hands, sitting atop the blanket, were well perfused, a good blood supply. Ellen looked at one, then the other. She picked up his right hand – looking at the color, the skin. Lines crisscrossed the palms, swirled around the fingertips. Even now, the muscles and tendons under the surface were drawn tightly, their sharp edges visible through the skin; no hint of weakness in these hands. Ellen looked at her own right hand, smooth, soft, the sinews hidden in the tissues. She looked back at Brink's hand.

That hand could only belong to Roland Brink. It was as singular as his face. Watching Brink in the OR in the past, she'd always considered his remarkable hands – hands that cut, cauterized, tied; hands that never wasted a motion – a reflection of the surgeon. Did she get it backwards? Was the surgeon a reflection of his hands?

She stared at the right hand for a moment more, then set it down gently on the bedcover and turned to leave.

But Brink reached out with that right hand, catching Ellen's arm. He slid his hand down her arm to her wrist and, for a few seconds, his fingers held her lower arm.

Ellen closed her eyes, making no attempt to move. She sensed he was staring at her, almost felt the gaze impaling her, burning into her, so she wasn't surprised when she opened her eyes and saw the intensity of his look. She looked away.

After a few moments, he released his grip and put the right hand back at his side.

Ellen was almost afraid to look at the surgeon's face again, but as she turned to go out, her eyes met his. Dark, unvanquished, they were fixed on her with startling intensity.

Ellen broke his gaze and walked out. She tried to chat nonchalantly with the nurse for a moment, then stole a quick look into the room. Brink's head was straight ahead, the eyes open, watching the wall.

Her notes finished, she began to leave.

The old woman from the waiting area approached as she left the ICU.

"Are you one of Roland's doctors?" she asked.

It was a face that looked as if it had finished fighting its battles and now had only the wrinkles of resignation. All except for the eyes, dark and unvanquished.

And the hands. The muscles and tendons ran lean and sharp; everything about these hands was unambiguous.

The hands and the eyes defined her, reaching past the wrinkles on the face, the stooping posture.

Ellen knew who this old woman was.

"How did you find out he was here?" Ellen asked. "He is so secretive."

"His secretary called me."

"He's very sick, you know," Ellen said, looking for a chair.

"I swore I'd never see him again," the old lady said, harshness in the voice. "But," her voice softening now, "it's hard when your own son is dying." She looked at Ellen. "He *is* dying, isn't he?"

"I...I'm only the medical student," Ellen began. "You'd really have to ask his doctors."

The old woman looked at Ellen.

"He *is* dying, isn't he," she repeated in the same voice.

"I..." Ellen stopped. "Yes," she said slowly, "he is dying. But there's still a small chance...." She didn't finish.

The two of them sat alone in the small waiting room. A security guard walked by and nodded . Ellen didn't quite know where to look, but whenever she turned her head she found the old woman's eyes fixed on her.

After a while, Ellen spoke. "Have you been in to see him yet?"

Mrs. Brink shook her head no. "And I'm not sure I will. I may just watch him from afar, where he can't see me."

"I think you should see him."

For a moment, the old woman's look softened, the eyes softened, the hands softened. But only for a moment.

"That's my business," she said, getting up and walking away.

CHAPTER 26

Ellen looked around the psychiatrist's small waiting room. The decor was spartan but adequate. A few chairs, two small tables, some magazines. A door lead to the doctor's office on the far wall. She leafed through Newsweek but couldn't get interested, so she set it down, leaned back in the slightly uncomfortable wooden chair, and closed her eyes.

Images of her teenage years kept coming to mind more and more these days. She was sitting on the bedroom floor with her best friend, looking through magazines, talking about boys and about their stupid school teachers.

Now, here she was, thirty-something years later, divorced, her son behind the doors in a psychiatrist's office, an insecure medical student with an unclear future, uncertain motives, undefined goals.

The door to the psychiatrist's room opened. Dr. Witherspoon pointed to an empty chair.

"Now Brent, as we discussed, I'm going to be talking to your mother for a few minutes. No secrets, I promise you." Brent found his way to the chair, his gaze catching Ellen's for a moment.

"Mrs. White," Witherspoon said.

Ellen followed him into the small office. His chair was a large brown leather swivel seat behind a good sized mahogany desk. A couple of comfortable living-room type chairs were opposite. The walls were painted beige and a few prints of horses were hung around the small space. A bookcase was filled with journals and volumes on psychiatry. A window admitted a dull gray light.

Ellen felt claustrophobic.

She sat across from the psychiatrist, shifting a few times in the chair. She adjusted her skirt, pulling it down an inch or two. It had been a long time since she'd worn this rusty brown suit. Somehow it had seemed appropriate to get out of her jeans for this interview.

Witherspoon rustled a few papers for some moments, then sat down, folding his hands.

"You're a medical student?" he said. "Brent was just telling me."

Ellen nodded.

"He's very proud of you," Witherspoon said. "Very proud."

Ellen caught her eyes stinging again. She took a few hesitant breaths.

"And I'm very proud of him," her voice cracking. "He's a wonderful kid."

Witherspoon shook his head up and down. "I agree. He seems like a nice young man, very sincere, mature for his years."

Ellen looked around the room. How was it possible that she was here, in this room, talking to a child psychiatrist? She looked up at Witherspoon, shifted a bit in her seat again and readjusted her skirt length slightly.

"What do you think?" she asked.

"You've taken your psychiatry rotation?"

"Yes."

"Well, I don't see a great mystery here. A nice well-adjusted young man, but his defenses have been overwhelmed. The separation from his father, the divorce, are just too much for him, so he's somatisized some of his distress."

"Do you think my absences are making it worse?"

"There's no sense in trying to blame yourself," Witherspoon said in a not unkindly way. "There are so many possible answers and..." he started to drone on. Ellen tuned him out, even as a vision of Brink came to mind. Be direct, he was telling her.

Ellen leaned forward, putting her hands on the psychiatrist's desk. "Dr. Witherspoon, I know you have an opinion. Please tell me."

"Well," he said, "your absences aren't helping things, but, Mrs. White, psychiatry isn't black and white. You're a medical student; you understand that things doctors say often carry great weight with patients, perhaps a disproportionate weight. So, if I say 'yes,' I think your studies are making things worse for him, you might change your whole outlook, change your lifestyle. But I could be wrong. I could do you and Brent a grave disservice with a snap judgment."

"What do you propose then?"

"I want to see the boy pretty regularly. Maybe twice a week to start. In a few weeks, I'll have a much better idea."

"And for now?"

"I'd like to try him on an antidepressant, in a low dose."

They discussed the pros and cons of various drugs.

"What will your endpoint be?" Ellen asked.

"Again, it's hard to know. A certain gestalt I think. When he has more energy, when he feels more like eating again, when his stomach aches go away."

The meeting over, Ellen took Brent shopping for some new clothes, then for dinner.

"Does he think I'm crazy?" Brent asked as they drove to the mall.

"No, not at all."

"What does he think then?"

"Dr. Witherspoon thinks you're depressed. The divorce, not seeing your father very often, and me being unavailable so much of the time."

Brent looked ahead at the road. "I'm not depressed."

"The mind's a funny thing," Ellen said. "It's hard to really understand yourself sometimes."

"I understand myself just fine," Brent said. "I'm not depressed."

"In any case," Ellen said, "my oncology rotation is almost over and then I have two weeks off before my next rotation."

"What's that?"

"Obstetrics and gynecology. You know, delivering babies. Stuff like that."

Brent picked out some new clothes. Ellen bought them slightly large because he'd lost about four or five pounds in the last month, and she hoped he'd be growing into them soon. Brent seemed pretty pleased with his selections, standing in front of the mirrors and twirling around.

"It's nice to see you smiling," Ellen said.

Dinner was a different affair.

"Where to?" Ellen had asked. "I want to go someplace really special. You'll be my date, okay?" She'd winked at Brent.

"Your choice," Brent had said. "Maybe a nice restaurant, a Mom kind of place."

Ellen chose one of her favorites.

"This is a real adult restaurant," Ellen said, smiling at her dinner companion. "It's not the kind of place I would've taken you when you were still a kid."

Brent was the only patron dressed in baggy jeans, oversized shirt and AirJordans. He carefully looked over the menu, asking what some of the various dishes were, many with French names. After some negotiations with the waiter, Brent settled for something familiar.

Brent bit into a roll. Ellen didn't say anything when the rubble of the hard crust ended up all over the table and Brent. He drank his Coca Cola slowly, admiring the crystal glass. When the main course arrived, the waiter served Ellen's fillet of sole, then unobtrusively cleaned the bread crumbs. With a flourish, he set down the hamburger in front of Brent.

"Bon appetit," he said.

Brent pushed the salad around a bit, then went to the main course. Ellen knew that Brent was trying to eat but couldn't finish anything. After a few mouthfuls of the burger, he just shrugged and put it down.

After their outing, Ellen took Brent home. She asked him about the Baltimore Orioles team and their pennant chances.

"You've never been interested in baseball before," Brent answered.

"It's going to be a new hobby. Maybe we'll get up to Camden Yards for a few games this summer."

As soon as they got home, Ellen ran upstairs and changed into her whites, and left for the hospital. Brent waved from the window as she pulled out the driveway.

Well, that was a huge success, Ellen decided as she sped down River Road. First we see the shrink, then I watch him try to eat, and finally I leave him alone at home to do his homework. Real quality time with my kid.

Ellen arrived at the hospital and headed down the hall, almost tripping over wheelchair with a young woman holding a newborn. A grandmotherly nurse, right out of casting central, was pushing them along, while the new father followed behind, holding a small suitcase. He almost fell over the wheelchair as he ran ahead to get the door.

It was almost the same twenty years ago when Deb was born. Ellen was in a wheelchair and Jeff, flustered, dutifully ran alongside. How little had changed. Mothers and fathers with the new baby.

No. Everything had changed. Jeff, now polished and never flappable, was gone. Jeff, who used to let his hair go wild before grudgingly going to the barber; Jeff, who used to hold a knife and fork as if they were instruments of war; Jeff, who used to play PacMan for hours. Now, an elegant and polished lawyer, hair cut by a 'stylist'; manners impeccable enough to dine with the Queen; and whose favorite game was playing the stock market.

Had he left because Ellen was too busy with her children to spend enough time with him? Was it because she didn't work at being slinky and seductive enough? Had she failed him as a wife?

Ellen walked quickly through the hospital to the ICU. Brink was stable but still not quite ready to have the breathing tube removed. He'd been on the respirator for a week, and the consultants were beginning to write notes about possibly needing a tracheostomy if things didn't get better. Ellen knew that after ten days on a respirator, the tube through the mouth can cause too much damage to the throat and windpipe, so a permanent, "gentler" method is desirable.

She flipped from page to page in the chart. Notes in various clear hands alternated with nearly indecipherable musings. Some notes were short, direct; others were lengthy, almost chatty. Everything was in the third person.

Maybe Roland Brink had lived his life in the third person, Ellen wondered. Could he really be as impersonal as he seemed? She may have detested Brink, but she knew it from the start; he had no hidden face. He was what he appeared to be. Not like Jeff.

The curtain remained closed around Brink's room. Ellen set the chart down and got up to look at the chest X-ray. The pneumonia was clearly a lot better. Where there'd been a whitish haze the week before, now a lot of normal lung peeked through. The oxygenation was getting better, but the patient still wasn't better enough...

The last few times that Ellen had visited Brink she was impressed that the surgeon's stare had changed, had moderated; not the same harsh stare that had peered over the mask in the OR. Of course, it was hard to say much of anything, with that tube stuck in his mouth and another tube going through his nose into his stomach to give him nutrition. Still, even with all that facial distortion, Ellen thought she read almost – what was it? – a softening perhaps in the surgeon's face. The eyes burned clear and bright as ever but with a slightly more muted fire.

But Ellen still didn't like him; that was clear enough. Maybe she'd stopped detesting him, but that was very different from liking him. If, on a few occasions recently she'd felt more sympathetic and maybe even a bit empathetic, obviously that was because she was fulfilling her role as the compassionate healer. Only because she was a medical professional had she been able to rise above her personal feelings. She was behaving as Tucker had instructed her to, right?

Funny though. A few times, when she'd been examining him, Brink had reached down and grasped her hand for a few moments. Once his hand had even 'slipped' onto her thigh, but plainly that was an accident; Ellen had moved back immediately.

Ellen had only seen Brink's mother one more time, however the nurses said she would come and go, ask a few questions, but never stay.

Looking across the hall at the closed curtain to Brink's room, Ellen tried to find an image of the surgeon only a few months before when he'd been so arrogant and proud. Now he was... what? Not quite so arrogant perhaps, but still – if the eyes and hands said anything – just as proud.

She sat quietly at the nursing station for a couple of minutes more, sometimes staring at the drawn curtain and sometimes looking abstractly around the Intensive Care Unit. At last, she stood up, straightened her white coat, and went to see the patient.

Ellen pulled the curtain back a few inches and looked in. On the chair next to the bed, in the half-darkened room, she had no trouble immediately making out the figure of Mrs. Brink, sitting stiffly next to her son, near his feet. The surgeon lay in the bed, staring at the wall, his chest moving up and down in concert with the bellows.

Both heads turned at the same moment. It was the same face. The same eyes, the same forehead, cheeks, nose. The wrinkles of time in the woman, the tubes in the mouth and nose in the man couldn't blot out the likeness. Mother and son.

"Oh," Ellen said, starting to turn, "excuse me."

The surgeon's right hand motioned to her, waving her back.

"I can come back later," Ellen said.

No, Roland Brink's head nodded, and he pointed down. Stay now.

Ellen approached him with a few small steps.

"How are you?" she asked in her most self-conscious voice.

Fine, he mouthed.

After a few more questions, she examined him. Mrs. Brink sat quietly, saying nothing.

"His secretary told him I was here," the older woman said.

"You don't have to apologize," Ellen said. "He's your son."

"Yeah. My son."

Brink reached out and grasped Ellen's hand, squeezing it tightly, remarkably so for a man this incapacitated. Ellen looked at the respirator, as if it suddenly contained some news of great interest. She knew the surgeon was watching her and when she turned at last to look at him, she found the newer, less harsh look.

After a few seconds, Ellen excused herself, although it took some effort to free up her hand.

"I hope to see you tomorrow," she said to Mrs. Brink.

The older woman nodded.

Ellen went outside and wrote a brief note in the chart, looking up occasionally at the closed curtain. She could still feel the impression of his hand.

"Two days," she heard a voice behind her say.

She turned around to look at George Tucker.

"Two days?"

"The tube comes out in two days. I want to avoid a tracheostomy."

"His mother's in there, you know."

"Of course. I told her he was here."

"You? But I thought your secretary...."

"Technically yes, I told Theresa to bring her in, but it was my idea. In case Roland was feeling hostile, I wanted his anger directed towards my secretary instead of me. Doctor-patient relationship, you know. But his mother was looking for an entr'acte to get in, so I had to give it to her."

"But she said..."

"Bah," Tucker said, scratching his head. "She didn't come here just to sit in the waiting room. She's probably been looking for rapprochement with him for a long time."

"If it's okay with you," Ellen said, "I'd like to continue to follow him even after I finish my oncology rotation in two days."

Tucker smiled. "I knew you would. By the way," he went on, "I'm giving you an 'A' for your oncology rotation. So, how would you like to join me at a little cafe in Georgetown for coffee and dessert?"

George Tucker?

Ellen looked at the curtain, then at Tucker. His expression had changed, almost imperceptibly. It was not the face of the oncologist now, but a man asking a woman out to coffee.

"I'd love to join you," Ellen said.

CHAPTER 27

There was a crowd in Brink's room as they got ready to pull out the endotracheal tube. With the temperature normal, the chest X-ray almost clear, and the oxygenation good, the long process of weaning from the respirator was about to end.

Ellen chose a spot in the corner. Tucker was somewhat closer, but the real work would be shared by the anesthesiologist and the Chief of Intensive Care, Dr. Pendleton.

Brink had already been breathing through the endotracheal tube, unassisted by the respirator, for nearly twelve hours.

"Roland, I'm going to deflate the cuff in a few moments, then I'll take out the tube," Pendleton was saying. "The nurses will suction you after that. Ready?"

Brink nodded yes.

The balloon was deflated and the tube came out smoothly. Brink coughed for a moment, then opened his mouth while all the accumulated mucus in the throat was sucked out.

The electrocardiographic monitor showed a steady heart rate. The blood pressure remained stable. Pendleton pushed a couple of buttons on the side of the bed and Brink's head was elevated to a 45° angle.

"How are you?" Pendleton asked.

"Fine," Brink said, his voice thicker than a bullfrog's; he coughed a few times.

An humidified oxygen mask was plopped over his face. Some of the staff listened to his heart and lungs. The oxygen saturation remained stable, pulse and respirations steady.

Within a few minutes, almost everybody was out of the room. It had been wall-to-wall people, standing room only; the excitement over, the crowds moved on to something else. Only the nurse, Tucker, and Ellen remained.

"I'll be back in about an hour, Roland," Tucker said, "after things have settled down a bit."

Tucker stepped back to let Ellen walk out the door first. This was her last day on the oncology rotation.

She turned her head back to see Brink just before going through the door. The surgeon was lying quietly, humidified mask over his face, arms at his side.

Their eyes met for a moment.

"Lunch?" Tucker asked as he and Ellen reached the nursing station. "Somebody told me about a nice place in Georgetown."

On arrival at the hospital parking lot, Tucker discovered he'd misplaced his car. After walking back and forth a few times, Ellen following, he remembered the car was in the small lot near the ER, on the other side of the hospital.

Scratching his head for a moment, he plotted a course of action.

"Let's walk instead to that Italian place on Wisconsin Avenue," Ellen suggested.

It was a short walk to the restaurant and they were seated right away.

"What's next for your star patient?" Ellen asked a few minutes later as she poured on the salad dressing and began mixing it into the lettuce.

"Roland?"

Ellen nodded.

"His blood counts are actually doing well," Tucker said. "His bone marrow has recovered nicely from the last round of chemo, so I expect he can probably go home in a few days."

"A few days? After being so sick?"

"Once we're sure that his lungs are okay, then his biggest problem is going to be getting him up and walking around, to recover his energy. We've got to be sure to keep him well fed."

"And then?"

"As soon as he's better, then…" Tucker paused, "….then we whack him with chemo again." The oncologist shook his head. "This is a hell of a profession. These patients – it's like a game. Build them up, knock them down. Supposedly for some abstract greater good I guess."

"What do you think his chances are? Realistically?" Ellen shifted slightly in her seat.

"For the record, they're okay. Off the record, I'm quite pessimistic. His tumor is extraordinarily aggressive. I'm sure he's got a lot of cancer left, and that's probably why we had such trouble getting him off the respirator."

"Will you give him the same chemotherapy?"

"Yes. The only difference is I'll cut back on the bleomycin a bit, because it's toxic to the lungs. And I'll put him on an oral sulfa prep to prevent another round of pneumocystis, just like they do with the AIDS patients."

Tucker took a big forkful of pasta and then watched it roll back onto the plate before he'd even gotten it near his mouth.

"Have you enjoyed the oncology rotation?" he asked, this time restraining the pasta on the fork with his knife.

"Enjoyed? I'm not sure that's the word. But it's been very interesting, that's for sure. I doubt I could ever be an oncologist. So few answers, so many questions."

"That's what being a doctor's about. I hope you'll give oncology some thought, because you'd make a terrific cancer doctor." Tucker successfully negotiated all obstacles and the pasta ended safely in his mouth. "You have the patience and humanity needed to be successful."

Ellen took a mouthful of salad.

"How's your son?" Tucker asked.

Ellen seemed surprised by the question. "Brent's about the same," she said when she'd finished chewing. "He's on Zoloft. His appetite does seem a little better, but he still has a stomachache and no energy."

"Did his pediatrician work him up?"

"Yes. In fact, he saw a gastroenterologist, had a barium enema and an abdominal CT scan. Everything checks out there."

"What's his father say?"

"Jeff? He's been over a couple of times to check up on Brent. Full of good cheer. Hey, let's go to a ballgame. Can I buy you a new CD player? Be sure to do your homework. Hmmph." She scowled. "Helpful stuff like that."

"And?"

"He's got a new CD player, but he doesn't look any better." She set her fork down. "And, he got to met Jeff's girlfriend." Ellen shook her head. "Like rubbing it in his face. But I'm sure Jeff was wearing a really nice cashmere sweater or something similar."

For a moment, they sat there, saying nothing.

"What does the shrink say?" Tucker asked at last.

"Lots of issues to work out, stuff lurking around from when Brent was just a little kid. Family problems are internalized over a long time. Sounds like the kind of things I used to read about on my psych rotation." She paused. "Witherspoon and Brent are meeting twice a week to work it all out. It's, well, very unnerving and a bit frightening."

Talk and pills, Dr. White. Talk and pills.

Brink on the surgical ward, holding the door open for her, followed by an image of Witherspoon's office: two sessions a week with the psychiatrist and Zoloft. *Talk and pills.*

"If I can help, please let me know." Tucker's voice, sudden and unexpected, briefly startled Ellen.

"That's very sweet," she said, coming back to the present, "because I know you really mean it." She squeezed his hand for just a second. "Thank you."

Tucker coughed and pushed his pasta around a bit on the plate.

"Ellen," he said slowly, measuring each word, "would you like to go to the Kennedy Center with me in a couple of nights to hear the National Symphony? Mozart, Brahms, and somebody I never heard of."

Ellen started to laugh, but stifled it when she saw the almost childlike look of expectation on Tucker's face. How long had he been planning this? How long to get up the courage to ask?

"Thank you, George," she said. "I'd love to."

CHAPTER 28

Suddenly George Tucker felt young again.

When Ellen White had first come into his office, she was just another student. Bright, affable, hard-working. Nothing more. George had gone on daily rounds with her at the hospital and had shared his office patients with her.

But it wasn't until the fourth week or so of her rotation that he'd actually *noticed* her. Attractive? He'd already known that, had no trouble seeing past her rumply white coat filled with stethoscopes, pens, handbooks. But suddenly the blue eyes clicked; the soft curves of the shoulders and hips looked different; all at once the whole woman became evident.

And George knew that the physical attractiveness was only part of her appeal. There was something else she had to offer, a kind of ripeness, almost a world view, that only a mature woman could have. And when those feelings gelled, George suddenly knew.

And he had a date. Tonight at the Symphony. He'd been trying for the past two weeks – ever since he'd made the discovery – to act the same as always, not to let Ellen know that he saw her in a new light. Until, that is, the six week oncology elective was over. Then he could approach her differently.

Tonight he had a date.

The office schedule was filled as always with cancer patients, but almost as if some deity knew he had a special night – his first date since Cathy had died – the day was filled with easy patients, patients who were doing well. Happy patients, grateful patients. George couldn't remember a more genial day.

Even the patients seemed to note his upbeat mood. He smiled more, his step was livelier. The cherry blossoms outside his office window tossed the sunlight around, the light flickering on and off the wall in his room.

He decided to leave work early – a rarity – to go home and search his closet for a nice outfit. There wasn't enough time to buy new spring clothes, but he took out his best suit – the only one without shiny shoulders and elbows – and resolved to buy a new tie, even thinking to bring the suit jacket with him.

The salesman admired the tie George selected, then tactfully suggested a different one. "It's better when the colors complement each other," he pointed out, and then also suggested a new shirt.

George hummed to himself as he showered. He was going to look pretty snazzy.

The car! He felt a sudden chill. What a mess! He threw on a robe, ran downstairs, then back upstairs to get some shoes. Furiously, he cleaned out the front and back seats with a hand-held vacuum. The ever-present assortment of books and journals was retired to the trunk.

Still plenty of time. He looked in the cabinet at cologne someone had given him one Christmas. George had never used anything like that in his life. He unscrewed the top and sniffed.

Not bad.

Maybe just the slightest dab. Should he?

He took out the pins from his new shirt and tried it on, then put a bandage over the small puncture wound where he'd missed a pin. Then on with the suit and new tie. He carefully combed his hair.

It would take him about 25 minutes to get to Ellen's, but he'd leave a few minutes early. George didn't want to be late.

Still humming, he turned on the lights in the living room and kitchen and headed to the garage.

The telephone rang.

I'll ignore it, he thought. Let the answering machine take it.

But....what if it was Ellen?

He'd wait just to hear the message, but wouldn't pick up the phone.

The third ring. The fourth ring.

His recorded message.

"Dr. Tucker," he heard the woman's voice say over the phone, "this is Grace Olsen. I'm sorry to bother you at home. I mean, I'm sorry to bother your answering machine."

Grace Olsen paused.

"It's just that, well, Curt had a terrible seizure a few minutes ago. I called 911 and they're coming." She began to cry. "Dr. Tucker, I'm so afraid. He looks terrible." Another short whimper. "I'm sorry to call you at home. I know you're busy. I can call the answering service and get your covering doctor."

George stood at the door. He was no longer humming.

"Oh God, Dr. Tucker, I'm so frightened. I..." She couldn't continue.

Curt Olsen, age eighteen, dying of a highly malignant brain tumor. The boy had been through hell, had shown extraordinary courage. His mother had been with him from the start, his support, his ally. George had gotten to know them very well in the four months since the diagnosis. In all that time, he'd never heard Grace Olsen cry. Now he heard the terror in her voice. This was her son. Not some stranger, not some friend, but the child she'd brought into the world. The child she'd nurtured and read to, the child she'd driven to soccer and basketball games. The child she loved. Her son.

The on call doctor – a nice guy, empathetic. But he didn't know the Olsens.

For another minute, George stood at the door, then he picked up the phone.

"You've reached the White residence," Ellen's voice said. "Please leave a message."

George knew Ellen would understand. He left a message. He'd try to pick her up as soon as possible. At least they could go out to a small cafe, even if they missed the Symphony.

George got in his car and headed to Cleveland Park Hospital. He'd be there for Grace and Curt Olsen.

CHAPTER 29

At first, Ellen laughed when she opened the front door. A delivery van was parked in front.

"Ellen White?"

He handed her a bottle of Dom Perignon elegantly wrapped with a single rose lying across the box.

Even before looking at the card, she knew who had sent this. It would never have occurred to George Tucker, so there was only one possibility.

"I hope you don't forget me," the small typed note said. "My plans are shaping up and I hope to return to Washington soon. Fondly, Dave."

* * *

Fondly, Dave.

Ellen bent over to pick up another fallen branch. It was sunny outside, and Ellen wanted to test the early spring warmth. Short khaki pants with a hand-knotted belt, a pale pink polo, and a floppy straw hat, her hair streaming out from underneath – she'd tried barefoot but the ground was still too cold, so she settled for old docksides. Early spring was the time to clean the yard of the winter debris. Twigs and broken branches, piles of dead leaves, littered the lawn, resting atop straw-brown grass. Impatient to get spring moving, dandelion patches staked out their positions, bright yellow flowers atop full green leaves, triumphant in the sunlight undiminished by the leafless branches.

Fondly, Dave.

Ellen walked into the small patch of woods behind her house and threw the sticks in. The leaves were still hidden in the twigs above; sunlight poured onto the litter of leaves on the woods floor. Ellen bent over to admire a small flower. Spring beauties, pale pinkish-white petals traversed by reddish veins. Five leaflets.

He loves me, he loves me not, he... .

Five: she stopped. No room for those kinds of thoughts.

Dave Longacre seemed interested....again. Or was it still? George Tucker, tripping over his own feet and his own words, seemed interested. After a drought, now....if not a deluge, at least a drizzle.

Fondly, Roland.

No! Ellen stamped hard on a dead oak branch, cracking it.

Not Roland! Dave!

A cloud moved in front of the sun, instantly muting its brilliance. The landscape, a moment ago in stark relief, the blacks and whites of shadows cutting sharply, now dulled into grays, edges fuzzy, perspectives foreshortened. The dandelions, so recently exultant, now listlessly hugged the ground in drab greens and yellows.

Not Roland! Dave!

* * *

"You sure seem fussy," Jill said later in the day when she came over to visit.

"Why?" Ellen asked.

"Because that's at least the fourth time you've washed off the kitchen counter. I think it's clean by now."

Ellen put the sponge away. "Better?"

"What's bothering you anyway? You said Brent's better today."

"Uh huh. He's been at school all day. He called me at lunch and said he was feeling okay. Hardly any stomachache at all." She took off the apron and hung it in the closet. Late afternoon sun poured in golden orange through the skylight.

"What's the shrink think?" Jill asked.

"The same. Ambivalence towards his father. Instead of taking it 'to heart', he's taking it 'to stomach.' Witherspoon's idea of a joke, I think."

"Not too funny."

"No, he's okay. Witherspoon's really quite simpático. He says this kind of adjustment reaction isn't unusual and he's convinced that Brent will get over it soon enough."

Jill leaned over the table, looking at her friend. "So what's bothering you then?"

"Not sure. Maybe it's the Dom Perignon."

"I think that's pretty exciting. Suave, powerful lawyer in Asia puts moves on ordinary woman in Washington." Jill paused. "Sorry. That came out wrong."

"I have so much on my plate that it's hard to get worked up," Ellen said, "but when he returns, I may get more excited. I still feel kind of let down however."

"So what else is bugging you?"

"Who knows," Ellen shrugged. "But, I still feel badly about that date the other night."

"What time did George finally pick you up?" Jill asked.

"About ten. We went out for a quick dessert, then went home. Somehow I was expecting, well, to have more fun."

"He was pretty upset about this sick child with the brain tumor, wasn't he?"

Ellen nodded. "I'm really proud to know someone like George. He did the right thing, going to the hospital."

"You know these people?"

"The Olsens? Sure, I followed them with George during my rotation. It's..." She stopped.

Jill said nothing.

"There but for the grace of God...." Ellen said. "I'm sure you're right. George was just too overwhelmed by the tragedy. How could he just go out and have a good time?" She sighed. "There but for the grace of God...." she repeated.

Jill remained quiet. The sun was setting and the kitchen getting cooler. Ellen went to the laundry room and found a pair of jeans. She slipped out of her shorts and into the jeans, her right knee peering through the shredded denim.

The automatic ice maker broke the silence with a brief low whir.

"And....there's something else," Ellen said in a low voice. "I keep thinking about Brink. This man, all alone in his house in McLean, with this horrible disease. Too proud or too stubborn to request help, to have a few friends."

"Or too stupid?"

Ellen sat down. "No, not that," she said. "He's anything but stupid." A vision of the OR, Brink mobilizing intestine as Ellen held a retractor, steel gray-blue eyes intermittently peering over the mask at the student. "No, anything but stupid," she repeated... .. There was Brink upbraiding her for letting a piece of tissue slip, telling her to scrub pots and pans.

An almost acrid smile. "The most impossible person I've ever met", Ellen said. "Hmmph." A pause. "Did I tell you he had a fight with his mother and told her to go back to New Jersey." Ellen shook her head again. "What an impossible man."

Jill looked over the top of her glasses. "Why don't you call him to see if he needs some help."

"My oncology rotation is over."

Jill sat motionless, still looking over her glasses.

"Maybe you're right," Ellen said slowly, getting up to take out the dustpan to sweep the corner.

Maybe she's right, Ellen wondered after Jill had left. Maybe I *should* call him. After all, he's so sick.

Ellen picked up the receiver, surprising herself by knowing Brink's home phone number from memory.

"Hello," the voice answered, a familiar voice. As the voice rolled through her, Ellen felt a sense of calm. It may have been weaker, but the voice projected strength and maybe even a sense of, what was it? Security? Reassurance? A vision of his hands came to her.

"This is Ellen. I, um, was wondering how you're doing."

A pause. "Ah," the voice said a few moments later, "Dr. Ellen White. I'm doing fine."

Ellen looked for something to say. "Do you have any pain?"

"No."

"How's your breathing?"

"Fine."

"Oh come on," Ellen said, suddenly laughing. "How are you?"

He returned the laugh. "Weak as hell. I spend most of the time in bed and it damn near kills me."

"Are you eating?"

"I get the local grocery store to deliver food."

Ellen's mouth dropped. "You're home alone and preparing your own food?"

"George came over to see me yesterday and said I'm doing fine."

Ellen spoke with Tucker every day but didn't know that. "I'm appalled," she said. "I'm coming over to visit and make sure you're getting enough food."

Brink said nothing.

"And anyway," Ellen continued, "you need some company."

"Why?"

"Because I said so."

A pause. "Dr. White, I would be glad for the company."

"Good God, you're impossible. Either that or you're stupid." She shook her head. "You call me 'Ellen' or I'm not coming."

Another pause. Then, "Just tweaking you. Ellen, I'd be glad for some company. I'll go downstairs and wait for you."

Ellen looked at her jeans. Perfectly respectable, no question. But maybe it would be appropriate to put on something a little nicer. More in the doctor image.

She found a casual skirt and top Deb had bought her a few years ago for Mother's Day. Lightweight and springy, maybe too much so for an early spring evening, but it looked good on her, flattered her.

She put on an L.L.Beans parka, then went to the local grocery and picked up some food. She bought some daisies for his bedroom. Something to brighten his life a little, she mumbled as she bought them.

After crossing Chain Bridge into Virginia and getting stuck in a traffic jam, she rang the door. Brink answered in a moment. It had only been one week since Ellen had last seen him, but he looked ever paler and thinner. Somehow she'd expected him to be improving.

"Come in Ellen," Brink said, his tone quiet.

"Where shall I put the groceries?" She took off the parka.

Brink watched her set out some food. Suddenly remembering the daisies she ran out to the car.

"I need a vase," she announced, swirling around slightly, the skirt following slightly behind.

Brink shrugged. "I don't have one."

Without saying a word, Ellen went to the kitchen and, finding a crystal water pitcher, arranged the daisies in it. In the living room again, she set the flowers down on a side table, next to a small beautifully lacquered model of an old car. It reminded her of the model Brink had on his desk at the hospital office - she remembered it as the only splash of color in the otherwise austere room.

Ellen looked around the living room. It was modern, angular, mostly blacks and whites. The crystalline chess board blended in so well that Ellen missed it on her first survey.

Roland watched her. "I decorated the room myself," confirming what Ellen already knew.

The conversation stumbled along in short snatches, bits and pieces here and there. Ellen was surprised to find the surgeon making an effort to keep a discussion going, although not with great success.

"Do you play chess?" he asked.

Ellen nodded negatively.

"Too bad," the surgeon said in tones so quiet that Ellen wondered how she heard them.

Brink sat quietly in a chair of black leather and chrome, trying to maintain his upright posture, but at times sinking into the harsh angles of the seat. Ellen surveyed the room for the most comfortable place to sit, but it was too far away, so she settled for a rigid all white and chrome upright chair.

Brink struggled to stay upright. Sometimes he closed his eyes, othertimes he would watch Ellen. Maybe the skin drooping on his face looked as if had given up, but not the eyes – still uncompromising, strong, sinewy. The hands, though somewhat wasted, radiated their own brilliance.

"Tell me about your most difficult surgery," Ellen said, leaning towards Brink after a lull in the conversation. "Even a great surgeon must have a tough case sometimes."

"One of my first cases," Brink said immediately, "just after I'd finished my training, was a modified Whipple procedure." At once he changed. He sat upright in the chair, now easily mastering its angular dissonances. The patient no longer, the surgeon once again. The skin on his face suddenly came to life, filling with color; his voice grew with each word. *He* was Roland Brink, *the* surgeon. Confident, arrogant, proud, he recounted the procedure, the great triumph of the surgery, a surgery against all odds, a surgery others had said was too dangerous. But not for him. The hands gestured, sometimes moving as if to cut, to cauterize, to sew. Face bright, motions energetic, his voice rose at the climactic moment. Roland Brink had triumphed where others might have failed.

Ellen sat breathless, pulled into the swirl of the story, following its crescendos and decrescendos as the surgeon took on the odds, fought the enemy, and emerged triumphant. Ellen's pulse sped up as the adventure unfolded until the dramatic conclusion.

And then, the story finished, Brink slid back into the chair, the energy spent, the battery discharged. The effort of telling the story had depleted him. The 78 rpm record slowed to 33 rpm.

They sat quietly for a minute, Brink's eyes closed.

"Can I ask you a question?" Ellen said softly.

Brink opened his eyes.

"Well?" he said after a few seconds.

Ellen coughed twice and shifted in the chair.

"I've sometimes wondered..." She shifted again.

'Well?"

"I…"

"Out with it," Brink said.

"What's the skull and crossbones mean?"

"That's none of your…" He stopped and closed his eyes. Tilting his head further back, he shut his eyes even tighter. For a long minute he sat immobile, chest barely moving. The room was silent; in the far distance was the faint buzzing of a lawnmower.

"I grew up poor in New Jersey," he said, speaking more slowly than Ellen could remember. "I was an outsider, someone who never fit in. My mother made me stay home to help with chores or to study or help my brother with his schoolwork. My clothes were all hand-me-downs from some distant cousin. And athletics? I couldn't run to first base without tripping. But…," he picked up his head and looked at Ellen, "…I wanted to fit in. Can you understand what it was like for me? No friends, living at home with a mother I detested and a weak-willed brother. Can you understand?"

The surgeon took several deep breaths, still looking at Ellen through glassine blue eyes.

"One Saturday, in my last year at high school, some other kids – the cool kids, the fashionable kids, the kids with more money – invited me to join them at a party. I was excited, flattered; I desperately wanted some friends. I made up some excuse and got out of the house."

The surgeon closed his eyes again. "They got me drunk," he said in a barely audible voice.

He opened his eyes and leaned forward. "They got me drunk because they wanted to make me look like a fool. They didn't want to be my friend. They wanted to humiliate me."

The room was quiet except for the sound of the forced hot air through the ducts.

"And do you know what happened?" Brink spat it out. "They took me, drunk, to a local whore. And they all watched me; they were an audience. And when I was finished with her, with the whore, they took me to get a tattoo." He pointed to his arm. "This tattoo."

Ellen sat breathless, neither able nor willing to move.

"But worse than the tattoo," he sneered, "I'd made a fool of myself, humiliating myself with that whore in front of an audience. An audience!"

He stopped for a moment, eyes shut, reliving it.

"The next day, while I was in bed with a terrible headache, my mother

172

found out about the tattoo – I don't know if she ever found out about the whore – and she started hitting me, pounding me. I didn't put up any resistance."

Brink sat on the edge of the chair, muscles rigid, veins on his head overwhelming the rest of his face.

"At that moment," he spat out, "I swore I'd never lose control again." He stopped for a few seconds. "I could've had the tattoo removed but I've left it there as a reminder."

The surgeon's sneer deepened. "I won't even tell you what it was like when I got to school on Monday; they ridiculed, they mocked me. Even some of the high school girls laughed at me."

Brink closed his eyes again and leaned back.

"I've *never* lost control again," he whispered. "*Never*."

Ellen watched the surgeon, saying nothing, not moving, hardly breathing. Had she really once detested him?

"I think you'll have to go now," Brink said at last, slouching forward, shoulders hunched. The voice, so energized a moment before, now was used up, thinner. "I need to get some rest."

"Can I help you upstairs?" Ellen said.

One last spark from the battery. The surgeon's eyes flashed. "No," he said, finding the firmness in his voice again. "I can make it by myself." He walked to the stairs, stopped, then slowly turning around, held out his hand. Ellen advanced to shake it.

"Thanks for coming," he said, not letting go of her hand. "Maybe..." he paused, "...you'll come again," releasing her hand. He reached out towards her, then pulled his arms back.

Ellen closed the door behind her. Roland Brink, she thought, the victor in the operating room, the loser with the whore, now fighting a far greater battle. Would he win this one too?

CHAPTER 30

Breathless, Ellen reached the telephone on the fourth ring.

"Hold on," she yelled into the phone even as the answering machine began its appointed rounds. Ellen listened to herself precisely doling out the prerecorded message. In a world of change, her set speech was invariant.

The beep.

"I'm still here," she said.

There was a pause.

"Hello?" Ellen said.

"Ellen," the voice said, "I'm back."

A pause. "Oh. That's nice," she said.

"You do know who this is, don't you?"

"Of course. Dave."

A laugh, a deep rich laugh, just like she remembered it. "Don't sound so excited," Dave said and laughed again.

"No, no. It's just that I wasn't expecting you."

"I'm in Los Angeles, but I'm coming back in a few days, and I wanted to invite you to join me at something rather special. But, before we get to that, tell me how you are. How's Washington's outstanding medical student? Saved any lives lately?"

Ellen thought of Roland.

"No," she drawled. A brief pause. "But, what's this special thing?"

The deep rich laugh. "Cut to the chase, eh?"

"No, no," she fumbled. "So tell me, how are you?"

"Tired," she heard, and the abrupt change in his voice confirmed it. "Travelling to Bangkok to get involved in a securities deal that I wasn't interested in. Crooks on all sides; it came down to which side was less crooked. Not the reason I went to law school."

"I didn't even know you were going to Thailand," Ellen said.

"Neither did I until the last moment. To keep the other side from knowing what we were up to, I wasn't even supposed to let anyone know where I was going. All sub rosa. Hush, hush, like an old John le Carre novel."

"But you did send me those beautiful roses and that wonderful champagne from there."

"After a few days of that nonsense, I figured 'what the hell.' What did it matter if my charming friend knew where I was? You weren't going to go to the Wall Street Journal with a breaking story."

Ellen laughed. "Thanks for your wonderful gifts. They meant a lot to me." She laughed again. "But, what's this special deal?"

"Not to be denied," Dave laughed. "I've been chosen to receive an award from the President. One of ten people being honored, and I'm allowed to invite a few friends."

"That's exciting! What's the award for?"

"Before I came to Washington, I used to do a lot of pro bono work. Mostly first amendment stuff, for people whose rights had been abused but couldn't afford a lawyer. When I was in Denver, I used to billet a couple of months a year for that. It drove my partners crazy and made some of my clients nuts, but I was so successful otherwise that nobody could argue with me."

"But aren't you a securities lawyer?"

"Only one of a number of hats." He chuckled. "But, you haven't told me: do you accept? Will you go as my date to the White House?"

Except for the standard run-'em-in run-'em-out tours, Ellen had never been to the White House.

"But…" Ellen stumbled, her heart racing, "I don't have anything to wear."

Dave laughed again. "What about that beautiful black suit with the mabe pearl earrings that you wore to the art gallery? I thought it was lovely."

Ellen thought about George Tucker for a moment; he wouldn't even notice if her clothes matched. But this guy…

She looked at her watch. Tonight's date was picking her up in a hour and she hadn't even washed and blown dry her hair.

"Okay," she said. "If you can stand to be seen with me, I'd be honored to accompany you."

They spoke only a couple of minutes more, then Ellen begged off.

"The White House!" She swirled around in her terrycloth robe and caught her image in the front hall mirror. "Hmmph!"

* * *

"The swordfish," Ellen said, "and the house salad with a vinaigrette dressing."

The waiter nodded then turned to George Tucker, who gave his order.

"Anyway," George said, "as I was saying, this new drug Gemzar has already helped a few of my patients with pancreatic cancer. You remember

175

Mrs. Dillon?"

Ellen nodded.

"After just a couple of doses, her abdominal pain is better and she's had virtually no toxicity." Ellen took a sip of the wine, then, putting her elbows on the table, rested her head on the hands.

"This is a nice restaurant," she said. "Like a small Paris bistro right here in Georgetown. Do you come here often?"

George tilted his head slightly and smiled. "No. Actually this is my first time. One of my patients recommended it."

Ellen thought of how awkward George had been when they arrived. They were seated in the back near the kitchen entrance. The maitre d' was solicitous, smiled a bit, hung around for a minute, then abruptly left. To Ellen it was obvious that the maitre d' was looking for a tip to give them a nicer table, but George was oblivious.

"It's been a long time since I've been to Paris," Ellen said. "And you?"

"I only went once, on my honeymoon. Very beautiful. Spent a lot of time at the Louvre. Lots of wonderful stuff."

Ellen nodded. "Jeff and I used to go there…"

She took another sip of the wine.

"Do you get to the National Gallery very often?" she asked.

"You mean the one here in Washington?"

Ellen shook her head up and down.

"No," Tucker said, "it's been many years."

George picked up a roll. He looked over at Ellen who was staring off in the distance for a moment. She turned towards him and smiled.

"Did you see that article in Oncology about using levamisole and tamoxifen in ovarian cancer?" he asked.

"No."

"Oh, well it looks promising. I've got a couple of people I'm thinking of trying it on. Especially Jane Arbadian. She's not done well with the Taxol, you know, and this might at least give her a little breathing room." George finished buttering his roll and took a bite.

"She's very nice," Ellen said. "I hope she does well."

The waiter arrived with the salads.

Ellen chuckled. "In France, I once had a fight with a waiter who refused to serve my salad with the meal."

"Oh?"

"Yes. In France, salad is served after the main course."

"Oh." George went to work again on his roll.

Ellen watched as a couple was seated on the opposite side of the restaurant.

"I really admire your dedication to your work," Ellen said. "How do you find the time to do everything?" Now it was George's turn to look across the restaurant. "After my wife died," he said, "I needed to work even harder, to fill my life with work."

"How do you relax?" Ellen asked after a long silence. "Do you have any hobbies you especially like?"

George said nothing as he continued chewing.

"No," he said finally, "no real hobbies. My work takes so much of my time. I guess you could say it's my hobby. And you?"

"Well, medical school and a kid at home consume most of my time, although these past two weeks, before I start my Ob-Gyn rotation, have been a nice breather. I've managed to read a couple of novels."

"That's good."

"You like novels?"

"Sure," he said. "Cathy used to read a lot of them, but I just don't have enough time."

"Ellen," a voice called out from across the restaurant. An older man approached them. Well-dressed, slightly ruddy complected, a trim white moustache, he leaned over and gave Ellen a brief peck on the cheek.

"George," Ellen said, "I want you to meet Bob McMasters, a friend from way back."

Tucker and McMasters shook hands.

"Bob and his wife are subscribers at the University of Maryland Choral Society," Ellen said. "They always take me to hear Handel oratorios."

"You ever go?" McMasters asked George.

The oncologist nodded no.

"We'll have to take you next time," McMasters said. "You like Handel?"

"Don't know much about him," George said, "but I do love The Messiah. I always hear it on the radio at Christmas."

McMasters pulled up a chair and ordered wine. He and Ellen talked about many different things. McMasters had just finished a biography of Winston Churchill and was anxious to talk about it. Ellen laughed when he told how he'd gotten drenched at an early springtime Baltimore Orioles baseball game. McMasters admired the wine as he talked about his recent trip to Bordeaux. Tucker sat quietly, listening.

"Say," McMasters said, "how's your daughter's piano playing coming?"

Ellen smiled gently. "She gave it up for a long time, but recently started playing again… but she hasn't admitted it to me yet."

"I remember coming to your house many years back, and being so captivated by her playing."

"Well," Ellen said, smiling, "now you have an excuse to visit again. Maybe you can get her to acknowledge that she's playing."

"Why the secrecy?" McMasters asked.

"Not sure, but perhaps she's trying to avoid an 'I told you so,'" Ellen said. She paused. "I think Deb feels she was a 'quitter,' and now has to prove herself."

"Well, call me when she's gone public. I'll come over to play some duets with her," McMasters said. He turned to Tucker.

"You play?" he asked.

Greorge nodded no.

"Well, then I want you to come hear our four hand concerts," McMasters said and laughed.

They spoke several minutes longer before McMasters looked at his watch and begged off.

"Interesting guy," Ellen said. "Retired lawyer, always busy."

George bit into his roast duckling.

"Say, did I tell you that Mr. O'Rourke's biopsy came back negative. I promised him I'd tell you." Another bite of the duck. "That was one happy man. I really thought he was going to kiss me."

The food was agreeable enough, and after they'd had dessert, Ellen and George went out to M Street to look in the Georgetown shops. Saturday night and there was plenty of activity. It was beginning to mist and George stopped a few times to wipe off the droplets on his glasses. The moisture didn't seem to bother a man dressed in a clown outfit juggling a half dozen beer cans. Ellen and George joined a crowd watching him; they didn't stay to see the argument after a policeman told the juggling clown to move. The Georgetown streets were filled with people, some standing in lines to get into bars, others eating in trendy little restaurants, still others going into holes-in-the-wall. The stores were all open, their bright fluorescence lighting the street. Cars were bumper to bumper, horns blowing, people yelling. At the intersection of M Street and Wisconsin Avenue, a policeman was desperately trying to make order out of the chaos. Pedestrians ran across the streets, dodging cars.

As they walked in and out many different stores, George spoke about some newer cancer therapies as well as how some of the patients were doing. For the most part, Ellen was quiet, walking with her hands in her raincoat. By the time they reached George's car it was beginning to drizzle.

The ride home was uneventful. After George briefly mentioned some recent studies using monoclonal antibodies in melanoma, the car fell silent. Ellen watched the rain out the side window. George turned on the radio. The car splashed through a few new puddles just before turning onto Ellen's street.

"Thanks for a lovely evening," Ellen said at her front door. "It was a lot of fun."

A few moments later, Ellen closed the door. The television was blaring; Brent was sound asleep in front of "Saturday Night Live."

She kissed Brent; he didn't move. A stronger nudge and he opened an eye. "How are you?"

"Maybe a little better," he said. "A small stomach ache, but at least no diarrhea."

"Did you take your medicines?"

Brent nodded yes. Ellen turned off the TV and walked her son upstairs. They stepped over books, clothes, and other assorted things Brent had dropped on his bedroom floor.

"Did you have a good time?" Brent asked as Ellen tucked him in.

She bent over and stroked his head gently, then kissed him. "I think so," she answered.

Ellen looked at herself in the full-length bedroom mirror. She'd never have dressed like this for Dave Longacre, in a tired old dress that was tight across the middle. She'd known George wouldn't notice, and her wardrobe was really thin. She got into her silk nightgown, a recent birthday gift from Jill, and returned to the mirror. Better, she smiled. Even though skin tight, it seemed to hide most of the sags.

She got into bed and pulled up the covers. The sound of the rain on the roof grew louder.

For a long time, she lay quietly thinking about the White House, the Louvre, the National Gallery, the Choral Society. Dave Longacre, George Tucker, Roland Brink. Tomorrow was the last free day before starting her Ob-Gyn rotation. There'd be lots of long days and late nights to follow.

She'd visit her "patient," Roland Brink, tomorrow morning.

Then she'd spent the rest of the day with Brent.

New drug for pancreatic cancer, negative biopsy, monoclonal antibodies. Handel, Louvre. Reading fiction.

The intensity of the rain increased. The sound in her ears, Ellen fell asleep at last.

CHAPTER 31

One last look in the mirror. Ellen made a face as she pushed her hair back, being certain to cover her ears; then she added a little eyeliner.

I'd do this for anybody, she assured herself. And anyway, it's Sunday and I should look my best when going out.

She decided not to wear the same clothes she'd worn last night with George; something a little fresher would be more suitable. This was one of her nicest outfits, very bright and springy.

Ellen stopped downstairs where Deb was at the Chickering. She'd finally admitted to Ellen that she'd been playing "a little."

"I don't recognize that," Ellen said, during a pause.

"A sonata by Scarlatti," Deb answered. "I thought I'd try something new." She adjusted the music. "Something easy."

"It's nice to have you playing again," Ellen said.

"You look nice," Deb said. "Going anywhere special?"

Ellen shook her head 'no.'

"Well, I hope that surgeon appreciates how good you look," Deb said, turning her head forward and starting up with a staccato chord.

Ellen bit her lip, and went to the car.

The trip across Chain Bridge was quick on the weekend morning and soon she turned onto Roland Brink's street. The spring morning odors saturated the air with special sweetness, even as flowers invaded the visual senses. Singing morning birds proclaimed their territories to anyone who would listen.

Each of the houses on the street had carefully maintained front lawns, nicely trimmed lawns and bushes, Mercedes and Jaguars in the driveways. All that was missing was people.

Parking her Chevy Impala in the driveway, Ellen looked once in the mirror on the back of the sun visor, and freshened her lipstick. After all, it was Sunday.

Ellen looked around as pushed the doorbell. Every corner of the earth seemed filled with spring, life's annual renaissance. It took a long time for Roland to answer the door, and Ellen watched a muscular jogger sweep across the landscape. The door opened. As always, Roland was dressed, but now the clothes dripped from his frame. His face had been commandeered by deep creases surrounded by grays, and where once there'd been a pinkish complexion, now his skin had the tone of unripe mustard, in places suggesting it had quit the battle of trying to remain attached to his body. The once thick head of hair now showed large patches of scalp between thin strands, a souvenir of chemotherapy.

But, as always, he was clean shaven.

Ellen reached into the bag she'd brought, producing a small chocolate cake.

"Baked it myself. It's part of your nutrition therapy," she said.

Roland walked slowly, working hard to maintain his balance, watching each small step fall in line after the last, declining any help from Ellen as he carefully made his way to the kitchen. After pouring black coffee for each of them, he sat down across the table from Ellen and leaned slightly over the steaming liquid, staring into its center.

"I hadn't expected to be knocked quite so flat by the chemo," he said. "George told me I'd tolerate it pretty well, but it's really done me in."

Still watching the coffee, Brink probably didn't notice the surprised look in Ellen's face. An admission of fallibility? But not a humiliation. He would *never* be humiliated again.

"You get your next chemo tomorrow?" Ellen said.

Brink nodded. "Will you be there?" he asked.

"No," Ellen said, "I'm starting my Gyn rotation in the morning. But I'll call you tomorrow night to see how it went."

"I'd like that," he said slowly. "And I like the chocolate cake," he said, biting into it. "I hope you'll come over often." He took a bite. "Sorry. What I meant was, I hope you'll bring me a chocolate cake whenever you…" He stopped. In the distance was the hum of a leaf blower.

"No," he said. "What I meant was what I said the first time. I hope you'll come over often." He looked at Ellen. "Even if you don't bring a cake."

He cut another small piece.

"George told me this should be the last chemo, at least for now," Roland said. "He says it may take me two months to recover and get my strength back. Maybe longer."

"Is it hard, not working?"

The surgeon smiled vaguely as he nodded yes. "I can't believe I'm not working. It's been my ethic since I can remember." He took a sip of his coffee and made a face. "Damn near kills me not to work."

There was a pause during which neither said anything. At last, Brink asked Ellen about the upcoming gynecology rotation.

"They – the gynecologists, that is – think they're surgeons," Brink said, "but – between us – they really aren't. I've scrubbed in with them numerous times on complicated procedures, and I wish I could teach them how to operate."

A faint smile on Ellen's lips. "I've actually given some thought to going into Ob-Gyn."

"No," Brink said, "can't see it. You're too…" He stopped, and resumed staring at his coffee.

"Too what?"

No answer for a moment. "Nothing. The thought left me."

"No it didn't. Too what?"

Brink looked up. "Too intellectually sharp. All those women coming in to complain about their irregular periods or their morning sickness would drive you crazy."

Ellen said nothing.

"Really," Brink said, "I'm not a misogynist. Believe me. But I *am* a realist."

"Let's agree to disagree on that," Ellen said.

"What? That I'm not a misogynist or that I am a realist."

"I'll leave you to make your own judgment," Ellen smiled.

Roland got up and poured a little more coffee, but this time he sat down in the chair next to Ellen.

"Are you remembering to take all your medicines?" Ellen asked.

"Of course. I always do exactly what my doctor tells me to do. I'm a good patient."

He reached over and touched her hand. Ellen looked down. The surgeon's hand still conveyed its strength, as if untouched by the disease or its treatment, but also there was a gentleness she hadn't expected.

For a few moments they sat there, holding hands. Then, suddenly looking impatient, Roland stood up. "Come with me," he said, leading to an area off the kitchen. A door lead down to the basement. Turning on the light, he grabbed the banister and began one step after another to descend. Faltering slightly, Ellen ran down next to him and put her arm under his shoulder. At first it seemed as if the surgeon would shake her off, then he didn't; she helped him down the stairs.

"Over here," he said as they walked across the basement to a small room. Roland pushed open the door and flipped on the lights.

On a table were perhaps ten small car replicas. At once they reminded Ellen of the polished models she'd seen upstairs in the living room and in Roland's office, the only splashes of color in either place. There was an immaculately clean workbench with tools carefully hung on pegs. A high wooden stool sat off to the side. A panel of switches appeared to control a host of spotlights and lamps. Perhaps twenty or twenty-five more model cars were behind glass partitions in a display case on the far wall.

"My hobby," Roland said. "I made each one myself."

"I never knew."

"Nobody does. It's my secret. There's a public Roland Brink, but there's also a private one." He swept his hand slowly across the workbench. "It takes me at least three or four months to make each one, every part made by hand. I carve each model from wood." He opened a drawer and took out a set of knife blades each carefully placed in an assigned spot. "After it's been carved and sanded carefully, I put on the chrome, shape the windows, make the headlights and steering wheel. I lacquer each car."

He went to the display case, carefully opened the glass panel and picked up a model, the one in the center. It was no bigger than his hand. "This is my first, a 1954 Packard."

"It's...beautiful," Ellen said.

Brink held the Packard up to the light, turning it around and over. He caressed the model with a gentleness that somehow didn't seem at variance with those still-strong hands. The only sound was the quiet electric buzz of the display case lights.

"When I was a kid," Brink said at last, "I was walking down the street in my hometown, and I passed the Packard dealership. The salesman saw me looking in through the window and invited me in. He told me the '54 Packard was the finest car ever made and he let me sit in it." Brink turned the model around. "It was an obvious choice."

He set the Packard down.

"Each of these models is my friend. Each one has its own history."

Ellen started to say something but stopped before the first words got out.

"At night, after a long day," Roland said, "I occasionally just have a Johnnie Walker and then go to bed. But more often than not, I come down here and work." He picked up another car. "I look forward to this all day. No matter how tired I am, this energizes me. Here, in my small studio, with my cars, carefully working on each one, as a jeweler would work so meticulously on a fine watch."

"I never knew…" Ellen said again.

"Why would you? I've never shown this to anybody before." Brink set the car down. "It's our secret now," he said. "Please respect my privacy."

"Of course," Ellen said, not quite knowing what to say.

Brink pulled over the stool and sat down, as Ellen tried to get comfortable on the edge of a box filled with small pieces of wood. Brink showed her each model, carefully describing each car, explaining why he elected to make that model, how he chose which woods, what type of paint and lacquer he used, how he designed each part.

"Are you bored and tired of this?" he asked after a while.

"I've never been so awake in my life," Ellen answered.

The last car was put back in its place.

Brink's head was slightly bowed forward, and he sat quietly, looking as much at the floor as anything else. Neither of them said anything. The surgeon turned slowly to look at Ellen. After another minute punctuated only by the unending hum of the lights, Brink raised his left hand and rested it on Ellen's leg.

Ellen looked down at the hand, but didn't withdraw. The two of them sat unmoving on their wooden stools.

"I'm tired now," Brink said a few minutes later. "I need to go upstairs and lie down."

Ellen put her arm under his shoulder once again and helped him up the stairs.

They went to the living room and crossed over to the sofa, the one seat that Ellen decided would be at least tolerably comfortable, and sat on opposite ends.

"Your mother looks just like you," Ellen said after they'd been sitting for a while.

"I'm sorry to hear that," Brink said.

"Why?"

The surgeon looked sharply at Ellen. "I already told you enough about her," he said.

They sat there for a couple of minutes, Brink looking out the window, Ellen trying to discretely watch him.

"She drove my father to his grave," he said at last, still looking out the window. "She was harsh, uncompromising, inflexible; he could never stand up to her. He died when I was seven years old." He stopped for a few seconds. "I remember a fishing trip with him and going to a baseball game, but little else. I…"

The surgeon stood up, slowly and with great difficulty, and walked next to Ellen.

"Would you like to learn to play chess?" he asked, sitting down and putting his arm around her waist.

"I never…" Ellen stopped. "Yes, I would. Will you teach me?"

Roland nodded his head up and down. "Not now," he said softly. "When I'm better." He stopped. "But you can keep coming over. I…" A pause "…I wait for to your visits. They give me something to look forward to. Maybe, they're even…" He stopped.

"Even what?" Ellen asked.

For a long while, Brink said nothing, looking abstractedly at the floor.

"Even part of my therapy," he said at last, voice just above a whisper.

He pulled her in closer.

"I… want to get better," he said. "I… will get better." He turned to Ellen, then lay back slightly on the angular chair. Ellen nuzzled in against him.

"I have to rest," he said several minutes later, pulling his arm back and turning to look at her. "Thank you for coming."

He got up slowly.

"Can I help you upstairs?" Ellen asked.

"I don't think so," the surgeon answered.

He walked her to the door. Ellen reached out and held his hand.

"Well," Brink said, "maybe you could steady me a little up to the stair landing."

Ellen put her arm around his waist. With the surgeon holding on to the railing, and Ellen pushing, he got to the top of the stairs. For a moment, they stared at each other.

"Good luck with the chemo tomorrow," she said.

"Thanks." His words lingered a moment. "Ellen, I…" He stopped.

"Yes?"

"Have you…" A pause. "Have you ever thought of becoming a surgeon?"

Ellen laughed, her first of the day.

"No," she drawled. "There are many things, but not a surgeon. Never a surgeon."

Roland nodded. "Think about it."

"I have," she said, squeezing his hand tighter. "It's not for me."

She let his hand go. Brink reached over and gave her a brief hug, then an even briefer kiss.

"Good luck tomorrow," Ellen said before heading back downstairs.

CHAPTER 32

The telephone was ringing just as Ellen opened the garage door. She flew into the kitchen, picking up the receiver just before her recorded message.

"Pretty exciting isn't it?" Jill said by way of starting.

The only image Ellen could conjure was Roland Brink, gently picking up a model blue sports sedan – what was it again?- caressing it as he turned it over and around, the reflection of the ceiling light in the lacquer almost blinding Ellen.

"What's exciting?" Ellen asked.

"What's exciting? Earth to Ellen. Have you ever been invited to a White House reception before, let alone met the President?"

"Oh that."

"Oh that? That's the best you can do? *I've* never been there, and *I'm* expecting a full report. Remember, I set you up with him, so you owe it to me."

A silence.

"Are you still there?" Jill asked.

"Sorry. I just got back from visiting Brink. I find him so inexplicable. Here was one guy who was black and white; I had him figured out. But now I find out there's more to him than I ever imagined." She paused. "Only because of this illness."

Another silence.

"And do you know what? He told me I should become a surgeon. Surely that's the highest compliment he can pay anyone." Another silence. "A surgeon. Can you imagine."

They spoke a few minutes more. Jill did most of the talking, filling Ellen in on details of her family adventures. It was cheerful; things had been going well with Jill's relatives.

"And," Jill added, "here's some more good news."

"Okay."

"Look, I'm really trying to be upbeat. I'm going to take you shopping for an elegant new outfit to wear to the White House. That should cheer you up!"

"Who's paying for it?" Ellen asked.

Jill laughed. "You are, of course. That's why money is no object."

"What kind of elegant?"

"A beautiful sleeve length black gown."

"But...I have no really beautiful jewelry to go with this pretentious outfit you're buying me?"

"No, *you're* buying it. It's way beyond my budget. But, don't worry about the jewelry. I'll think of something."

"Like robbing Tiffany's?"

"Whatever it takes. Listen, there'll be official photographers; there always are at these White House affairs. Ten thousand years from now, some future historian will see your picture. Long after I'm dead and forgotten, you'll still be alive.

> 'So long as men can breathe or eyes can see,
> So long lives this, and this gives life to thee.'

And you'll have *me* to thank for this immortality, because you're going to go out and buy a magnificent outfit, and have a really good time, and stop feeling sorry for yourself."

"I'm not feeling sorry for myself."

"Of course you are. But, no matter. Dave really likes you. He told Rick that you are 'enchanting.' That's a direct quote."

"He said that?"

"*If* you believe Rick."

"Well, it might be fun. I suppose it really is pretty unusual to get invited to a really fancy affair."

"Maybe I should go in your place," Jill said. "Dave shows up at your house, and I'm there. 'Sorry,' I says, 'she got called away on an emergency, so I'm her stand in.' And I'm dressed up all fancy."

Ellen tried to imagine an elegant black sack cloth.

"I hear you laughing," Jill said, "and I choose to ignore it."

"Well... you know, it might really be fun. Interesting. Different." She paused. "He really said he found me 'enchanting?'"

"*If* you believe Rick."

"Hmmph. They really do have official photographers there, don't they? 'Who was that beautiful mystery woman at the White House the other night?' I'll be on every gossip columnist's lips." She laughed. "Okay. Let's go for it."

"The enchantress at last!" Jill said.

"*If* I believe Rick."

CHAPTER 33

Monday. George Tucker looked in the mirror again as he brought the razor up to his face, then washed off the remaining shaving cream.

Monday. Every patient who'd been waiting all weekend to speak to him would phone in early and await the oncologist's return call. A weekend of mounting fears and uncertainties would all be on the telephone by nine o'clock.

George looked in the mirror once more. He started to count the lines advancing across the forehead and cheeks, then quickly shook it off.

He'd been surprised by his Saturday night date. Ellen had been charming and engaging but somehow he felt – what was the word? – clunky. He'd been pretty good with the ladies, he told himself, when he was young, but now he seemed out of practice. Had his life been so restricted to oncology that he'd lost the art of small talk?

Ellen had been so attractive, so appealing, and…Damn! How her face had lit up when she saw that Handel guy. She'd suddenly come alive and sparkled; her whole demeanor had changed.

George caught another glimpse of himself in the mirror just before turning off the bathroom light. He'd always been young, spirited, but now he saw a weary old man. He'd dedicated so much to his work that he'd forgotten how to be a human. Well, George decided, I'm not going to give up on myself… or on Ellen. The next time will be different.

He ate a quick breakfast of dried cereal and slightly soured milk, then drove to the office. He'd been despondent all Sunday thinking about that date. Getting to work would be a relief from being alone with himself.

Then he remembered all those phone calls that would be waiting.

So be it. Left foot, right foot. He'd get through the day just like he always had before.

Several piles of papers awaited him scattered around his desk. George had worked for a few hours Saturday but left early for his date and…Damn! Couldn't he get that out of his thoughts? How Ellen's whole demeanor had changed when that Handel guy appeared. Damn!

He looked at the schedule. The first few patients seemed easy enough, except for Mrs. Garcia with her metastatic breast cancer. He was trying to get her into a new NIH protocol, but she just didn't quite fit their criteria. Still, with a bit of arm twisting, Tucker hoped he'd land a spot for her, because he had nothing else he could offer her.

At ten o'clock he was seeing Roland Brink. George knew things were getting worse with the surgeon, and he'd decided on a new plan. The lymphoma was just too damned aggressive. It had been ten days since George had seen Brink, but the phone calls he'd been making hardly were encouraging. And Ellen had been going out to see him and reported the surgeon looked pretty frail.

Ellen. There she was again. The excitement and disappointment over Ellen converged simultaneously. Couldn't she leave him in peace even for a short while?

Theresa was on vacation for a few days, and her replacement, a kid, bounced in at eight o'clock. George pushed aside a pile of papers and looked at his secretary for this week. *She* seemed happy.

"Ready, Dr. Tucker?" she said. "It's Monday!" A big bright smile, which quickly changed. "Are you alright?" she asked. "You look kinda down."

"No, I'm fine. You look like you had a good weekend."

"My boyfriend and I went to the beach. We had a lot of fun."

"Wasn't it kind of cold for the beach?" George asked.

"Probably," she answered, "but we never got that far."

The phones began ringing and George got to work. He saw patients every twenty minutes, and used the intervening free times to talk on the phone.

"I'm sorry," he said "but the final pathology report still isn't back. I promise to call you as soon as I learn anything."

"The bone scan looked fine. Really good news!"

"Dr. Delaney just called to tell me that the tissue margins were clear of tumor. Congratulations!"

"I'm worried about your weight loss too. I think you'd better come in for a look see."

"You really can't ignore a fever like that. I want you to go to the hospital now, and I'll see you during lunch."

"It doesn't look good. The CT scan showed a mass in the neck."

A storm was threatening outside, heavy gray clouds rolling in from the northwest, ready to throttle Washington with an encore of the cold winter just passed. George barely paid it any mind as he went from room to room, phone call to phone call.

His ten o'clock patient sat down in the office. "I've felt better," Roland Brink said, "but I'm hanging in there and I'm ready for my next chemo."

Tucker looked at the surgeon. His hair had almost completely fallen out, only a few wisps hanging on at the back and sides. The gray face, the sunken cheeks with the skin now drooping below the jaw.

George felt ashamed. How could he be feeling sorry for himself?

Roland's eyes burned bright, the head held upright.

Tucker brought the surgeon to the examining room. He checked the blood pressure, felt for lymph glands, listened to the lungs, palpated the abdomen. Brink was just getting dressed when there was a knock at the door.

"Ellen," Tucker said, his pulse suddenly doubling. "I thought you were on your gynecology rotation."

"I am," she said, "but we had our first lecture and now I'm going to cut the afternoon activities because I've got something very important to do. So I thought I'd stop over here first to see how our patient is doing."

"Let's go into my office," Tucker said, and he, Brink, and Ellen went next door. The oncologist cleared a space on each of the chairs for the other two, then sat on the edge of his desk.

"Roland," Tucker said, "there are some things we need to discuss. I'm not quite sure how to address this, but…"

Brink held up his hand.

"Please just tell me. I'm a big boy."

"Alright then," George said, looking at the surgeon and then the medical student. He leafed through a few sheets of paper on his desk. "Your tumor is still growing," he said, looking up, "in spite of all the chemotherapy you've received." Tucker spoke softly but clearly. "Your spleen is bigger than it was even ten days ago, and I can feel your liver for the first time. You've also developed some glands in the supraclavicular area."

"I know," Brink said.

"Clearly our present course isn't working. I have some ideas, but I think maybe you'd like to get another opinion."

"Are your consultants smarter than you?"

George smiled. "Probably not, but you might feel more comfortable with another perspective."

"No," Brink said, shaking his head. "I don't need reassurance. You're my doctor."

"Well, let me know if you reconsider."

A silence.

"And the bottom line is…?" Brink said.

"The bottom line: I think you need a bone marrow transplant."

Brink sat impassive, but Ellen gasped.

She reached over and grasped his hand, squeezing it for a few moments before letting go.

But in those few moments, George saw it, and he knew. Ellen would not be his.

The oncologist coughed and went on. "The idea is to give you much more potent doses of the chemotherapy, but in the process, not only would we hopefully wipe out the tumor but we also would destroy your own immune system. You'd need a transplant to save you."

"Where would I get a donor?"

"Don't you have a brother? We could type him. If he didn't match, there's a large pool of random donors we could try and match."

"My brother's out of the question," Brink said.

"Why?" Ellen asked.

"We haven't spoken in years."

"Suppose," Ellen said, "Suppose your brother came to you and told you *he* needed a bone marrow transplant. Would you give it to him?"

"Of course. But this is different."

"No it isn't. I will call him if you won't."

George looked at the surgeon and for a moment, the briefest speck of time, he saw a look of uncertainty he'd never seen before in his face. But that moment of weakness, if that's what it was, was controlled in an instant. And, as if sensing that his weakness had been exposed, the surgeon sat up straighter and taller than before.

"When do we start?" he asked.

"Let me give your some idea about the statistics first. I think it's important that you understand what…"

"Are there other options?" Brink interrupted.

"No, I don't think so."

"Then the statistics don't matter, do they? When do we start?"

"As soon as a donor is lined up, then we'll start you on EPOCH. It's a lot like the CHOP regimen you had but in stronger doses. And I'll give you some radiation to reduce some of the bulk disease, like your spleen and the periaortic lymph nodes."

"Let's get started."

"Nothing for a few days. You need a CT scan of the abdomen and chest today…"

"And?"

"And we need to learn about your brother."

Tucker spoke briefly and made a few phone calls, then arranged to meet with Brink later in the day, after the preliminary tests were completed.

When Tucker left, Roland stood up, carefully and cautiously. "Come," he said to Ellen, even as he wobbled a bit, "give me a hand and I'll buy you a cup of coffee."

Ellen looked at her watch. "I'm supposed to meet someone to buy a fancy new dress," she said.

"Maybe another time then," Brink said, stumbling slightly to the left.

Ellen looked at her watch again. "Just a minute," she said. "Let me make a call, and then we'll have that cup of coffee."

* * *

"It's magnificent," Ellen said twirling from side to side, looking in and out of the mirror, "but it's too pricey."

"You look, how shall I say, brilliant. It was made for you. And," the saleslady said, lowering her voice, "you can pay with your credit card."

Ellen laughed as she turned again, rubbing her hands down over the hips, caressing the black silk. "And, who's going to pay my credit card bill? Hmmph."

"I think a pearl necklace would go beautifully with this," the saleslady said, indicating the desired length with her hands.

Ellen laughed again.

"She'll take it," Jill said. "It needs to be ready by the end of the week."

After a few 'my dears' and one 'oh my,' the saleslady disappeared into a back room. Ellen shook her head. "I really can't afford it, but…"

"You already have the necklace, and your pearl earrings will be perfect," Jill said.

Ellen sat down on a nearby chair, hands on knees, head on hands.

"Hmmph. My emotional life is a roller coaster. One minute I'm with an overwhelmingly sick man, and a few hours later I'm here buying the nicest dress I've ever owned. The hospital one day, a sick man's home the next, the White House the third. I'm glad I have you to help me remain at least nominally sane."

Jill came over and put her arms around her friend. "And I'm glad you still have some room in your life to enjoy it."

CHAPTER 34

The calendar had changed to May as Dr. Everett Danker pushed again on the abdomen, gently and carefully pushing on the upper and lower areas.

"Deep breath," the pediatric gastroenterologist said.

Looking at Danker through wide open eyes, Brent complied.

"Again."

Another deep breath, this time with a slight wince.

"That hurt?" Danker asked in his quiet, gentle voice.

"Yes sir, a little."

Danker made a few "hmmm" noises, then bent over Brent's head at the front of the examining table.

"Why don't you get dressed," he pointed to the pile of clothes Brent had dropped on the floor, "and come back into my office."

Brent nodded. Danker, very tall and broad, pushed back his dark black hair and stepped ahead to open the door for Ellen and the two of them walked into his office. A bright springtime sun was shining through the window, landing directly on a picture of Danker and his family on a motorboat, their hair flying behind them. Danker went over and pulled the shades part way down.

"Tough problem," he said. "Pediatric gastroenterology is never easy, but when Warner Millstone sends me patients it's particularly challenging, because he's already ruled out the easy stuff." The gastroenterologist adjusted the shades once again.

"It's frustrating," Ellen said, sitting down in a straight-backed wooden chair. "He just doesn't seem to eat, and he has so much less energy than usual."

Brent walked in and looked around, first at his mother then at the gastroenterologist. Danker pointed to the other wooden chair, then he sat down in his large swivel chair behind the desk.

"I've reviewed your X-rays, Brent," he said, pointing to a fluorescent view box on the wall opposite. The films were spread across the four view box panels; still others lay in the tan folders on a side table. "The barium enema looks fine," Danker said, sweeping his hand towards the X-rays, "and the abdominal CT scan also is perfectly normal."

"Isn't he a little anemic?" Ellen asked.

Danker nodded. "I can't readily explain that. I'm thinking it may all be nutritional, not getting enough vitamins and iron in his diet. He really hasn't eaten very well in the past few weeks."

"When I took pediatrics," Ellen said, "they said that doesn't happen very often, especially in boys."

"True enough," Danker said, "but sometimes the textbooks aren't always applicable to real human beings." He turned to Brent. "You've been under a lot of stress, haven't you?"

"I suppose," he answered. "That's what everybody keeps telling me."

"It's hard to have your father away, isn't it?" Danker bent forward trying to get down to Brent's height, trying to affect a grandfatherly smile. "I think you may be internalizing a lot of your anger and hostility, and your belly seems to be your weak spot." He stood up to his full height and swept his arm towards the X-rays again.

"Isn't the Zoloft supposed to help?" Brent asked

"Sure, but sometimes it takes more than a pill, Brent. I really think you should stay with your psychiatrist and keep working on these things."

Danker resumed his seat in the swivel chair. "I think it's only a matter of time," he said, turning towards Ellen. "I've seen this lots of times, and usually once the acute stress is over, things have a way of working themselves out. In the meantime, Brent," he said, looking at the boy and wagging a friendly finger, "I want you to promise me you'll follow through on all those nutritional supplements we've been talking about."

After a few more questions and answers, the gastroenterologist stood up and walked towards the office door. "I want to see you back in two weeks," he said, "and I'm counting on you to gain five pounds by then." He stuck out his hand. "Deal?"

"I'll do the best I can," Brent said, weakly shaking Danker's hand while turning to look at his mother.

Ellen and Brent left.

"He really is trying to be helpful," Ellen said. "I feel reassured, don't you?" She turned to look at her son. Brent was walking along, head slightly bent, watching the sidewalk, trying to avoid the cracks.

Ellen opened the door to the Chevy Impala. The passenger's side door was chronically slightly stuck. Brent pulled hard on the handle a couple of times until the door finally yielded.

"Mom," he said as they pulled out of the parking lot, "why does everybody think it's in my head? Don't you think I'm strong enough to deal with Dad leaving us? I'm not a baby, you know."

Ellen paid the parking lot attendant and pulled out onto Massachusetts Avenue just above Scott Circle. They drove to Wisconsin Avenue, stopping at a fast food restaurant. Brent heroically tried to eat a Philly Cheesesteak, but only managed slightly more than half. He eyed the french fries and ate a few, Ellen watching every bite.

There were a few messages on the answering machine when they got home. Another medical student wanting some lecture notes; a very cheery promotional man trying to sell something or other; the plumber trying to set up an appointment to fix the leaky shower.

"Ellen," the fourth and last message said, "this is Roland returning your call."

"I was at the pediatric gastroenterologist," she explained when she called Roland.

"What about your gynecology rotation?" the surgeon asked.

"I had to duck out. My son comes first. Anyway, it's a slow day on the wards." She twirled a strand of hair near the ear.

"What's wrong with your son?" His voice was quiet, measured.

"Like I told you," Ellen answered, "he has a stomach ache and doesn't feel like eating, so he's dropped almost ten pounds."

A pause. "What did the pediatric gastroenterologist say?" Thinner than it had been, Roland's voice still had its challenging tone

"He agrees with everyone else. An adjustment reaction."

"And what the hell is an adjustment reaction?" Roland asked.

"The stress from the separation from his father."

"And that..." Roland paused. "That's causing his stomachache and weight loss?"

"That's what they all say," Ellen answered, twirling the hair strand furiously.

There was a long silence. "Why don't you bring the boy around to see me," Roland said. "Bring all the X-rays with you."

"That's very kind," Ellen said, her voice faltering a little, "but it might be too much of a strain on you."

The voice that shot through the phone was vintage Roland Brink. "I wouldn't have offered if I weren't up to it," he said. Then, quietly: "Bring your son over."

Brent was lying in bed. It had been nearly a week since he'd been to school.

At Ellen's prompting, he got into the car.

"I already saw one doctor today," he said.

Ellen explained about Roland. "He's doing this as a favor to me."

A favor to me, she repeated under her breath. The whole damned profession can't do anything to help this dying man, yet he wants to try to help me and my son.

The trip to McLean went quickly. Everywhere flowers were shining, trees greening. The sweet spring air brought news of the south.

Two men were mowing Roland's front lawn while another was trimming bushes.

Roland spent most of the day in bed, too weak to come downstairs but refusing to go into the hospital. A full time nurse was staying with him.

Ellen and Brent walked into the room. Roland lay in one of the two beds; the other, its cover carefully pulled down, sat alone, unused. The large round nurse sat uncomfortably in a sloping angular black chair, and seemed glad to stand up when the pair entered.

It was only yesterday that Ellen had last seen the surgeon, but the change astounded her. If Brink noted her surprise, he didn't say anything. The flesh was hanging even more, ribs sticking out further, the eyes in full retreat into their sockets – the man was all bones.

"Has George seen you like this?" Ellen asked. She put her hands up to her face. "I'm sorry, that came out wrong."

Brink's smile was weak but unmistakable.

Ellen went over to his bed, reached for his hand, and stood there for a good minute before moving. Brink lay in bed, watching her. At last she set his hand down and then…slowly… bent over and kissed him on the head. "You need to be in the hospital," she said softly. "You can't go on like this at home."

"That's what I keep telling him," the nurse put in.

Brink squinted at the nurse. "Would you excuse us please," he said, his voice now sharp, clean. Roland Brink in charge.

The surgeon carefully swung his legs over the side of the bed and sat up. Streaming golden through the windows, the late afternoon sun enhanced the sharp staccatos of the furniture.

"Come over here, son," he said to Brent.

Taking a few small steps forward, Brent stopped five feet from the surgeon who eyed him carefully, top to bottom. Brent shifted from one foot to the other.

"Tell me what's going on," Brink said.

"He's had nausea and pain," Ellen said, "and…"

Brink held up his hand. "I think he can speak for himself."

Brent related his story in brief detail, Brink interrupting with some questions. The interview took only five minutes.

The surgeon pointed to the empty bed. "Lie down over there," he said. As Ellen listened and watched, the bedroom, the furniture, the pictures on the wall faded away: there was Brink on the ward. She looked at those still piercing eyes, and suddenly the flesh on his face was no longer hanging, the hair was no longer sparse, the cheeks no longer sunken.

"Pull down your trousers," Brink said as Brent began to lie down.

Brent hesitated, looking over at his mother.

"It's your mother, for God's sake," the surgeon said. Brent wavered a moment then, as Ellen looked away, stripped to his underpants.

Brink sat on the edge of the bed, silk pajamas hanging loosely from his frame. He reached over for his bathrobe, then closing both eyes for a second, leaned forward and stood up, shunning any help from Ellen who hurried over. Walking over to Brent, only a few feet away, the surgeon moved slowly, not because he wanted to, but because he had to. He sat on the edge and motioned for Brent to lie down.

For a full minute, the surgeon did nothing but look at his new patient's abdomen. Then gently he put his right hand on the belly. Carefully, patiently, sometimes using only his right hand, other times using both, he pushed, palpated, prodded the abdomen.

Ellen watched from a distance. The surgeon's hands were firm, strong, certain.

Brink continued to push with exquisite slowness, sometimes with eyes open, other times closed, sometimes pushing very deliberately, other times resting one or both hands on the abdomen before palpating again.

At last he turned towards Ellen. "Let's see the X-rays," he commanded.

Ellen started to walk out to pick them up in the front hall. "Do you have a viewbox?" she asked.

"The sunlight is better than any viewbox," Brink announced.

The X-rays were produced. Slowly but stubbornly the surgeon walked to the window, looked around for a moment, then carefully pulled up a small chair. He took out the first X-ray and pushed the film directly against the glass. His arm quivered as he tried to hold it; uncertain, Ellen stayed back for a moment, then came over and held it for him. He reached down and picked up more films, holding each up to the window. The warm May sunlight shone through the blacks and whites of the CT scans and barium enema.

For ten minutes, he moved among the various films, sometimes asking Ellen to hold one up next to that he was holding. Back and forth his eyes went, from X-ray to X-ray, looking at one, then another, sometimes for the third or fourth time.

Brent got dressed and sat wordlessly on the bed.

Finally the surgeon set the films down and cautiously walked to Brent, sitting down next to the boy.

"Do you think the Zoloft has helped you, son?" the surgeon asked.

"Well…"

"Be honest."

"No sir, I don't think it's helped."

It was a thin smile on the surgeon's face, but it was unmistakable. Ellen had seen that smile before on the wards. The smile of triumph.

"Young man," he said, still not appearing to know Brent's name, "have you ever heard of Burrill B. Crohn?"

"No sir."

Brink turned to Ellen. "And you?" he asked.

"No," Ellen said.

"In 1932," the surgeon said, sitting up straighter, head nodding slightly up and down, "Dr. Burrill B. Crohn described a disease, regional enteritis, which bears his name. Crohn's Disease. He separated it from another serious intestinal disease, ulcerative colitis."

He looked at Ellen, then turned back to Brent.

"You can stop the Zoloft, son. It has no place in the treatment of Crohn's Disease."

* * *

For nearly a minute, no one said anything. Brink turned to look out the window while Ellen and Brent looked at each other.

"Crohn's Disease?" she said at last.

The surgeon nodded. "On careful palpation, I had no trouble feeling an inflammatory intestinal mass in the right lower quadrant. Clear as day. And then, of course, I knew where to look on the barium enema."

"But," Ellen said, "the radiologist didn't see anything."

"Because he didn't know where to look. It's right there in the terminal ileum, a subtle distortion showing edema and irregularity." He rocked back slightly on the edge of the bed. "Clear as day."

Looking at the surgeon, Ellen didn't see wasted muscles or skin hanging from the emaciated frame. She saw sharp eyes, strong hands; she heard the certain voice.

"Don't worry, young fellow," Brink said. "I'll call Dr. Danker and tell him. You'll be feeling better soon. Maybe even a little bit better by tomorrow."

"I would always hit the ground running," Mr. Rigby said. "Nothing could keep me down." Up and down went his head slowly. "I used to be a man. Now," he said, his voice trailing off, "I'm a nothing."

"That's not true," Ellen said.

"Of course it's true," Mr. Rigby said, his voice now so feeble he could barely whisper. "I'm so weak..." He began to cry softly, a thick strange muffled sound coming from the back of his throat.

Ellen squeezed his hand harder.

CHAPTER 35

Nobody would miss her if she skipped out a few minutes. George Tucker had paged Ellen and asked her to come over; he wouldn't say why. Obviously something to do with Roland.

Roland. Every time Ellen saw Roland, he seemed worse. Weaker. But still somehow ... inexplicably... strong. The weakness almost highlighted his strength.

When was he going to get better? Ellen had listened…and listened…as Tucker recommended this therapy or that, gave these or those odds, followed one or another blood test, X-ray, scan, physical sign.

And yet the man only seemed to get worse.

When she wasn't awake on the obstetrical wards delivering babies, Ellen was spending the nights in her bed – alone in her bed – seeing only the dark ceiling, turning left, then right, then…

George. Full of ideas, new therapies; fiddling with the dose of this medicine or that. Try this for Roland. Or maybe that. And what was there to show for it?

What in hell was there to show for it?

Alone in her bed. Hadn't she so recently pitied Roland for being alone in that hospital room, on the respirator, surrounded by so many, yet so alone.

Here was Ellen, busy on the wards, son and daughter nearby…

Alone, she shivered. So very alone.

She'd been seeing the surgeon as often as she had time on the busy gynecology rotation. Exhausted, running on nervous energy, Ellen tried to see her patient most nights. But tonight she wouldn't be visiting the surgeon; tonight she'd be going to the White House. She'd find the stamina to stay awake, to be charming, gracious.

And tomorrow she was on-call. But for now, George Tucker had asked her to come to his office as soon as possible.

Ellen finished writing a note in a chart, then hurried down the hall. She didn't look in the room with the newborns in their plastic bassinets; she didn't see the gynecology nursing station as she sped by; she almost knocked over an orderly as she careered around a corner. "Sorry," she muttered and pressed on.

The elevator would take too long. Pushing the staircase doors open, Ellen almost jogged down. She moved down the main corridor of the hall towards the parking lot, not hearing a friend call out to her. The Chevy was waiting in the parking lot. The clock on the dashboard was long defunct; Ellen checked her watch. Bringing the car to the exit ramp, she hurried to catch the green light, just missing it. Her fingers drummed back and forth on the top of the steering wheel.

Five minutes later she pulled into parking lot of the building overlooking the Whitehurst Freeway. In the distance, an airplane was practically skimming the Potomac as it began its final descent into the airport, but Ellen didn't notice. Nor did she see the carefully planted flower bed brimming with tulips, just outside the building's entrance.

The gynecology rotation was busy, far busier actually, than she'd expected. Days filled with surgery in the mornings, patients on the wards, gynecology clinic, obstetrics clinic, lectures. And every third night, she'd be up much – or once, all – of the night delivering babies. Or more correctly, staying with the resident and attending physicians learning how to deliver babies. And now, she still had two post-ops to see and an admission note to write on another patient, then she'd rush to Tony to get hair done, sprint home, feed Brent, and get ready for her big night out at the White House…somehow. The new sleeveless gown was stunning. Her first really nice new clothes in – how long was it anyhow?

Still, nobody would notice if she skipped out for only a few minutes. Would they?

Bursting into George Tucker's waiting room, two patients looked up as she headed to the door leading to the oncologist's office. She took a few hurried steps, then stopped. Slower, she said. Pace yourself. Theresa, back from her trip, watched the abrupt change in her gait and smiled.

"Come in," Tucker said to the breathless medical student standing at the open door. The oncologist was sitting behind his desk, piled high, as always, with charts, X-rays, reports, journals, and seemingly random pieces of paper.

George was not alone. Sitting across from him in one of the office chairs was a man who seemed vaguely familiar. Why did she know him?

But if the man recognized her, he certainly didn't show any sign of it.

"Ellen," George said, "I want you to meet Carter Brink, Roland's brother."

Ellen had spoken to him several times on the phone, had even helped arrange for him to get his cells typed for the possible bone marrow transplant.

The cells had matched.

Ellen knew Carter Brink would be coming to D.C. sometime in the next few days but hadn't realized until now that he'd arrived.

"Nice to meet you," Ellen said, extending her hand slowly and deliberately even as her pulse was still racing.

Carter appeared to be a few years younger than his brother. He extended his hand almost self-consciously, the expression on his face one of uncertainty. "Nice to meet you too," he muttered. He may have looked something like Roland Brink, but he sure didn't act like Roland Brink.

Ellen cleared a space on the remaining unoccupied chair, and sat down just as Tucker answered the phone. The oncologist was trying to sound reassuring to an obviously frightened patient. There were long pauses as the oncologist listened, then tried to respond. Tucker looked over at Ellen who was drumming her fingers.

She stopped.

At last the conversation was over. "So," Ellen said, turning to Carter as soon as the phone was back in its cradle, "you've come to donate the bone marrow. I think that's terrific."

Carter Brink appeared puzzled as he looked towards Tucker.

"No," George said very slowly, measuring each word, "he's not going to donate the marrow."

"But…" Ellen sputtered, looking at Carter. "He's your brother. How can you not…?"

George held up his hand, cutting off Ellen's stammer. The oncologist's face was drawn and gray, the lines almost flattened out with sags in the skin, eye creases turned down, corners of lips drooping.

"Ellen," the oncologist said after a short sigh, "nobody is going to donate anything."

"But…has Roland refused?" Ellen said hurriedly. "I don't understand."

"I went out to see him last night, apparently only a few minutes after you left. You know what he looks like."

Ellen nodded. "The transplant's his only chance," she said, voice slightly shaky.

"No," George answered. "He has no chance. I've never seen a lymphoma like this. For a transplant to be successful, the tumor has to show at least some respect for the chemotherapy. Even after he had that episode of massive necrosis, his tumor was back, worse than before, in a short time. The lymphoma has just laughed off the first two courses of chemo. The cancer has come back more aggressive than ever." He turned to look at Carter Brink, then back to Ellen. "The radiation and the high dose we'd give him before the transplant would kill him immediately."

"Well," Ellen said, voice rising slightly, "then...what do you plan to do?"

"Make him as comfortable as possible," George said.

Ellen slumped slightly in the chair, the remaining color draining from her face. She looked quickly at the oncologist, then Carter, then back to Tucker again.

For a long moment, nobody said anything. At last, Ellen turned to Carter. "Why did you come here?" she stuttered, voice barely a whisper.

"Because he's my brother," Carter said.

* * *

"Mrs. Sorrel brought something for you," Brent said when Ellen walked in the door at 4:30. "She said it would go really well with your new dress tonight."

What would Jill have brought her? Ellen opened the small box her friend had left. And gasped. A diamond stick pin looked back at her.

This was Jill's most special possession, given by her father. It was a special present when she graduated college. He was so proud of her, and they went out to buy this special diamond stick pin. Jill only wore it on the most special occasions. She'd never lent it to anyone before.

Ellen gingerly picked it up and brought it near a window. The diamonds caught the sunlight like the glitter of a summer sun on the ocean.

She went upstairs to get dressed, stopping by Brent's room. He'd gone upstairs after mumbling indistinctly about how nice the diamond stick pin was; now he was in his room playing some CDs. It had only been one week since Brink had diagnosed Crohn's Disease, but already Brent was feeling much better. The disease, which could cause so much intestinal inflammation, with variable amounts of abdominal pain, and often with the weight loss, lassitude, and generalized symptoms that had so plagued Brent, was responding to a cortisone derivative Danker had started. Soon enough, Brent would start other drugs while trying to get off the steroid, but for now he felt the best he had in months. The belly ache was gone, the appetite dramatically better, the energy level almost normal.

It would be a long haul, Dr. Danker had told them, but things were looking up for Brent... and without Zoloft.

The new black dress was the most beautiful thing she'd ever owned. Banished was the tired middle aged woman in the white lab coat with the pockets filled with pens and papers and notes and cards, gone the lifeless hair flying in every direction, cast off the flats that scuffed the hospital floors.

The black dress restored something she'd forgotten; the new Bruno Magli shoes, also at Jill's urging, atop the sheer stockings made her feel twenty years younger; the styling by Tony just an hour before gave her hair a life it hadn't seen in years; and he'd even helped her with some makeup ("I don't do this for just anyone," Tony had said). The pearl necklace, the mabe pearl earrings, and most special of all, the diamond stick pin.

Tonight would be a special night. The President, the White House. Maybe the start of a relationship with Dave? If she could somehow find the spirit, that is.

"Did you get the message on the answering machine?" Brent asked as he came by. Even he admired his mother's outfit

Message? Ellen pushed the playback button.

"Ellen," said Roland's thin and quiet voice, "I don't want to bother you, but if, well, you had some time tonight, I'd really enjoy having company." A pause. "Only if you're not busy of course."

She'd never told him about the White House.

The black dress drooped, the dress shoes got heavy, the stick pin went dull. Here was a sick man, her patient.

Her friend.

She sat down on the bedroom chair and looked out the window. Two squirrels were chasing each other, leaping from branch to branch. More than once it looked like one of the squirrels would miss a branch and fall, but their acrobatics always saved them to continue their pursuit. From downstairs, Ellen could hear the Scarlatti sonata, its phrases rising and falling on the Chickering.

Tucker canceling his date to see Carl Olsen and his mother at the hospital.

Brink in the ICU, surrounded by so many, yet so alone.

Brink working patiently carefully in his basement room, alone with his model cars.

The 1954 Packard.

No bone marrow transplant.

As comfortable as possible.

Ellen...surrounded by so many, yet so alone.

She picked up the phone and pushed the buttons slowly.

"Hello Dave," she said, "this is Ellen. I really have been looking forward to tonight. One of the most special nights of my life. But something else special has come up and…" she faltered, "…Dave, this is really hard to say, but I just can't join you tonight."

They spoke only two or three minutes longer. Ellen set the receiver gently in its cradle and looked out the window again. The squirrels were gone.

She called Roland's house and asked the nurse if there were anything she could bring with her. She'd try to get there by seven o'clock.

Slowly she took off the black dress and put on a light cotton weight skirt. Sandals replaced the Bruno Maglis. The diamond stick pin was carefully set in its box and put away in a drawer.

The phone rang. It was the nurse. "Dr. Brink wants you to bring your son with you," was all the nurse would say.

Bring Brent to see the surgeon again. Ellen stopped brushing her hair for a moment. Roland must have wanted to see how his patient was doing. *His patient.* The slightest hint of a smile played on Ellen's lips. Brent was, after all, Brink's triumph. One last chance to gloat. *Dr. Brink wants you to bring your son with you.*

Ellen did some really fast explaining to a very confused Brent, threw together something for him to eat, rounded up his homework to bring with them, and started for the car.

Oh my God, she thought, as she got into the garage. I'd better call Jill!

* * *

"Sorry," Ellen said as they stopped short. "I'm just very upset."

"About what?" Brent asked.

The light turned green.

"About…" she stopped, looked over her shoulder and changed lanes.

"About missing the White House thing?"

"Yes." She stopped. "I mean, no. I mean, I'm very unhappy about Dr. Brink." She looked at her son. "Can you understand?" she asked. "This man's dying, and my profession can't do a damned thing. What's the sense in being a healer if you can't heal?"

She slammed her right fist onto the steering wheel.

"You're angry, Mom?"

"Yes I'm angry. Angry and tired and fed up. This whole profession is nothing more than game playing." She hit the horn as a man cut her off. "I'm going to quit! I'm tired of the emotional drain, tired of fighting."

"I'm so weak..." Mr. Rigby started again, "...that I can't even put up a fight anymore."

"You'd quit, after all your effort?" Brent looked away. "You'd never let me be a quitter," he said softly.

Deb banged her fists on the keyboard. 'I quit!' she said.

'You can't just quit!' Ellen said.

Ellen pulled into the driveway. For a long time, she sat in the driver's seat, looking ahead. Brent started to ask her what she was doing, then stopped.

Slowly, Ellen's left hand reached for the car door, ands she stepped out, almost shuffling to the front of the house.

The nurse opened the door. Except for the foyer, the downstairs was dark. Looking up the staircase, Ellen saw the light at the top.

"Dr. Brink's mother and brother just left," the nurse said, "along with that cancer doctor."

Ellen went into the living room and turning on a light, settled Brent in a chair with one of his school books.

As she reached the stairs, Ellen turned back to look at her son studying. Her heart was pounding, prickles of sweat beading up under the blouse, stinging her forehead.

"Where's the boy?" Brink asked when Ellen walked in the room. Without a word, the nurse went downstairs to get Brent.

Roland Brink lay in the bed, his yellowish-gray skin dripping over the bones that stuck out, now even visible through the bedsheets. Previously, whenever he'd had visitors, the surgeon would rise to greet them; this time, he turned onto his side, not even trying to sit up.

"Pardon my rudeness," he said, as Brent walked into the room, "but I don't have the strength to get up just now."

The surgeon extended his hand, and Brent edged over to the bed. Ellen gave him a slight nudge, and Brent reached out to shake Brink's hand.

"Young man," the surgeon said, voice animated, "when you shake somebody's hand, make it worth their while. Don't give a wet fish."

"Now," he commanded, "give me a handshake."

Brent squeezed firmly.

For a moment, Brink said nothing, grasping the boy's hand, his eye bright, his grip firm.

"Better," he said.

The glow in his eyes, the strength in his hands, Ellen decided. That was the essence of the man.

Ellen sat on the bed, lightly kissing the dying man's forehead, holding his hand – now soft and gentle.

They chatted a few minutes, but soon Roland's voice began to weaken.

"I think maybe he needs some rest," the nurse said. Ellen waited for Brink's protest, but there was none. Ellen and Brent turned to leave.

"Young man," the surgeon said abruptly, voice strong again. "In the basement – your mother will show you where – are my model cars. I want you to have them. In a small cabinet on the right is a half completed model of a 1931 Bugati Type 41 Royale. I had hoped to finish it, but I can't. It requires great care if it's to be done properly. I hope you can do it justice."

CHAPTER 36

Ellen didn't have much free time after Roland's funeral seven days later. She had to rush back to the hospital to scrub in on a difficult gynecologic case.

One of the senior surgeons was scrubbing to help the gynecologist actually doing the case.

Ellen put a little phisoHex on her glasses to prevent fogging, then adjusted the clip on the frame to keep them from falling from her face. Going to the sink she carefully began the ritual of scrubbing her arms and hands with Betadine solution.

"Have you taken your surgery rotation yet?" the senior surgeon asked as he rinsed his arms in the water.

"Yes," Ellen answered.

"Good," the surgeon answered. "These gynecology guys really don't know how to operate. They're damned lucky I had the time to help them out." He shook his head, then began to towel his arms. "Damned lucky."

"You gonna become a gynecologist?" the surgeon asked. "A lot of women are going into gynecology these days."

Ellen washed off the Betadine, then began to towel her arms dry.

"Actually," she said slowly, shifting the towel to her other hand, "I'm thinking about becoming a surgeon."

Ellen left the sink, stepping on the automatic door release. The electric door to the OR opened. She hummed a few notes of the Scarlatti sonata.

Washing off the Betadine a moment later, the senior surgeon dried his arms, and followed Ellen into the operating room.

The End

Printed in the United States
1023500004B